# THE
# FALANO
# FINDINGS

## By James Robert Fuller

## A Myrtle Beach
## Crime Thriller
## Book III

# Dedicated to:

# All the friends who allow me to use their names in my books.

# Other Myrtle Beach Crime Thrillers by James Robert Fuller

## Paradise: Disturbed

*I love the twists and turns. Fun to read about all the places I'm familiar with in Myrtle Beach."*... Pat Gurley

*I enjoy the dialogue between FBI agents, Ron Lee and Tim Pond. The constant ragging on each other makes me laugh. Great characters*... John Coughenour

*Poor Ernie! I loved that character*... Bill Jackson

*I just finished Paradise Disturbed, which I must say I had a hard time putting it down. I thoroughly enjoyed the story. I can't wait to start The Scale Tippers*... Tere Harper

## The Scale Tippers

*All I can say is I really enjoyed the 1st book of your new series... and then, the second was even better. I had to throw away a couple of shirts due to salivating down the front of myself while reading all of Agent Ron Lee's donut adventures*... Joe Saffran

*The books are gripping, I can't put them down. Everything stops until I finish. My wife is still waiting for the lawn to be mowed...when is the next one?*... Gary Whittaker

*Lay off the donut comments!*... Ron Lee

*I have read the 2nd book and thoroughly enjoyed it. I can't wait to read the third one. They are great!*... Tere Harper

# THE FALANO FINDINGS

## A Myrtle Beach Crime Thriller

### Book III

**Authored by**

**JAMES ROBERT FULLER**

**FIRST EDITION**

December 2019

**ISBN: 978-0-359-94962-5**

# THE BAY HOLLOW THRILLERS
## by Ron Wing

*Murphy's Thicket – Book I* **
*The Dare – Book II* **
*Rebecca's Watch – Book III* **
*The Half Doubloon – Book IV* **

*Windfall – Book V*
*HoBo's Lagoon – Book VI*
*Silhouette Road – Book VII*
*The Ottoman Dagger – Book VIII*

*The Hangman – Book IX*
*Red Eyes – Book X*
*Gator's Gold – Book XI*
*Drinkwater – Book XII*
*Baker's Dozen – Book XIII*

Illustrated Poem Books by the author:
*Bert's House* ***
*Poems by Mort* ***

**     Recommended for ages 8-11
***    Recommended for ages 3-7

# THE MYRTLE BEACH CRIME THRILLERS
## By James Robert Fuller

*Paradise: Disturbed – Book I*
*The Scale Tippers – Book II*
*The Falano Findings  - Book III*
*The Combos – Book IV – Summer of 2020*

FOLLOW BOTH SERIES AT:
www.lulu.com/spotlight/BAY_HOLLOW_THRILLERS

Contact the author at:
RONWING44@GMAIL.COM

# TABLE
# OF CONTENTS

# PROLOGUE

**Only those present** could hear the *"whack! - whack! - whack!"* The old home's wine cellar, built deep below the main floor, was soundproof. It was far from being in tip-top shape with walls seeping water that collected in small puddles, and rafters that were dry-rotted or weakened by years of seepage. It was, however, safe enough to carry on the present doings.

A wine cabinet's remains, long ago turned to dust by termites, lay about the 10x15 enclosure. The floor was hard scrabble dug out by slaves who served their master some 200 years earlier. Its center was much darker than that around it, the result of the many bloody beatings that had come before their current counterpart.

Two kerosene lanterns illuminated the room. One hung near the closed doorway, the other dangled from a small hook in a ceiling beam. Its light, nudged by the backswing of the tool causing the "whacking" sound, wavered back and forth, enhancing the menacing feel of the enclosure.

Tied up and hung upside-down on a hook in the ceiling was the target of the beating, one Horace Simpson. A blackjack meeting flesh accounted for the constant whacking sounds. A face, so badly mutilated his own mother would never recognize him, was only a hint of the man's suffering. Blows to his body had broken a half-dozen ribs, made his scrotum forever useless, and had crushed both knees. His hands were nothing but useless dangling pulp.

Three other men occupied the enclosure. Two of them stood near the walls so the splashes of blood would not hit them. They watched the proceedings in silence while smoking aromatic cigars. The third man, his face streaked with blood, administered the beating. He looked almost as horrific as the victim as he stood in the man's blood with his clothing saturated in gore and sweat.

"So Horace, was it worth it?" asked Cameron Driscoll, the taller of the two men standing against the wall. "Was it worth the $5000 you held back on your last delivery?"

Horace couldn't have answered if he wanted to. They had broken his jaw, most of his teeth were missing, and his tongue was nothing more than a piece of hamburger.

"I think he has had it, boss," said Jocko Moritz, the man who was administering the beating.

"I believe you are right. Finish it and then get rid of the body in the usual manner. I will see you tomorrow. I need to find someone to fill Horace's position."

As Bruno Lorenza, Driscoll's top lieutenant in his organization, opened the door leading to the upstairs, Jocko put a bullet in the brain of Horace Simpson, ending his employment in the Driscoll drug cartel.

You don't screw with the family, and Simpson had been a family member in the truest sense.

Horace was Cameron Driscoll's brother-in-law.

# CHAPTER 1

**Manny's Deli, on** South Kings Highway, was a huge favorite of locals and tourists. Known for his sumptuous subs, the deli was seldom without activity.

If you passed by at certain hours of the day, you would notice it was also a favorite eatery of law enforcement. It was not uncommon to see three or four police vehicles parked in front of the establishment around noon and at six in the evening.

On the night of January 8th, any passerby might have noticed a pair of Horry County Sheriff vehicles sandwiching a South Carolina state trooper cruiser belonging to Cpl. Jesse Bennington.

Having arrived about 10 minutes before the two sheriff's deputies, Jessie placed his order for the 8-inch Godfather sub. Manny was making Jessie's sandwich when the deputies arrived.

"Hey, Manny," called out Deputy Bob Maury. "Throw a meatball sub together for me."

"Will do, Bob. What will you have, Carl?"

"I'll have the Italian, Manny. No onions, please," answered the second deputy, Carl Malone, a huge man by anyone's standards.

They both sat down at Jesse's table and the three of them chatted about things not related to work. Being polite, Jesse waited to eat his sandwich until Manny had served the other two officers.

"The Coastal basketball team sucks," spurted Maury. "There are better high school teams in the area."

"You'll get no argument from me," agreed Carl, a former player for the Myrtle Beach High School.

"I'd like to stick around fellas, but the job calls. My lieutenant likes to roam the area to see if we are doing our jobs. I need another citation like I need a hole-in-the-head,"

3

said Jesse, referring to two incidents involving women who he had pulled over on traffic violations. Both reported he had made suggestive remarks that inferred their traffic transgression would go away if they agreed to his offer.

Since it was a case of "she says, he says" the court dismissed the charges, but the stains remained on his record. Another of its kind, or any other egregious complaint, would end his law enforcement career.

"Okay, Jesse. We'll see you tomorrow night at the Sundown," called out Deputy Maury.

It was 7:20 when the deputies paid for their meal and said goodnight to Manny. As they exited the restaurant, they saw Jessie's cruiser still parked between their vehicles.

"What the hell," barked Carl. "He left 20 minutes ago, at least. Why is his car still here?"

"Something ain't right, Carl," murmured Officer Maury, as he unsnapped his holster and approached the vehicle with his hand close to his firearm.

Officer Malone mimicked Maury's actions, but swung around behind his vehicle and approached the trooper car from the rear.

Maury, using extreme caution, moved toward the driver's window. He had advanced to within three steps of the driver's door, when he stopped and bellowed, "Something shattered the side window, Carl!"

Three steps later he screamed into his mic the dreaded words, "Officer down! Officer down!"

Stretched out on the front seat was Trooper Jesse Bennington. A hole, the size of a tennis ball, had replaced the left side of his head. His left eye wasn't where it should have been, and much of his splintered forehead occupied the passenger window. Jesse's blood, brains, and bone also covered the seat, the dashboard, and the onboard computer.

Cpl. Jesse Bennington wouldn't be receiving any more unwanted citations, but he did get that unwanted hole-in-the-head.

# CHAPTER 2

**"Has someone contacted** his wife?" asked Special Agent Ron Lee of the FBI.

"Yeah, Ron," answered Captain Bill Baxter, commander of the South Carolina State Police. "The wife was hosting a card night. There were three other women in attendance."

"Well, at least she had friends there for support," replied Ron.

Seeing that the victim was a law enforcement officer, Baxter had to notify the FBI. Ron and his partner, Agent Tim Pond, having little on their "to-do-list," caught the case.

"Yeah, and that's a nice alibi, too," added Pond.

Soon after the FBI agents' arrival, the two Horry County deputies, Maury and Malone, briefed them on the specifics that led to finding the body.

"What kind of record did this guy have, Bill?"

"He was a woman chaser, Ron. He had two misconduct charges involving women he had pulled over."

"Oh! Was his wife aware of those charges?" asked Tim.

"Yeah, she was. I heard she threatened to leave him, but he convinced her the two women were lying."

"Were they?" asked Ron.

"I don't think so," answered Baxter, "but they couldn't prove anything. It was their word against his."

"Are they married women?" asked Tim.

"Yeah, both of them. When the rendering came down, the husbands didn't seem pleased."

"We'll need their names."

"The two women?"

"Yeah, and those of the husbands."

"You think one of them may have done this, Ron?"

"It's possible."

"Check to see if either has a registered gun, Bill," added Tim. "It looks like a .45 may have caused this carnage."

"Agreed partner," nodded Ron. "That's a helluva big hole in the side of his head. It appears as if the killer stepped up to the window, put the gun barrel against the glass, and pulled the trigger. Officer Bennington never saw it coming."

"Nobody sees it coming, Ron," muttered Baxter.

"A cop can have lots of enemies, Bill," said Tim. "Did this guy have any heavy cases in his career?"

"None that I recall," answered Baxter. "He caught a few heists, but nothing big time. I'm guessing he broke up his share of family feuds, as do most cops."

"No drug cartel involvement?" asked Pond.

"None."

"How about hostile traffic stops?" Ron asked.

"I'd have to check on that, but other than the two women I mentioned… I can't recall anything that might lead to this."

"Could it be just a random killing, Ron?"

"I guess that's possible, Tim, but I'm thinking it's not."

"Well, someone didn't care for him, that's for sure," claimed Tim.

"It's clear that whoever killed him knew he would be here. They waited for him to leave the restaurant. Once he got in his car, they walked over, and 'bang', they took him out."

"Professional?" asked Tim.

"Could be, but why would a pro kill a state trooper?" answered Ron. "Bill, are you sure he had no involvement with anything related to organized crime?"

"Jesse, setting aside the thing with the two women, was a good trooper," claimed Baxter. "We keep watch on these guys and he had no known affiliation with anyone on the wrong side of the law."

"If that is true, and I'm sure you're right, Bill, then it had to be something personal between him and another individual. Let's go talk with the wife. Bill, get us the names of the two women and their husbands. I'll want to talk with them as soon as possible."

The two agents left the scene and headed toward the Bennington home in Market Commons, just a mile down the road.

"Any immediate thoughts, Ron?"

"It was a cold-blooded murder, that's for sure. The thing that sticks in my craw, is the killer knew his location. How many people would know that, Tim? A handful, maybe? What are your thoughts?"

"Plenty of cops stop there, Ron."

"You ever been in there?"

"Hell, yes. Great subs. They are way too much to eat… although I doubt you would find it's too much of a challenge."

"Up yours, partner."

"I'm guessing his wife might know," offered Tim.

"No doubt. What's her name?"

"Sheila. She's 29. They married five years ago. No kids."

"That's good."

"Here's a bit of info that might perk your interest, Ron. She served in ROTC in college."

"She might know how to use a gun, is what you're implying."

"Yeah, but we know she didn't do it. She has that card game going for her. That's a solid alibi."

"There's little doubt about that," murmured Ron.

"Little doubt? What the hell does that mean?"

"Think about it, Tim. What are the chances the night your husband gets knocked off is the same night you're home playing cards, surrounded by three witnesses? Most people can't prove where they were during the commission of a crime. They are home alone, asleep in front of the tv."

"I think you're reaching, Ron."

"Yeah, you're right. I still wonder if she knew he would be at Manny's Deli tonight. Let's be real here, Tim. She had a motive."

"What? Her husband putting the moves on some women he pulled over for speeding?"

"Yeah. How many moves do you think he put on women just sitting in a bar? I bet it crossed... what's her name again?"

"Sheila," reminded Tim.

"I bet it crossed Sheila's mind once or twice."

"You have a deceitful mind, Ron. I suspect that suspicion, rather than blood, courses through your veins."

Ron was smiling at his partner's assessment when something caught his eye.

"Hey, partner. You just passed a donut shop."

"That's right, Ron, with 'passed' being the operative word. I'm looking out for you, partner."

"Looking out for me? How's that?"

"You have your physical coming up in two weeks. I'd like to think you might have a slim... wait, slim seems inappropriate given the subject. How about... prayer! Yeah, prayer fits. I'd like to think you have a prayer of passing."

"I'm calling in sick that day," replied Ron. "Screw that physical."

"Wow! I must admit, Ron, that is a brilliant call. The day of your physical, you'll call in sick. What a marvelous idea. Genius is what it is! But wait! Is there something wrong with this picture?"

"Keep driving, Tim-o-thy."

# CHAPTER 3

**Ninety miles from** Havana is the city of Matanzas, the capital of Matanzas Province. It was here in 1977 that a future legend was born. His name would be Ramon Ruiz, the only child of Raul, the governor of the province, and Felicia Ruiz.

After taking full advantage of all the cultural benefits the Province provided, Ramon attended the University of Havana, where he graduated in three years with a law degree.

In the late fall of 2000, Castro declared Ramon's parents dissidents and had them imprisoned. Envisioning what was to come, his parents sent him off to an uncle who lived in the Sierra Cristal Mountains.

Intending to break his parents out of prison, Ramon organized and trained a group of guerrilla fighters, all young men and women orphaned by Castro's policies.

The Castro regime had converted El Morro Castle, originally built as a fortress to guard the entrance to Havana Bay, into a prison for political prisoners.

The incarcerated, numbering well over 500, included men, women, and children. They were guarded 24/7 by two squads of soldiers under the command of Luiz Delgado, a man who embraced torture and murder. Under Delgado's thumb, death for a prisoner was just a small misstep away.

It was a mid-May evening, under a moonless sky, when a small armada of Ramon-led guerrilla fighters slinked into Havana Bay. Their destination was the notorious El Morro Castle.

The attack and takeover of the castle was clinical. Killed in the attack were twenty-five of the guards, while only three of Ramon's guerillas fell. Ramon himself ended the reign of Luiz Delgado with a slice of his knife across the sadistic commander's jugular.

They quickly gathered the freed prisoners into small sailing boats that silently made their way out of the harbor to make the sea-crossing to the southern Florida coastline. Freedom in the United States was only 90 miles away.

They were 30 miles from their target when the Cuban navy appeared on the horizon. Their gunboats would be on them in mere minutes, and if not killed in the water, the prisoners would face execution on their return to Havana.

Although Ramon's guerrillas were well-armed, he knew they stood no chance against the gunboats. He had to admit defeat.

"I'm sorry, Papa," he said, turning to his father who held Ramon's frail mother in his arms.

"Nothing to be sorry for, son," replied the proud father.

Unknown to the inhabitants of the armada, there were some among them the U.S. government had a vested interest in seeing they made it safely to its shores.

The situation was being closely monitored by southern Florida's Homestead Air Force Base.

Seeing that the Cuban gunboats were about to intercept the armada, the base commander ordered four helicopter gunships to intercept them.

Their orders were brief and simple: "Blow them out of the damn water, if need be."

Just as one of Ramon's lieutenants yelled, "What should we do, Ramon?" the squad of gunships passed overhead and headed directly toward the Cuban gunboats.

The Cubans, realizing they were no match for the battle-ready helicopters, quickly abandoned their interest in the armada, and reversed their course.

Shouting wildly, the refugees waved scarfs and hats upon seeing the gunboats make a hasty retreat toward Cuban waters.

"Damn!" said Ramon in total admiration.

Now protected by the U.S. Air Force, the armada sailed safely into U.S. waters.

Hours later, the small armada reached the Florida coastline.

During the moments that the inhabitants were being helped from their vessels and taken to a hospital for medical attention, a U.S. Army captain approached Ramon.

"Sir, I am Captain Jim Leslie of the U.S. Army. I understand that you are responsible for this rescue. Is that correct?"

Ramon, surprised that the man knew this, answered, "I trained the guerillas and planned the assault. This is true."

"What is your name, senor?"

"Ramon. Ramon Ruiz."

"Well, Ramon Ruiz, there is someone who would like to speak with you."

"And who might that be, Captain?"

"He is someone that would like to offer you a job."

"A job? What kind of job?"

"I'm sorry, Mr. Ruiz, but I'm not at liberty to say. I can tell you it takes a special person to fulfill the job's requirements and they think enough of you to offer you the position."

"They?"

Ignoring Ramon's reply, Leslie merely said, "Take care of your family and get them settled, Mr. Ruiz. I'll come by your hotel on Wednesday at 9:00am to pick you up."

"Hotel? What hotel?"

"We have taken care of everything, sir. Your parents will get the medical attention they need. Afterward, someone will escort the three of you to your temporary living quarters. I'll see you on Wednesday."

"Hey, I didn't say I'd take this job, whatever it is!"

"Oh, you will, sir. You won't let this slip through your fingers, I assure you. See you on Wednesday at 9:00am sharp."

And with that pronouncement, the captain turned and walked away, replaced by two men dressed in U.S. Army uniforms.

"Sir, we have a vehicle ready to take you and your parents to the medical treatment facility."

"Sure," said Ramon, following the uniformed men to a military vehicle. His head was still spinning at what had transpired as he stepped into the vehicle and was whisked away.

After being cleared by medical personnel, they escorted Ramon and his parents to the Hyatt Regency Hotel in downtown Miami.

They gave his parents a room on the fifth floor, while affording Ramon a suite on the 23rd, overlooking the Miami River.

Room service came knocking within the hour and the waiter provided Ramon a meal of prime rib and crab. Although presented with various liquors for his choosing, Ramon opted for a cold beer.

A few hours later, the phone rang.

"Hello."

*"Mr. Ruiz, this is Captain Leslie. I trust you found everything to your satisfaction?"*

"Yes, it is all very nice. Thank you, sir."

*"Oh, you're more than welcome, sir. If there is anything you or your parents require, just call the front desk and request it."*

"Thank you, but I can't think of anything at the moment."

*"If you check your closet, Mr. Ruiz, you'll find clothing. I think you'll find the sizes to be correct. We have also provided your parents with new clothing, sir."*

Ramon, at a loss for words, sputtered, "How do you know our clothing sizes?"

Leslie ignored Ramon's question, saying, *"I will be by in the morning to pick you up. I'll be waiting in the lobby at 9:00am sharp."*

"What's this all about, Captain?"

*"Patience, Mr. Ruiz. Patience."*

The phone clicked off, leaving Ramon staring at the phone in his hand and wondering what the hell this was all about.

*************

Dressed in a pair of tan slacks and a white button-down shirt, Ramon was waiting in the lobby when Captain Leslie walked in at 9:00am sharp.

"Ahh, I see that the clothes we selected for you were the correct size. Are you comfortable?"

"I'm fine. Let's get on with this, Captain. Take me to whoever I'm supposed to meet about this job."

"There is a car waiting outside. We only have a short distance to the meeting place. I think you'll find this opportunity to your liking, Mr. Ruiz."

"Please, call me Ramon."

"Very well, Ramon. Follow me."

Ten minutes later, the black Cadillac pulled into a driveway that led to a parking place under a building in downtown Miami.

"I didn't notice what building this was," said Ramon.

"It's the headquarters of the FBI," answered Leslie.

"The FBI? Is that who I'm here to see?"

"Yes. You'll be speaking with Michael Anderson, the Bureau Chief."

Ten minutes later and 12 floors higher, Ramon was sitting in a leather chair opposite a man of slim stature but wearing a face that radiated seriousness.

Leslie introduced Ramon to Michael Anderson.

"Please sit, Ramon. I would like you to listen to what I have to say. If what I say doesn't appeal to you, you may leave. No questions asked. Fair enough?

Ramon, with a nod, agreed, then sat and listened to what the man had to say.

Twenty minutes later, Ramon spoke for the first time.

"Thank you, sir. I accept the job."

When Ramon left the office, his name was no longer Ramon Ruiz. It was Carlos Moyà. He was no longer a Cuban refugee. Carlos Moyà was now an undercover agent in training for the FBI.

# CHAPTER 4

**The woman answered** the ringing of the doorbell within seconds of Ron's pressing of the buzzer. Dark-haired, blue-eyed, and looking like she was in her late twenties, she opened the door, saying, "Yes? Can I help you?"

"Ma'am, I'm Special Agent Ron Lee of the FBI, and this is my partner Agent Tim Pond. We'd like to speak with Mrs. Bennington."

"Please come in. I'm Molly Darby, one of Sheila's friends. I was with her when she received the news."

"How is she taking it, Miss Darby?" asked Ron.

"It's Mrs. Darby, and she's not taking it well, as expected."

"I understand you were playing cards."

"Yes. We were playing bridge."

"Is this something you do weekly?"

"We intended it to be a bi-weekly affair."

"Intended? What does that mean?" queried Ron.

"This was our first get together. We planned to play every two weeks, rotating homes. Sheila volunteered to host this week."

"Bad opening bid," remarked Tim.

"Yes, it is. I'm guessing we won't be playing again, at least for the foreseeable future," added Molly Darby.

"Who's idea was it to start a card club, if you will?"

"It was Sheila's, I believe. Why?"

"Just wondering," answered Ron.

Darby led them to a living room near the rear of the house. As they entered the room, they saw two women consoling the new widow as the three sat on a flowered cloth couch.

"Sheila, these are FBI agents Lee and Pond. They have asked to speak with you."

"FBI?" said the blonde beauty who was now a grieving widow. "Why is the FBI involved?"

Strange question to ask based on the circumstances, thought Ron.

"The FBI always gets the call when a member of law enforcement goes down when on duty, ma'am," responded Pond.

"I see," said Sheila, dabbing her eyes. "Please sit down, gentlemen."

"Thank you, ma'am. We are sorry for your loss."

"Thank you. Jesse was a wonderful husband. Who did this?" asked a crying Sheila.

"That's what we intend to find out, ma'am. Do you know if your husband had received any threats as of late? Did he mention any trouble he was having with anyone?"

"We would often talk about his work but no, he mentioned nothing about receiving threats."

"Someone killed him at Manny's Deli. Do you know of it, ma'am?" queried Tim.

"Oh, yes, I know it. We often had lunch there. Good sandwiches. I'm not too crazy about the coleslaw though."

Ron, hearing her answer, made a notation in his notepad.

"Was it his habit to eat there on Tuesdays, ma'am?" asked Tim.

"I believe so," answered Sheila. "He also ate there on Fridays. Tomorrow he would have gone to the Sundown Restaurant in Surfside. Do you know where that is?"

"Yes, ma'am, we do," answered Tim, remembering the man named Ernie who fell victim to the serial killer known as Ichabod.

"Mrs. Darby told us that this was your first night for your card club, Mrs. Bennington."

"Yes. We planned on rotating the hosting every two weeks."

"Mrs. Darby said that this was your idea."

"Yes, it was. Jesse worked the middle shift… that's 3:00pm to 11:00pm every other week. It's lonely without him around, so I thought playing cards one night when he was working would… fill in the time."

"I see," said Ron. "Are you other ladies married to cops also?"

A chorus of "no's" filled the air.

"Well, we will leave now, Mrs. Bennington," announced Ron, rising from his seat. "We'll do our best to catch your husband's killer. Here is my card. We'll be in touch."

"Thank you, gentlemen. If I can think of anything that might be of help, I'll call you."

\*\*\*\*\*\*\*\*\*\*\*\*\*

Ten days later, on the night of January 18th, Sheriff's Officer Jimmy Patterson was sitting alone in his squad car parked beside Painter's Homemade Ice Cream Parlor. The business, on the corner of Business 17 and Calhoun Road in Garden City, was closed for the winter, but the location offered an excellent spot for catching speeders.

Patterson had his radar on and although many cars passed at speeds exceeding the 45mph speed zone, he paid no attention. He was talking to someone on his cell phone when the bullet blew the base of his skull off.

When the car door opened, a woman's voice screamed from the fallen cell, now lying at the feet of the dead police officer.

*"Jimmy! Jimmy! Are you there? Jim! What's happening? What was that noise, Jimmy! It sounded like a gunshot!"*

Retrieving the phone from the floor, the killer glanced at the caller's name before tossing the phone back onto the floor. Then, as the car door was closed, the caller heard, "you got what a dirty cop deserves."

# CHAPTER 5

**Ramon Ruiz spent** a dozen harrowing years in Florida working as an undercover agent for the FBI. All too often he came close to being unmasked.

Knowing that twelve years was way beyond the shelf life of an undercover agent, the FBI moved Ramon to Myrtle Beach, South Carolina.

The Driscoll drug ring controlled the flow of all drugs along the state of South Carolina's coastline. The ring had grown powerful, and the FBI needed someone inside the organization. The overwhelming choice for the job was Ramon.

Placing him under the jurisdiction of the South Carolina Law Enforcement Division, better known as SLED, they sent him in as Hector Falano, a former Cuban drug runner. It was an unbreakable cover built specifically for him.

Three months after his arrival, Ramon, with little effort and minimal resistance, infiltrated the cartel.

After assimilating himself into the Driscoll organization, it took Hector three short years to make the climb to lieutenant, but it wasn't easy or lawful.

Over the course of those years, Hector had to prove himself on multiple occasions by committing unlawful acts.

The most unlawful was killing a traitor in the organization.

Knowing the traitor as a vicious killer who had killed two of its agents, SLED had no qualms in giving Hector the go-ahead.

The kill sealed the cartel's trust in Hector. They rewarded him the coveted position of a cartel lieutenant.

Along with the promotion came the responsibility of running the northern region, which included all of Horry

County, the state's largest in square miles and 4th in population.

Ralph's Beach Supply store, in North Myrtle Beach, was nothing more than a front to launder the cartel's drug money. It was from here that Hector ran his operation.

Over the next three months, Hector gained unlimited access to significant facts about the ring, including its distributors' names and locales, and most important, the flow of drug money.

Although this information was of significant value, it paled in comparison to what Hector's hacking skills had uncovered.

Using those skills, Hector hacked his way into Driscoll's encrypted computer files. There he found evidence of payoffs to those who had the power and the influence to protect the drug ring.

Realizing the importance of what he had found, Ramon copied the data onto a flash drive and hid it where no one would ever think to look.

He had the evidence that would take down the Driscoll organization and he would present it to his superiors on Saturday, just two days from now.

For three dangerous years, Hector had avoided making a mistake while building trust with Driscoll's organization. It took a single ill-advised phone call to undo all that and place him in harm's way.

Driscoll had the wherewithal to have most of his phones tapped. When people paid to listen in on Driscoll's employees overheard Hector's call, he unknowingly signed and sealed his own death sentence.

Only the delivery remained, and it was afoot.

The door to the back room swung open and Bruno Lorenza, his boss, entered.

"Hector!" cried Lorenza, "How are we doing, my friend?"

"Doing well, Bruno. So far this week we have taken in $145,000 from the drop points from Little River to Main Street."

"Wow, that is extraordinary!" exclaimed Bruno. "Your crew has done well, Hector. You should be proud!"

"Thanks, Bruno."

"Hey, how about we take a break for lunch? I'm starving and I'm told there is a little Mexican restaurant that just opened on 45th that serves outstanding margaritas. I'm buying!"

"Sounds good, boss. Let me put this cash in the safe and I'll be ready to go."

"I'll bring the car around to the back," said Bruno.

A few minutes later, Hector stepped into the front passenger seat of Bruno's 2018 Mercedes. Sitting in the back were two of Bruno's men, Hector knew as Mike Cora and Jocko Moritz, both cold-blooded killers.

"Afternoon, guys," said a nervous Hector.

"How you doing, Hector?" asked Mike who was sitting behind Hector.

"I'd say everything is going even better than expected. We made a good haul this past week. Driscoll should be a happy man."

It was then that Hector noticed that Bruno had made a right turn onto Route 17.

"Bruno, 45th is the other way," said an alarmed Hector.

"I know. I have to make a quick stop in Little River. Won't take over ten minutes."

"Little River?"

"Yeah, there's an old home, well hidden in the marshes. Its owners left town leaving a mortgage. It's under foreclosure. Driscoll wants me to check it out to see if it may be of use to us."

Ten minutes later, Bruno pulled his Mercedes down a dirt road that led to a southern plantation type house.

"It looks interesting," remarked Hector.

Bruno stopped the car and turned off the ignition. Then turning to Hector, said, "Oh, it is interesting, Hector, that's for sure."

"What are you implying, Bruno?" asked a now nervous Hector.

"Mike has a gun. It's pointed at the back of your head. If I give the word, he will blow your brains all over the windshield and dashboard of my new Mercedes. Now, I must admit, I would find that infuriating, but, if that's what it takes, so be it."

"What's this all about, Bruno?" asked Hector, already knowing the answer.

"Where is the flash drive, Hector? Tell me, and we will make it quick. Don't, then you and your wife, will suffer slow and excruciating deaths."

"Corrina! She has nothing to do with this!"

"True, but if you don't talk, well, me and the boys will stop by your house, have a little fun, and then kill her, sparing her no pain."

"Don't you dare touch her!"

"Fine," said Bruno. "Just tell us where you hid the flash drive."

Hector spat in Bruno's face.

Big mistake.

# CHAPTER 6

**"What time was** he killed, Bill?" asked Ron.

"The coroner thinks it was between 7:30 and 8:00."

"What about a murder weapon?"

"The coroner, with an educated guess, says it was a .45 that did the trick. He'll know better after the autopsy."

"Any witnesses?" asked Tim, shivering in the low 30 degree temperatures.

"None."

"Who found the body?"

"When he didn't report in at 8:00, our dispatcher sent out a 10-97…"

"10-97?"

"That, Tim, is the code for a 'time and security check on patrol vehicles,'" answered Baxter.

"I knew that," Tim lied.

Smiling, Baxter continued with, "When he didn't respond, she dispatched another car in the area to his last reported location at 7:15… which was here."

"Is this a spot he used on a regular basis, Bill?"

"It is a popular spot, Ron. It's in shadows and it sits back a ways so it is tough to spot. I'm guessing he placed himself here each shift. I can check citations he has issued in the past and give you a count on how many were on this stretch. Why do you ask?"

"I doubt this was a random killing, Bill. Someone knew he'd be here. Question is, who?"

"I would guess there would be quite a few, Ron. Fellow officers for example."

"Who found him?"

"That would be Officer Clyde Garrett. He's over there, standing next to his patrol car," said Baxter while pointing over Ron's shoulder.

Garrett was seen huddled with other sheriff deputies who answered upon hearing Garrett's "officer down" call.

Ron, seeing Garrett's six- foot-three frame and his obviously well-cared for body, was taken aback by the man's white hair.

"Kind of old to be a cop, isn't he, Bill?"

"Who? Garrett?"

"Yeah, his hair is whiter than Santa's."

"He's only 34. Had white hair since he was in his early twenties. One of those gene things, I'm guessing."

"Did he touch anything, Bill?"

"Not a thing. The way he tells it, he pulled alongside Patterson's vehicle, and seeing the window blown out, exited his car. Using his flashlight, he saw Patterson lying across the seat. Seeing the body and the blood, he called in the 'officer down.'"

"He didn't help his fellow officer?"

A voice from behind answered Ron's question.

"I saw the back of his head was missing, sir. The amount of blood on the seat, and splattered on the window, told me there was nothing I could do to help Patterson."

Sheriff's Officer Cpl. Clyde Garrett, seeing Captain Baxter pointing at him, had made his way over toward the three men and heard Ron's question as he approached.

"I suppose, under the conditions, I would have done the same," admitted Ron. "No offense meant."

"None taken, sir."

"Did you know Officer Patterson, Garrett?"

"Oh, yeah. We went to high school together. After school, we spent a lot of our free time hanging out."

"Doing what?" asked Tim.

"Usual guy stuff. Fishing, drinking, and," he added with a smirk, "some hunting."

"What was it the two of you hunted?" asked Ron.

"Well, Jimmy had a taste for women, if you know what I mean."

"And you?"

"I guess I'm guilty of the same pleasures."

Turning to Bill, Ron asked, "Anything in the car that might be of value?"

"We found his cell phone on the floor between his feet. We checked and the last call he made was at 7:34 to a Loretta Small. Small broke off the connection."

"Where does she live?"

"Lives in Myrtle Beach on 38th Avenue North. House number is 44."

"We'll stop by and have a chat," said Ron. "How about Patterson? Was he married?"

"Yeah, he was. Six years. Wife's name is Peggy. They live just up the road here in Surfside. Their address is 109 Poplar. It's on the corner of 15th South. We sent someone over, but she wasn't home. There was a note on the door saying that she was at her mother's house."

"What did the note say?" Ron asked.

Baxter pulled a notepad from his jacket, flipped through a few pages, and then said, "It read, 'Jimmy, I'm over at mom's. I should be home by 10. Love, Peg.'"

"She hung the note on the outer door?" asked Ron.

"Yeah. Stuck there with a piece of Scotch tape."

"Where does mom live?" asked Tim.

"She lives a few blocks from her daughter's place. She's on Hollywood at the corner of Surfside Drive. The house number is 241."

"Have they notified her?"

"Yeah. From what I'm told, she fainted when the officers gave her the news."

"I wonder why she was at her mother's house."

"Get this, Ron. Her mom, who is a widow, was having a Tupperware party. I didn't even know people did that anymore!" exclaimed Baxter.

"So there are people who can corroborate her alibi when the murder of her husband occurred?"

"Yeah, about a half-dozen from my understanding," answered Baxter.

"I see he had his radar on," said Tim. "Does it record the speed of passing vehicles?"

"Yeah, it does, along with the time."

"Has anyone looked at it, Bill?"

"No. Why?"

"I'm curious if he was more interested in doing his job or talking with the Small woman."

"Are you implying what I think, Tim?"

"Depends on what you think I'm implying. If it's infidelity, then yes."

"Well, if that's true, then his wife isn't a suspect. She has an air-tight alibi backed by a half-dozen witnesses, including her mother."

"Convenient, isn't it?" chided Ron.

"Remind you of something, Ron?" Tim asked with a smile, knowing what Ron's reply would be.

"Seems like a 2 + 2 to me, Tim. Two cops killed on a weekday night. Both wives having airtight alibis with plenty of witnesses to corroborate. A .45 is the likely weapon of choice. Both husbands 'Romeo types.' Both killed while sitting in their cruisers."

"Could be a cop-killer, Ron."

"Yeah, you're right, Bill. It just might be but I doubt it. I have some questions for our new widow."

"She's still with her mother, Ron."

"That's fine. I'd like to speak to Loretta Small first. Do me a favor, Bill."

"What's that, Ron?"

"Check on tonight's whereabouts of the widow Bennington."

"Am I allowed to ask why?"

"Call me crazy, Bill, but there's this old idiom swimming around in my head."

"Would the old idiot like to share his idiom thoughts?" asked Tim with a smirk.

"Number one, it's an… old idiom. Second, I'm not an idiot. And third, I knew you couldn't handle a word longer than four letters."

"I noticed you didn't discount being old."

"Would you like to hear my thoughts or not?"

"Hey, Bill, we are about to hear idiom thoughts!"

"Do you want to hear it, Tim? Yes or no?" asked Ron with a snarl.

"Okay, give it to us, but be gentle, old fella."

After giving Tim 'I'd like to strangle you look,' Ron whispered, "One hand washes the other."

"Quid pro quo," whispered Tim back.

"If you rather," said Ron, nodding his head.

"Damn, Ron, you're not thinking…"

"Yes, I am, Bill."

"Do you want me to ask the Patterson woman where she was last week?"

"No! Do not!" barked Ron. "You might, however, want to check phone records to see if they have been communicating."

"Okay, Ron. I must admit, after giving it a moment's thought, it has potential."

"I'll call you after Tim and I have spoken to the Small woman. Oh, one other thing, Bill."

"What's that, Ron."

"Did the Patterson's have any children?"

"No."

"Geez, is everyone on the pill?" said Ron as he left the scene with Tim in tow.

# CHAPTER 7

**Ron's first thought** when Loretta Small opened the door, was, no one can accuse her breasts of being small. Ron estimated she was at least a 40. Tim would later admit to thinking she was a 44. As for the rest of her, Ron admitted to himself that if Patterson was cheating on his wife, he doubtless had excellent taste. Gorgeous blond hair, soft blue eyes, lips, red and moist, and a Hollywood body.

When she opened the door and saw Ron holding up his badge as he announced who he was, her first words were, "He's dead, isn't he?"

"Had half his head blown off, ma'am," said Ron, not averse to telling it like it is.

"Sweet Jesus!" cried Loretta. "I knew it!"

After she invited them in and they seated themselves in a beachy living room setting, Ron began asking questions.

"How long have you known Officer Patterson, ma'am?"

"Please call me Loretta, gentlemen. You're making me feel old with that ma'am crap."

"We can do that, Loretta," replied Ron.

"Thank you. Let's see, now. We've been hanging out together for about five weeks, maybe six. I met him at the Dead Dog Saloon. I was sitting at the bar and he offered to buy me a drink. One thing led to another and before I knew it we were… friendly."

"No need for those details," said Ron, not wanting the woman to expose personal secrets. "You were on the phone with him when it happened?"

"I was. He parked over on Calhoun. Right?"

"Correct," answered Tim.

"He always called me when he parked there. Referred to it as his quiet time," said the beauty as she wiped tears from eyes stained with mascara.

"What time was that, Loretta?"

"It was 7:30 when he called. He always called at 7:30 on the dot."

"Tell us what you heard," instructed Ron.

"We were talking about getting together after his shift when I heard this explosion! I screamed into the phone, asking Jimmy what the hell that sound was."

"It's obvious he didn't answer."

"No, he didn't. I kept asking him what that sound was, but I knew it was a gunshot. Don't ask me how I knew, I just did."

"Did you hear anything else, ma'am?"

"Yeah, I did. I heard what sounded like the car door opening. I think I could hear passing cars."

"You must have good hearing, ma'am. The road was some 40 yards away."

"A second or so later, the sounds got louder."

"How much louder?" asked Tim.

"Enough so that I could tell the difference," replied Loretta.

"Maybe the killer picked up the phone from wherever Patterson dropped it," said Tim.

"Yeah, that was my thinking too, partner."

"A moment or two later, the sounds became somewhat muted and then I heard the car door shut, but…" she paused, wondering if she should continue.

"But what?" asked Ron, leaning forward in his chair.

"I'm sorry but I'm not sure what I heard next."

"That's okay. Just tell us what you think you heard, Loretta."

"I heard someone say, 'you got what you deserved...' then the door closed and then I think I heard, 'dirty cop.'"

"Are you sure you heard 'dirty cop,' ma'am?"

"No, I'm not sure, but that's what it sounded like to me."

"Anything else?" asked Ron.

"No. I called out to Jimmy a few more times, but in my heart I knew he was dead."

"Did you call 9-1-1 to report what you thought you heard?" asked Tim.

"No, and I hope you know why."

Nodding his head, Tim asked no more questions.

"The voice you heard. What did it sound like?"

"I would call it a soft gruff."

"What, on God's green earth, does that mean?" asked Tim.

"It's how I would describe the voice. Gruff, but soft."

"Explain that description, Loretta," said Ron in a mellow tone.

"Listen mister, you have a deep voice and if you said those words they would sound menacing, but this voice didn't sound menacing. No offense, Agent Pond, but it sounded more like your voice... a much higher octave."

Tim, feeling uncomfortable by the woman's assertion, immediately changed his position in his chair and trying to sound rougher, growled, "Oh, yeah?"

"That's quite a comeback, you had there, partner," said Ron with a sly grin. Addressing Loretta, he asked, "Could it have been a woman's voice?"

"A woman's?" she asked, with a look of surprise. "I never thought of that."

Sitting for a moment and thinking on Ron's suggestion, she cleared her throat and with a much deeper voice said, "you got what you deserved."

Looking at Ron, she asked, "Did I sound menacing?"

"I can't say you did, Loretta, but I see what you meant by 'soft gruff.'"

"You think it might be a woman who shot Jimmy? His wife, maybe?"

"We're keeping all avenues open, Loretta. We don't think it was his wife as she has a solid alibi at his time of death."

"Well, at least she has someone who knows what she'll be going through."

"Why do you say that?" asked Tim.

"I'm sure you know about the cop shot to death about a week ago."

"Yeah, what about him?" asked Ron.

"Jimmy told me that his wife and the other cop's wife were high school classmates and best of friends."

# CHAPTER 8

**"Get this cocksucker** out of the car," roared Bruno, while wiping Hector's spit from his face.

Jocko exited the back seat and with remarkable agility for a 300-pound man, appeared to dance his way around the vehicle before stopping at Hector's door.

Throwing the door open, Jocko's enormous and powerful right hand grabbed Hector by the throat and pulled him from the car.

Having a firm grasp of his throat, Jocko held the gasping Hector high above his head, as if he were a trophy. Jocko regarded the undercover spy for a moment, before tossing him onto the white-stone driveway as if he were nothing but a child's broken and battered doll.

Hector's head hit the ground hard, face first. The sharp stones tore skin from his cheeks, nose, and forehead. As blood dripped down his face, he slowly rolled over into a sitting position. The first thing he saw was the silencer, attached to Mike's Glock, pointing at his head. Standing at his feet was Jocko, looking like a bigger version of King Kong. The blackjack in his right hand was smacking, *slap, slap, slap*, the palm of his left.

Hector knew it was the end. He also knew it would be painful. Excruciatingly so.

A car door slammed and moments later Bruno stepped from behind Jocko looking like a creature straight out of hell. The fury in his face turned Hector's blood cold.

"I don't like spitters!" roared Bruno as he lifted his right foot and slammed it down onto Hector's chest. The force of the blow was such that not a drop of air remained in Hector's lungs, nor could he gather the strength to take another breath.

Another right foot kick to Hector's right side shattered three ribs and now he was spitting up blood.

"I said I didn't like spitters!" screamed the infuriated Bruno, while kicking Hector in the face, and breaking his nose which resulted in even more blood staining the white stones.

"Get him into the room," ordered Bruno.

Minutes later, Hector, his hands tied behind his back, was hanging upside-down from the ceiling in a room resembling a small dungeon. Below him, Hector could see a large dark stain on the dirt floor. He recognized it as dried blood. Now his bleeding mouth and nose were adding to it. He knew before much longer, he would contribute much more.

A mellow sounding Bruno appeared, saying, "I'll tell you what, Hector. Tell us where the flash drive is and I'll have Mike put a bullet in your head. All this pain will end. But don't lie to us. If you do, we'll go to your home and after having some fun, we will do to Corrina what we've done to you. Lei capisce?"

"Go to hell, Bruno," Hector gurgled through spewing blood and broken teeth.

"I see," said Bruno, stepping back. "Okay, have it your way. I hate telling you this, Hector, but now it's Jocko's turn to have some fun."

Turning to the giant, Bruno said, "Go at it, Jocko, but don't kill him... please."

The blackjack dealt out unimaginable pain. Jocko delivered one blow after another to all regions of Hector's body. A blow to the face crushed Hector's left orb. Another smashed his jaw and removed a half-dozen teeth. It shattered knees, broke elbows, crushed feet and hands, and gruesomely beat Hector's manhood to an unrecognizable pulp.

The Jocko beating lasted but 10 minutes. When finished, Hector, barely conscious, was only minutes away from blissful death.

"Hector, can you hear me?" said Bruno softly. "Hector, I don't want to do this to your wife. Tell me where you hid the flash drive and we'll end this pain. Do this, and I give you my word that no harm will come to Corrina."

Opening his one remaining eye, Hector looked into Bruno's and whispered, "Someday, someone will come for you Bruno, and send you straight to hell."

His ire, raised by the dying man's condemnation, prompted Bruno to draw a knife from his coat and cut out Hector's tongue.

"Know this, Hector. Your silence has sealed Corrina's fate. She will suffer, that I swear to you. I promise she will curse you with her last dying breath."

Hector somehow extended the middle finger of his left hand.

"Kill this mother, Mike, but don't bury him. I want his body found. We need to send someone a message!"

A shot to the head, followed by two more, just for effect, ended the pain of Hector Falano.

The man known as Ramon Ruiz, was dead. Some knew him as a hero.

In time, others would also know Hector Falano as a hero.

# CHAPTER 9

**It was approaching** 9:30 when the two FBI agents rang the doorbell. Vivian Hanson, the mother of Peggy Patterson, wearing a blue robe over pink pajamas and a pair of white fluffy slippers, answered the door.

"Hello, ma'am. I'm Special Agent Ron Lee of the FBI. This is my partner, Agent Tim Pond. We are here to speak with Mrs. Peggy Patterson."

"I'm Peggy's mom, Vivian Hanson," replied the woman, who, for being 54-years-old, appeared to be much younger. Her face, free of wrinkles, was tight, blemished only by an obviously once-broken nose. Ron guessed that she was either wearing dentures or had some excellent work done on her front teeth. Her body, from what they could tell, was lean and supple, and her long black hair was free of any hint of gray. It was her eyes, however, that dispelled her age. They had a glint that said she could still play the game and play it well. "My daughter is, as one might expect, distraught, Agent Lee. Could you return at a later time?"

"We are sorry for what happened tonight, Mrs. Hanson…"

"Please, call me Vivian."

"Okay… Vivian. We understand what your daughter is going through, but it is important that we speak with her this evening."

"Very well. If you must. Please come in. Can I get you something to drink? I made a fresh pot of coffee just 20 minutes ago."

"I'll take a cup," said Tim, never showing shyness when it involved free food or drink. "Just cream, please."

"Okay, young man, I'll have that for you in just a minute. Peggy is in the sunroom, out back. Just follow this hallway toward the back of the house."

Ron noted the vestibule. He suspected the door on the right wall was a coat closet. Hugging the left wall was a small table holding a green tiffany lamp. Hanging on the wall above the table was a small plaque shaped like a large key. There were a half-dozen hooks embedded in the plaque, and all but one had keys dangling from them.

"Thank you, Vivian," said Ron as he hastened toward the rear of the house.

A minute later, the agents were sitting on a two seat couch. A small coffee table separated them from Peggy Patterson who occupied a recliner in the laid-back position. She had a cold compress on her forehead.

"We are sorry for your loss, Mrs. Patterson."

"Please, call me Peggy."

Peggy Patterson was her mother's child, no doubt. She had the same facial features, the body of a model, and the same look in her eyes that her mother exhibited.

*Why would Patterson cheat on this woman?* thought Tim. *She's drop-dead gorgeous.*

Ron was thinking the same thoughts but had questions that needed answering and so he asked, "Why did you leave the note on the outside door, Peggy?"

"What do you mean?" asked the woman, her eyes showing a momentary glimpse of being caught off-guard.

"Why not just leave a note inside where your husband would see it? That small table in the foyer would seem like the spot to leave a note. I'm guessing he hung his keys on the plague above the table. Correct?"

Peggy's eyes darted from Ron's to Tim's as she sought to find a plausible answer.

"Yes, I guess I could have done that, but... well, I don't know why I stuck the note on the outside door. I just did, is all! What in the hell does the positioning of the damn note have to do with my husband's murder?"

Ron avoided answering her question as he asked another of his own.

"Have you ever attended a Tupperware party before, Peggy?"

"No. Why?"

"Why did you go to this one?"

"It was my mom's party!"

"Did anyone else, your age, attend?"

"No. Other than myself, it was all of my mom's friends," she answered with a look of bewilderment. "What does my mom's party have to do with Jimmy's murder?"

"Where were you on the night of January 8th, Peggy?"

"I don't recall," she answered without giving it much thought. "Why?"

"I would think you could remember where you were when someone murdered a good friend's husband. That seems reasonable. Wouldn't you agree?"

"Yes... I would think so," she murmured, but then, after a short pause, blurted, "We were home!"

"We?"

"Yes, Jimmy and I. Tuesday is Jimmy's day off. We watched tv most of the night."

"What were you watching between 6:00 and 8:00 that night?" asked Tim.

"Let's see, we watched the local news..."

"Which local news? What channel?"

"Channel 10. We always watch Channel 10."

"What else?"

"I made dinner… macaroni and cheese and a slice of ham. Afterwards, we cleaned up the kitchen, and then we watched Family Feud and Jeopardy."

"The Feud and Jeopardy? Are you sure that was the night someone murdered Jesse Bennington?" asked Ron.

"Yes, because I remember the family, an Asian family… very smart… won $20,000 dollars on The Feud. And I had to listen to Jimmy bragging about getting the answer to the final Jeopardy question which was something about the space program. I think it was the name of an astronaut."

"Is there anyone who can verify you were home?" asked Ron.

"No, there isn't. The only person who could, my husband, is now dead! Where is this line of questioning going, Agent Lee? Do you think I had something to do with Jesse Bennington's murder?"

Ron's phone rang before he could reply. Seeing it was Bill Baxter calling, he excused himself and went into the living room where he could talk without being overheard.

"Yeah, what is it, Bill?"

*"Sheila Bennington, Ron."*

"Yeah, what about her? Can she account for her time tonight?"

*"Yeah, she can, Ron, and it's airtight."*

"Oh, how's that?"

*"She's in Charlotte."*

"Charlotte!"

*"Yeah. Her mom lives there. She's staying with her for a while."*

"Damn!" said Ron, as he hung up. His "one hand washing the other" theory, just went down the drain.

# CHAPTER 10

**As they drove** to their office, Tim asked, "What in the hell was that all about, Ron?"

"What do you mean?"

"Those questions you were asking her."

"Which questions?" replied an irritated Ron.

"The question concerning the note left on the outside door, for one."

"I was thinking she knew it wouldn't be her husband coming home, but more likely it would be someone to inform her of his death. Why else would she leave a note on the outside door? My wife left notes hanging on the fridge."

"Gee, what a surprise! You, heading to the fridge as soon as you walked in the house. Never would have guessed it."

"Oh, is that right? Well, can you guess I'm on the lookout for a new partner?" Then after a pause, Ron added, "A silent partner."

"What about the Tupperware question?" asked Tim, ignoring his partner's hollow threat.

"Did you know they had such things, anymore, Tim? I didn't."

"Neither did I, Ron. In fact, I never gave it a thought. I would have guessed though, that you would know more about Tupperware, since that's where your wife kept the food."

"You just never quit, do you? It's just my luck, that of all the guys who could have been my partner, I get stuck with the only asshole in the bunch."

"Is that a little Bogart I'm hearing?" asked Tim.

"What are you talking about?"

"I'm talking about a classic movie line."

"What classic movie line?"

"This one," said Tim, pausing a moment before beginning his impersonation of the old Hollywood star. "Of all the gin joints in all the towns, in all the world, she walks into mine."

"I'm right," said Ron with a big grin. "You are a dick of huge proportions."

"Wilma would disagree with you on that point. And I'm sorry to admit, she would win the argument. Now, what about the Tupperware party?"

"It's a perfect alibi, but it's an improbable situation. This young woman goes to a Tupperware party where the next youngest person is more than twice her age. What's the commonality? There is none! How does she converse with them? She doesn't. She can't!"

"Maybe," interrupted Tim, "she says things like, 'Hey, I see gravity hit those boobs hard, eh'? or 'What are you doing for those deep wrinkles in your cheeks?' or maybe even asking, 'How's that dry vagina thing working out for you'?"

"That's my point, Tim. Nothing in common. The whole thing doesn't add up. It's just too pat in my mind."

"Let's check out her story about being home watching tv. We can see if what she said about the winners of The Feud and Jeopardy's final question are true."

"We could, but it won't do us any good."

"Why not?" asked an annoyed Tim.

"They have a DVR. She could have recorded the shows and played them back to establish her alibi."

"Oh, yeah," said Tim, angry with himself for not thinking of something so obvious. "Maybe a lab technician could determine if she taped them," suggested Tim.

"I'm not sure if that's possible, but we'd need a damn strong case to get a warrant to look at her DVR. As it now stands, we have no case at all."

"How do we know if her husband was home, Ron? That other cop we met tonight…"

"Clyde Garrett?"

"Yeah, Clyde. He more or less admitted that Patterson was a skirt chaser. He may have been poon hunting the night Bennington got whacked."

"Yeah, Tim, that's a strong possibility. Let's contact lover-boy Clyde and ask him where Patterson liked to do his hunting."

"I'll get on it first thing tomorrow, Ron."

Tomorrow, however, would be too late.

# CHAPTER 11

**"What do you** mean he's dead!" shouted Cameron Driscoll. "Dead men can't talk, Bruno! He can't tell us where the flash drive is, you stupid asshole!"

"Sorry, boss, but Jocko got carried away with his blackjack."

"Jocko? Oh, so now you're blaming Jocko. You're the damn leader! You're the one responsible for making sure things don't get out of hand. Not that retarded asshole Jocko!"

"Ye... Ye... Yessir," Bruno stammered.

"Did you bury the body?"

Bruno, hearing the question and realizing he had made a huge mistake, turned as white as a ghost.

Driscoll, seeing Bruno's reaction, screamed, "WHAT! What's that look about? What the hell did you do with his goddam body, you ass wipe?"

"We dumped it in an abandoned parking garage in Cherry Grove. I thought you would want to send a message."

"You… you thought I… would want to send a message? Is that right? You thought I would want to send a message using the dead body of a SLED undercover agent? Are you out of your goddamn mind!"

"I thought…"

"You thought? You thought, Bruno? Just what the hell did you think? That I was an idiot! Is that what you thought!"

"No. No. I thought…"

"Shut the hell up! Do you know what you've done? The fucking FBI, along with SLED, and who knows who else... the damn U.S. Army, Navy, and Marine Corps will be all over and up our asses. Don't you realize that a body not found is a mystery? No one knows what the hell happened to the guy. He could have skipped town. He might have drowned in the damn ocean and carried out to sea where sharks ate him. Hell, who knows, maybe aliens abducted him and took him to fucking Mars! But no, that's not the case, is it, Bruno?"

Bruno, being scolded as if he were a five-year-old child, answered an almost inaudible, "No, boss."

"Thanks to your brilliance, everyone who is anyone knows that someone tortured and murdered an undercover SLED agent."

"Maybe," said a humiliated Bruno, "they haven't found the body yet. Maybe we could retrieve it and bury it."

"Yeah, why don't you go do that, Bruno. If the law is there, just walk right up to them, excuse yourself, and explain to them you're there to pick up a dead body. I'm sure they won't mind you taking a stiff off their hands."

"It might be worth a try, boss."

"Yeah," said Cameron, doubting their chances. "Go see if it's still there. If it is, you better get rid of it. Quick! If the FBI isn't there already, they soon will be. If that's the case, it's mandatory that we find that flash drive before they do or else we're all dead men."

"There's one more thing, boss," muttered Bruno, with a look of deep regret.

"Oh, and what might that be?"

"Hector's wife."

"Corrina? What did you do to Hector's wife?"

Bruno's eyes darted around the room and he tried to moisten his lips with a tongue that was dryer than sand.

"What about her, Bruno!"

"We took her out too."

"YOU WHAT!" screamed Cameron "Are you shitting me?"

"I thought she might know..."

"There you go thinking again, Bruno. I don't pay you to think! What did you do with her body?"

"We left it on the bed."

"You left it on the bed? On the bed! YOU LEFT HER BODY ON THE BED! JUST HOW STUPID ARE YOU?" screamed an apoplectic Cameron Driscoll.

"We thought she might know where he hid the drive."

"And?"

"No," Bruno admitted as his eyes found the floor.

"That's brilliant, Bruno. Just brilliant. Tell me, did you rape her? How about Jocko and Mike? Did they join in the fun? Did you torture her and leave blood everywhere? Were you thinking that I wanted to leave another message!"

Bruno, his eyes wide and terrified, nodded, yes.

"Yes? Yes what? You raped her?"

"Yes."

"Jocko and Mike?"

"Yes, they raped her."

"Let me guess. You tortured her and left blood everywhere?"

"Yeah."

"Get out of my office! You better go get her body because when the FBI gets your DNA... well, Bruno, I'd say, you're as good as dead."

As the door closed behind Bruno, Cameron Driscoll pulled his phone from the pocket of his $1500 tailored suit.

He punched in a three-digit code and within moments, without saying hello, he was speaking to someone.

"I'll be needing your services."

He paused, then said, "Three liquidations."

Following another pause, he said, "Two cops and a judge."

After two minutes of listening, he said, "Ten thousand each is much too steep, don't you think? How about $25,000 for all three, and I'll throw in some inside tidbits my undercover man passed on to me this week. I'm sure knowing this information would be to your benefit."

Hearing the contractor's acceptance of the terms, Driscoll replied, "Good. I'll send half the cash and the info over tonight. The rest you'll get when you have finished the job. Hey, here's some advice though. Don't make a mess of it."

# CHAPTER 12

**"Let's go, boys,** we need to get to Hector's house and clean up the mess we left."

"Hey, Bruno, it's still daylight. How are we getting the body out of the house without attracting attention?" asked Jocko.

Bruno checked his watch. It was 4:15. It wouldn't be dark until 5:30. He asked himself, *Can I afford to wait over an hour?* He answered himself with an emphatic, *No!*

"Mike, drive up to the garage and see if they have found Hector's body. Call me, but not on your phone. Use your burner. We'll park near Hector's house waiting for your call."

"If they haven't found his body, what do you want me to do?"

"Put him in your trunk and get him to the burial grounds. We'll meet you there."

"And if they have discovered the body?"

"Get the hell out of there! Wait for us at the burial grounds."

\*\*\*\*\*\*\*\*\*\*\*\*\*

Both parties had reached their destinations in less than 15 minutes.

Bruno, wanting to survey Hector's house for any police activity, had Jocko park a block away. Seeing none, Bruno gave thought they hadn't found Hector's body as yet. A minute later he received a call from Mike, confirming his suspicions.

"Get him in your car, Mike. We'll take care of business here. I'll see you in about an hour."

"Go!" Bruno barked to Jocko who already had the car's engine running.

Jocko made his way up the street and pulled into Hector's driveway.

"Jocko, back the car up tight to the garage door."

Bruno's thinking was having the garage attached to the house would give them some cover in getting Corrina's body into the car.

"How much time do we have, Bruno?"

"Let's assume not much. Grab the bags."

Jocko reached into the back seat and grabbed a box of 33 gallon garbage bags. They would hold Corrina's remains, and anything that had blood or incriminating body fluids on it, like sheets, blankets, and towels.

Exiting the car, the two men made their way to the rear door, all the while keeping their eyes peeled for nosy neighbors watching their movements. All seemed clear. They opened the unlocked door and entered. The smell of death had already permeated the house.

Ignoring a smell they knew well; they went to work.

************

Mike, after hanging up with Bruno, made a U-turn and drove back toward the parking garage entrance. He drove into the garage and up to the second level where they had left Hector's body. Turning the corner, he saw the body lying just where they had left it. He maneuvered his car so that the trunk was only a few feet from the body. Popping the trunk, he exited the vehicle and made his way to the rear of the car.

He had just bent down and lifted the body by the shoulders when he heard the sirens. Lots of sirens. As the first police car turned the corner, Mike dropped the body, and headed toward the open driver's door. A second car followed a moment later and then a third. All stopped a good 40 feet away with their drivers abandoning their vehicles and positioning themselves, with sidearms ready, behind each car.

"Put up your hands!" ordered one officer.

Mike realized they had him boxed in. He couldn't get out of the garage with the three police cruisers blocking the exit.

He decided he would talk his way out of the situation.

"I just found him. I was about to call for help."

"Why is your car positioned like that, sir? Why is your trunk open?" asked the officer. "I saw you lifting the body, sir. Get down on the ground! I want your hands clutching the back of your head. Do it now!"

Mike had spent 12 years in various jails and prisons. He promised himself that he'd never go back. He intended to keep that promise.

Edging his way toward the open driver's door, Mike pulled his Glock and squatted behind the half-way closed door. He was an expert marksman and his first shot wounded an officer in the shoulder. That, however, was Mike's only and last hurrah.

The three lawmen sent a hail of 18 bullets his way in a matter of seconds and Mike's body and head absorbed five of them. He was dead before his body hit the cement floor.

It wouldn't be like Driscoll said. Hector would not just up and disappear. He wouldn't leave town; he wouldn't get swept out to sea and eaten by sharks, nor would aliens abduct him and take him to Mars.

Someone had tortured and killed FBI Agent Hector Falano. It was now a whole new ballgame. Law and order still prevailed, but now revenge had joined the fray. If you wanted to play, you had better have your "A" game. Blood spilling was about to begin. There would be a great deal of blood spilled, with all sides making significant contributions.

\*\*\*\*\*\*\*\*\*\*\*\*\*

"You get her body in the bags, Jocko. I'll strip the bed and pick up any towels we used."

Although they tortured Corrina, it was nowhere near the magnitude of that inflicted on Hector. They had spilled Corrina's blood, but only in the bedroom with the sheets and mattress drenched with the sticky bodily fluid.

Ten tedious minutes passed with an anxious Bruno checking the front windows multiple times in hopes of not seeing a police car in the driveway.

The tension, even for these hardcore criminals, was unbearable.

Then Bruno heard Jocko's lament.

"Boss. I can't find one of her fingers."

The tension only got thicker.

They had clipped off two fingers on each of Corrina's hands in hopes of her giving up the flash drive's location, but it was to no avail. The woman was either tougher than they envisioned or she knew nothing of the device.

"Damn! Have you looked under the bed?"

"Yeah, I did. I searched the entire room. It's not here."

"What about the kitchen, Jocko? Isn't that where we started?"

"Not with the tough stuff, boss. That all occurred here in the bedroom."

"It has to be here somewhere, Jocko. I doubt it just got up and walked away on its own!"

"Maybe Mike took it as a souvenir," suggested Jocko.

"Now why would he do that?"

"I don't know. It's just a thought. Why don't you call him?"

The thought had already crossed Bruno's mind. He took his burner phone and dialed Mike's.

*"Hello,"* answered a voice that Bruno didn't recognize.

He immediately hung up.

"That wasn't Mike who answered."

"Oh-oh," mumbled Jocko. "That's not good."

"No. Not good at all," confirmed Bruno. "Get these bags into the garage, Jocko."

It was 4:58. It would be another 30 minutes before total darkness could cover their departure.

They stood in the garage with the bags containing Corrina's body and the bedding lying at their feet. Bruno stood peering out the small window in the door leading to the driveway. Their car, with its trunk cracked open an inch or two, sat just two or three steps away.

"How long should we wait, Bruno?"

Swimming through Bruno's mind were thoughts about when to leave, the missing finger, and how Mike's fate could be affecting theirs.

"I wish we had that damn finger, Jocko."

"I could go back inside, boss. Maybe I missed something."

"Did you look between the mattress and the bed, Jocko? Maybe it slipped between them. Go take a quick look."

"You remade the bed, boss. You would have seen it if it were there. Don't you think?"

Bruno had found some sheets in the bedroom's linen closet and remade the bed. On the outside, it looked like a professional bed-maker had made it. Underneath, however, lay a mattress stained with blood.

"Go look! When you come back, we'll leave."

It was 5:09 when Jocko returned empty-handed.

"No luck, boss."

"Damn! Okay, let's get this done. We're pressing our luck staying here any longer."

Bruno opened the door and with the bag of linens in hand, stepped out to the trunk of the car and opening it wide, tossed the bag inside.

Returning to the garage, he helped lift the bags containing Corrina's lifeless body and together they dropped it into the trunk.

Bruno closed the trunk while Jocko started the vehicle. Reaching the end of the driveway, Jocko made a right turn onto the street and drove away. They were only a dozen houses away when a police car passed going the opposite way. Jocko watched it turn into Hector's driveway. He saw headlights coming from the opposite way. They all converged on Hector's house.

As Bruno watched the gathering of police cars in his side-view mirror, he muttered, "Another minute, Jocko, and we'd be dead."

"Just like Mike," stated Jocko.

"Yeah, just like Mike," agreed Bruno, knowing they would never see him alive again.

# CHAPTER 13

**It was just** after 8:00am on a Saturday morning when Jim Braddock, the head of the Myrtle Beach branch of the FBI, called Ron and Tim into his office.

"Sit down, men."

"Morning, Jim," greeted Ron.

"You guys working on Saturday is surprising. Saved me the effort to call you in."

"We're working on the two cop killings," said Ron.

"Are you making any progress?" asked Braddock.

"We thought we had an angle, but it hit a snag."

"I'm sure you'll figure it out, Ron."

"Why did you call us in here, Jim? What's happening?"

"Dead people."

"Sounds serious."

"It is serious, Ron, and it's personal. There's bad news, and then it gets worse."

"We're listening."

"SLED has had… wait, let me correct that… SLED had a plant in the Driscoll organization for the past three years. His undercover name was Hector Falano."

"Those words, 'had and was,' don't resonate good vibes, Jim," remarked Tim.

"Yeah, you're right," agreed Braddock. "They don't, and for good reason."

"I'm guessing this is the bad news we're about to hear. Right?" asked Ron.

"Yeah, I'm afraid it is," responded a solemn Braddock. "The Horry County Sheriffs received a call yesterday afternoon that there was a man lying in an abandoned parking garage up in Cherry Grove. Three units responded to the call. They arrived in time to see a guy trying to lift the body into his car's open trunk. The officers called the guy out, but he resisted and started shooting. He wounded one cop, but they took him down. He's dead."

"Who was he, Bill?"

"His name is Mike Cora. He worked as a button man for the Mexican cartel. I'm guessing he was up here working for Driscoll's organization."

"I know that name," said Ron. "He came out of Mexico about ten years ago. We thought he did some damage in the Phoenix area when that area was going through a mini drug war."

Braddock nodded his head, and then continued, "The body was that of Hector Falano. Someone, I say someone, but I'm guessing it was more than just one individual, mutilated his body almost beyond recognition. After gouging out his eyes, they cut off his tongue and genitals. After all that, they put three .38 slugs into his head."

"Damn! They tortured him! Whatever he did pissed them off. That's for damn sure," stated Ron.

"You're right. What he had was a flash drive containing information on payoffs to anyone who has the juice to keep the heat off the Driscoll organization. Big names, who, if revealed, would be in jail. He told SLED that he'd deliver it to them today."

"So there goes a big bust, I take it."

"No."

"No? Whatever do you mean by that, Jim?"

"Here's where it gets worse, guys. After killing him, they went to his home. We believe they tortured and killed his wife."

"What do you mean, 'you believe' they killed his wife?" asked Tim.

"When our guys got to the house, they didn't find a body. They did, however, discover a finger in the toilet, and the bedroom mattress stained with blood."

"In the toilet?" Tim asked with a look of disgust.

"I'm guessing they tried to flush away the fact that something happened. The place was pretty well cleaned up. Someone made the bed and hung clean towels in the bathroom. Nothing looked disturbed."

"I'm guessing they threatened to kill his wife if he didn't reveal the whereabouts of the flash drive?"

"Yes, that's also my thinking, Ron."

"I'm also guessing he didn't talk."

"That seems to be the case," agreed Braddock.

"So he gave up his life, and that of his wife to keep them from getting the evidence. What does that tell us?" asked Tim.

"It tells me," said Braddock "he hid what amounts to a bombshell, some place where it may remain until hell freezes over."

"I'm assuming you have searched the obvious; his home, car, clothing."

"Yeah, Ron, and so did someone else long before we did."

"What about a safe deposit box? Did he even have one?"

"He did," responded Braddock, "and we had the bank manager open it up last night. It wasn't there."

"What makes you think the cartel hasn't found it?" Tim asked.

"Because," explained Braddock, "rumor has it they are out on the streets asking who knew Hector's hangouts and friends."

"If that's true, then there are people in harm's way," stated Tim. "Especially those who were acquaintances of Falano."

"You said earlier that it was personal. What did you mean by that, Jim?" asked a curious Ron.

"That, fellas, is the wild card in this scenario."

"And what would that be, Jim?"

"Hector was one of us."

There were a few seconds of pause before Ron ended it with, "He was FBI?"

"Yeah. He was on loan to SLED from our Miami division. I'm told it got too hot for him down there so they transferred him up here to get close to Driscoll's organization."

"It's obvious that he got too close," Tim murmured.

"You didn't know he was undercover, Jim?"

"Nope. A SLED official informed me just last night. I confirmed it with Miami earlier this morning."

"Damn, that's just wrong," voiced Ron with an emphatic pounding of his fist on Jim's desk.

"Maybe so. Regardless, it's in our jurisdiction and I want you guys to work it. Solve the damn case, and just between you and me... I also want bloody revenge."

"I was hoping you'd say that, Jim," stated Ron with a look of dead seriousness.

"Good. I'll talk with you later, fellas. Go get started. Let me know about anything important ASAP."

As they headed back toward their office, Tim said, "People will die, Ron. This is a ruthless bunch."

"Yeah, you're right, partner. Maybe we should call Driscoll to warn him not to let his life insurance lapse."

# CHAPTER 14

**The previous evening** Bruno had returned to his boss's home to report what had happened.

Hearing Bruno's explanation sent Cameron into a tirade.

"Just how stupid are you, Bruno?"

"I don't know but I think you're about to tell me, boss."

"Don't get cute with me, Bruno. Everyone is expendable."

Bruno swallowed hard and then apologized for his remark.

"Why did you bother going to his house? All you had to do is get rid of Hector's body. If someone can't find Hector, then nothing gets reported. Who would report him missing? His wife? No! She's dead. Us? Not unless we're total idiots."

"I wasn't thinking like that, boss. My thoughts centered on the DNA evidence we left behind."

"Yeah, I get it, Bruno, but if you had taken care of Hector first, then you would have had all the time you needed to deal with Corrina."

"Mike's dead."

"What!"

"I sent him to check on Hector. I don't know what happened, but when I called him, someone else answered his burner phone."

"Well, at least you had enough sense to use burner phones."

"There's something else," said Bruno, barely audible.

"Do I dare ask?"

"We couldn't find a finger."

"I… I… I'm sorry, Bruno, but say again."

"I'm afraid that Mike got a little carried away with Corrina. Hoping that she would reveal the drive's whereabouts, he cut off a few of her fingers. When we were bagging her body, Jocko noticed that a finger was missing. We searched everywhere but…"

"I'm blown away by your stupidity, Bruno."

"Yes, sir."

"How many fingers did Mike remove?"

"Four."

"Four? Is there someone amongst you that can count that high? Maybe you miscounted?"

"I don't think so," answered Bruno while boiling inside.

"Have you looked in the obvious locations to find that disk, Bruno?"

"I have already searched their house, cars and clothing, boss."

"Do you think that should impress me? I don't think so, Bruno. I recall that you can't find a finger you cut off a woman. Why would I think you're capable of finding that damn disk?"

"What do we do if we can't find it?"

"We will liquidate some of our assets, Bruno. I have already instructed The Ghost to get started. There are a few people who will fold early once it becomes known about the flash drive."

"What can Jocko and I do?"

"Oh, well for starters, Bruno, how about finding that damn flash drive! Start talking to his acquaintances. Ask about where he liked to hang out after work. Check on all his activities. I have someone who works for SLED who may provide us with some inside information that would help us uncover the flash drive's location."

"He may have kept it in a bank, boss."

"Yeah, I thought of that," said Cameron, annoyed that Bruno had also thought of it. "Nothing I can do about it though. We'll know soon enough if that's where it is."

"How's that, boss?"

"How's that? Because the goddamn law will beat down our doors, dumbass, that's how."

"Oh, yeah," said Bruno, feeling stupid for asking such an obvious question.

"Get out of my sight before I have Jocko hang you from a ceiling and beat your balls to a pulp. Find the damn drive, Bruno. When you get it, bring it to me on the double."

Bruno left and as he walked out to his car he mumbled to himself, "He shouldn't talk to me like that. It makes me mad."

# CHAPTER 15

**Driving to Conway** in January takes about a fourth the time than it does in July.

"I love this time of the year, Tim."

"Oh, and why is that, partner?"

"Why the hell do you think! Look around you. There ain't but a dozen cars out here on 501 compared to the two million you find every damn day in July. And, it's about 50 degrees cooler."

"You like it cool, Ron?"

"Yeah, I do."

"Then how come you got the heat set on 78 on your side, and the fans goin' full blast?"

Seeing a Dunkin' Donuts, Ron ignored Tim's question, saying, "Hey pull into the donut place. I'll buy you a small coffee."

"No."

"Okay, a medium coffee."

"No! You think you can buy me off with a cup of coffee? A small one at that, you cheap bastard."

"Everyone has a price, Tim. What's yours? You want a large, I'll buy you a large."

"Hey, I'm not stopping at any fast-food joint until you pass your physical. You want to kill yourself, do it on your own time. I won't be an accessory to your murder!"

"You may not be aware of this little known fact, Tim, but donuts are healthier than opioids."

"Yeah, well, so is a salad," Tim retorted.

"You're a prick. I hope you know that."

"My wife told me that long ago, and she repeats it much more often than you do, and it's usually accompanied with the word 'little.'"

Once again there was silence as the two bickering agents completed their journey to the county morgue.

They arrived at the Coroner's Office at 10:15, where Margie Haskins, the receptionist, greeted their unexpected arrival.

"Well, looky here, if it ain't the F-B-I. What brings you boys to town?"

"Dead bodies, Margie," replied Ron. "Why do you ask? Does the morgue now serve lunch?"

"First, that sounds disgusting. Second, if you keep talking to me like that, I'll offer you a dose of good old-fashioned wup ass."

"Yikes, I better unholster my gun, Tim. We got us a bad ass in our midst."

The three joked amongst themselves for few more minutes before Ron asked the whereabouts of Robert Edge, the longtime coroner of Horry county. Told he was autopsying a body, they said goodbye to Margie, and made their way to the morgue.

Entering through a pair of swinging doors, they saw Edge near the back of the room. He stood over a stainless steel gurney that held something that resembled a human being. Even from 30 feet away, the body of Hector Falano appeared grotesque.

Edge looked up to see the two agents, and said, "I'm guessing you are here to talk about this fella, Ron."

"Yes, if that's Hector Falano. How are you doing?"

"I've seen a lot of broken bodies come through here, Ron, the worst of which was that of Tanner Bruckman."

Edge was referring to the district attorney run over multiple times in the Conway City Hall parking lot the previous Thanksgiving eve.

"This guy, however, comes a close second."

"What can you tell us, Robert?"

"I can tell you that where they found Falano was not where they killed him."

"How's that?" asked Tim.

"Two reasons. First, his body is bled out. The blood in the garage was minimal. In fact, I believe they hung him upside down before killing him."

"What makes you say that?" Ron asked with more than a bit of curiosity.

"Well, they aerated his head with a three .38 slugs. That allowed most of the blood to flow from his body, but before they shot him, they tortured him."

Pulling back the sheet to expose Hectors entire body, Edge said, "See these blood trails along his torso."

"Yeah," the two agents replied in unison.

"They are not running down his body or even sideways. They are running from his crotch up toward his chest. Whoever did this, cut off his genitals. That bleeding caused these blood trails. He had to be hanging by the feet to have created those."

"You said there were two reasons the kill zone wasn't the garage, Bob. What's the second?"

"See these cuts on his face, Ron?"

"Yeah, what about them?"

"The garage's cement floor didn't do that. White marble stones caused these wounds."

"White marble?"

"Yeah, it's a decorative stone used around trees or in plant beds," Edge explained.

"I wonder how he got those?" asked Tim. "Someone must have thrown him facedown or maybe he tripped."

"There's little doubt in my mind that someone threw him down," Edge suggested with conviction.

"Why would you say that, Bob?"

"I found bruises on his throat, Ron. They suggest it was someone's fingers."

"He was being choked?" Tim asked.

"It's possible, but in most cases when someone is choking someone, they use two hands. A right hand caused these bruises. The direction of the bruised skin tells me that whoever did this held this man up by the neck."

"That, Robert, would take one strong son-of-a-bitch."

"Yes, Ron, it would. If you run into this guy, I suggest you shoot him before he gets his hands on you."

"I believe that is sound advice. We will adhere to your warning, my friend," Ron said while nodding his agreement.

"What about the other guy?" asked Tim.

"You mean the dumbass that tried to shoot it out with three cops and got shot five times for his trouble?"

"That's the one!" Tim exclaimed with false delight.

"Two things I can tell you," said Edge as he walked across the room where another gurney sat with a body covered by a white sheet.

"And they are?" asked Ron.

"He's the guy who cut off the woman's finger," Robert declared as he pulled back the sheet to reveal the naked, bullet ravaged body of Michael Cora.

"You know this, how?"

"The knife he used was in his jacket pocket and the blood on it matched the woman's."

"And the second thing?"

"I believe he used his gun to shoot your boy. It was a .38. There were no bullets in your boy's head, so a ballistics match is impossible, but the odds are..."

"What does this guy weigh, Bob?"

"He weighed in at 154."

"And what about Hector?"

"He weighed in at 173, but remember, he's missing some parts and his blood volume was near zero. I'm guessing he weighed close to 180."

"So Cora couldn't have handled Hector all by himself. Right?"

"Agreed, Ron. Also, in Hector's case, you're talking 'dead weight' in the truest sense of the word."

"Good point, Bob."

"This is also not the guy who bruised Hector's throat. He wouldn't have had the strength. Besides, although I haven't done a comparison, it looks like his hands are too small to have made those marks."

"Is there anything else you can tell us, Bob?"

"Yeah. Someone kicked your boy in the face wearing a black leather boot. It left bits of the boot imbedded in his nose. Whoever did that, also stomped on his chest leaving two outstanding details."

"I'm eager to hear what those two outstanding details are, Bob." Tim said as he jotted down almost every word Edge spoke.

"First, the man's shoe size is either an 11 or 12. I determined that by the size of the bruise on Hector's chest."

"And the second thing?"

"White marble particles."

"What about white marble particles, Bob?" asked Ron, annoyed by Edge's half-answers.

"White marble dust particles covered the bottom of the stomper's shoe," replied Edge. "It left a plethora of dust particles embedded in Hector's shirt."

"That means he was lying on the ground when they first started roughing him up."

"Most likely," agreed Edge.

"I have a friend who has beds filled with that marble stone," offered Tim.

"So?" asked Ron.

"Surrounding the beds is his driveway and his grassy lawn."

"What's your point, Tim?" asked a Ron, losing his patience.

"Patience, Ron. I'm formulating a question for Robert, not for you!"

"What's the question, Tim?" asked Robert smiling at the two bickering agents.

"You said dust particles covered the bottom of the shoe. Correct?"

"Yeah, that's right."

"Let's say I step off a driveway or grass into a bed of white marble stones and stomp someone. Would I leave notable dust particles on my victim's shirt?"

Edge pondered the question for a moment, before replying.

"If how you described it, Tim, was the full extent of contact with the stones, I would have to say no. There would only be traces. Where are you going with this?"

"Yeah, partner. What the hell is your point?"

"I'm wondering if the white marble area isn't a flower bed, but maybe a road or, more likely, a driveway."

"Now that's a strong possibility, partner. Why don't we, in our spare time, drive around the countryside and search for white marble driveways?"

"Maybe it won't take that much effort, Ron."

"Meaning?"

"I'll let you know after I've done some research."

"I'm sorry to interrupt this biting conversation, fellas," said an annoyed Robert, "but I need to get back to work. However, before I kick the two of you out of my office, there's one other thing you should know. Whoever inflicted this beating, did so with a blackjack."

"A blackjack? You're sure?"

"I'm positive, Ron."

"Thanks, Robert, for your time," Ron uttered. "It is my belief that over the course of the next few weeks, we'll be seeing a lot of you."

"Hey fellas," called Robert, stopping them before they reached the doorway.

"If you're going after whoever did this, and I hope you catch the son-of-a-bitches, you best be careful. These people aren't human. You'll be dealing with the devil incarnate. If, in fact, I see you two sooner rather than later, I would hope you are standing around my table, not lying on it."

Ron and Tim both absorbed Edge's ominous remark and nodding their heads, left without returning a reply.

# CHAPTER 16

**The drive from** Garden City to Hilton Head took almost four hours, with a stop for lunch, but The Ghost was in no hurry. He couldn't complete his task until late that evening, so time and distance was no factor. The expedient return home, however, required that the job went smoothly. He had calculated he would complete the task and be back on the road by midnight. If all went well, he'd be back in his bed by 4:00am and could catch a solid six hours of sleep before reporting to his job.

Sgt. Harold Sutcliff was tonight's target. Sutcliff was an 11-year veteran of the Beaufort County Sheriff's Office. He didn't work in the field, but he was an important cog in the Public Information Division. Sutcliff was in charge of the Evidence and Property Management division of the department.

Eight years earlier, Sutcliff was in dire financial straits and his $43,000 a year salary wasn't cutting it.

He was four payments behind on his mortgage, and three on his two-year-old car. Adding to those woes, he owed a large sum of money to a bookie who didn't play games with people who didn't pay, even if they were cops.

Married with two children, he was contemplating suicide. He had swallowed his firearm on two occasions but didn't have the balls to pull the trigger. He was, however, getting close. It was a hot, sticky August night in 2011, when Sutcliff set his mind to do it. But then along came Bruno Lorenza, a bartender at a bar in Bluffton, seven miles from Hilton Head. It was an oasis where guys like Sutcliff went to drown their sorrows and contemplate suicide.

"Hey, what's the matter, buddy? You seem down in the dumps," whispered Bruno, who already knew all there was to know about Sutcliff and his problems.

"Nothing you can help me with, Bruno."

"Try me. I might surprise you."

"Oh, yeah. Can you pay my mortgage for me, my car payments, or get a dangerous man off my back?"

"A dangerous man? Aren't you a cop?" asked Bruno, acting incredulous.

"Yeah, but this guy is out of my league. He doesn't care what you are. It's either pay him or…"

"Hmm, what if I could help you with all of that? What would it be worth to you, Harold, if I could relieve you of all your problems? What if I could do that… and, put some cash in your pocket so that this would never happen again."

"How, Bruno, with you being a bartender, could you do something, like what you're suggesting, for me?"

"I have a friend who needs a favor from a guy like you, Harold. A friend who would relieve you of your financial obligation problems and get that monkey in Beaufort off your back."

"It sounds illegal."

"Maybe it is, maybe it isn't. I'll tell you one thing though."

"What's that?"

"It's better than being dead."

And so, Sgt. Harold Sutcliff sold his soul to Cameron Driscoll. Occasionally, he would perform a favor. The favor was always the same. Make case evidence, against Driscoll associates, disappear or, better yet for Sutcliff, have it turn out to be false evidence.

For the next eight years, everything was fine. They only called upon Sutcliff for a 'favor' a half-dozen times and he always came through, as did the organization. Sutcliff's cop salary didn't go up much over the years, but he paid off his mortgage, bought a new car, and sent his son to The Citadel.

Sutcliff had a solid reputation of delivering favors, but his dossier contained a one-word note that sounded alarms.

The word was: suicidal.

They knew that Harold would jump ship if the boat were to take on water.

The hidden flash drive hung over the organization's head like a lead balloon leading them to believe it best to remove all risks. They considered Sutcliff to be a risk.

Sutcliff was working the 3:00 to 11:00 shift when early in the day he received a call that the organization needed a favor. He was to meet his contact at the usual spot.

The usual spot was the Pinckney Wildlife Preserve under the William Hilton Parkway on a piece of land known as Last End Point. It was desolate, difficult to get to, and dark. It was perfect for subterfuge.

What some would call subterfuge, others would call murder.

Sutcliff arrived at 11:20 and U-turned his car so it was pointing toward the exit. The road ended just a hundred yards behind him. He sat there in the darkness, his window cracked just enough to hear the animal and insect sounds emanating from the swamp that sandwiched his car.

An unexpected tap on the window caused Sutcliff's bladder to spit a small stream of urine.

"Damn!" he whispered.

Not wanting his contact to see his dampened pants, Sutcliff rolled down the window. Standing a few feet from his door stood an image whose face Harold could not see.

"Bob?" asked Harold.

"Bob couldn't make it tonight, Harold. Step out of the car."

"Where's Bob? Bob is the only contact I know. I don't know you. You could be anybody!"

"I could be, but I'm not. Step out of the car."

Now fear entered the picture. Seeing no other vehicle, Harold asked, "Hey, where's your car?"

The Ghost told Harold the truth.

"I parked up the road about a half-mile or so."

"I didn't see any car on the road."

"It's parked in the circular road on your left as you came in."

Harold knew the spot.

"Why?"

"Stop asking questions, Harold. Get out of the car."

"Why? I don't know you. I'm leaving!"

Harold's finger never made it to the button that would have started the car. The .22 bullet entered his left ear and split into multiple fragments as it passed through his brain, killing him instantly. Harold slumped sideways, with his ear spewing blood that ran down his cheek and neck onto the center console.

"Damn you, Harold," whispered The Ghost. "I was hoping not to get any blood on me. Maybe I can still do this so I won't."

Opening the car door, he pushed Harold's body over so his head, still gushing gobs of blood, was hanging above the passenger seat. Tipping Harold over gave The Ghost enough room to occupy the driver's seat. Putting his foot on the brake, he started the car and turned the steering wheel to the left as far as he could.

"Now the hard part," said The Ghost aloud.

Putting his foot on the brake, and grabbing the gearshift, he slid it downward from park toward drive. It stopped midway in the neutral position. It stopped because Harold's rib cage was pressing against it.

"Damn you, Harold!"

Leaving the car, The Ghost walked around to the other side, opened the passenger door, reached in and grabbed the 200 pound Harold by the shoulders and pulled. Harold didn't budge.

"Damn you, Harold!" cried The Ghost again, only this time in an octave much higher than his first damning of his victim.

Climbing into the car, he positioned his knees on the passenger seat. Taking Harold's left arm, which had wedged itself between the console and the driver's seat, he raised it while also pulling it toward the back seat. As he was doing this, he felt a warmness on his knees. Reaching down and feeling the sticky blood on his fingers, he realized that the wound in Harold's head had leaked blood onto the seat. The worst of it was that his pants were absorbing it like a sponge.

"I don't know who the bigger asshole is, Harold, you or me."

Lifting Harold's arm up over the back of the front seats resulted in Harold's ribs no longer pressing against the gearshift.

The Ghost began backing out of the front seat, but when he let Harold's arm go, the dead cop fell back into his original position. The gearshift was once again, immovable.

He sat there motionless for a moment. Driscoll's last words to him, *"Don't make a mess of it,"* rang loud and clear in his mind.

Repeating the lifting of his arm resulted in the same end, the blocked gear shift.

"Well, damn, I'm full of blood now, so what the hell," he said aloud to whatever critters might be listening.

He returned to the driver's side. Reaching in, he righted Harold, but in doing so, Harold's head flopped from the right to the left, showering The Ghost's face with blood and brain matter.

"Remind me not to do it this way ever again," he told his alter-ego.

With Harold sitting up straight and the car running, The Ghost reached in and put the car in drive. Like all cars, when the brake is not engaged, it began creeping forward. It found the swamp and a minute later was sinking fast. He watched until it disappeared. Satisfied that it would be some time before anyone would find the vehicle, he began the half-mile trek to his car.

It was already 12:30am when he got on the road back to Garden City. He had disposed of his blood-soaked pants in a section of woods far from the murder scene. A bottle of drinking water he carried in his car, cleansed the blood and brain particles from his face. Wearing only his underwear and a blood-blotch t-shirt, that he had turned inside-out, he drove home. He gave consideration to driving without a shirt but decided that it might attract unwanted attention.

Driving with the utmost of care, he hoped to avoid getting pulled over. He dreaded the thought of having to kill a guy on the job.

# CHAPTER 17

**"So who's the** guy we're looking for, Bruno?"

"His name is Jose Perez."

"Who is he supposed to be?" asked Jocko.

"I'm told he would know where Hector hung out in his free time and with whom."

They were driving down Business 17 around 3$^{rd}$ Avenue North when Bruno spotted the place he was looking for. It was 7:30am, and the roads were all but empty as expected in Myrtle Beach during the month of January.

"Pull in here, Jocko."

"Hey, a good choice, Bruno. I could go for a hot cup of joe and a donut."

"We're here on business, not to feed your face."

"Can't we kill two birds with one stone, Bruno?"

Ignoring Jocko, Bruno exited the car and entered the shop known as The Donut Man. The restaurant was roomy and clean. Both square and round tables filled the room. A dozen or more people sat enjoying a calorie-filled breakfast while either chatting, reading the paper, or watching the news on the large tv hanging on a wall.

Bruno, with Jocko right behind, marched to the counter and waited while a woman took five minutes to buy a half-dozen donuts. Seeing the vast donut selection, Bruno understood the delay. When the lady completed her purchase, the clerk, asked, "May I help you, sir?"

Deciding not to be outright blunt, Bruno ordered a glazed donut and a large black coffee.

"So much for business," sneered Jocko in a hush.

When the girl returned with his order, he asked, "Do you know a Jose Perez? I understand he's a regular customer of this establishment."

"Oh, yeah, he sure is. That's him sitting on the couch reading the paper."

Bruno glanced back over his shoulder and saw the man to whom the counter-girl was pointing.

"Ahh, yes, that's him. Thank you, miss."

Bruno began walking away when the girl said, "Excuse me, sir, but that will be $4.15 for the coffee and the donut."

"Oh, my friend here needs to order. He'll get it."

Jocko gave Bruno of look that spoke of a plethora of four-letter words.

"Okay," said the girl, "and what will you have, sir?"

Before ordering, Jocko leaned across the glass counter and whispered, "That man is a cheap prick."

Hearing this unexpected remark, the girl blanched, then recovering, nodded her head, while asking, "What would you like, sir?"

As Jocko was ordering, Bruno made his way to the couch where Jose Perez was sitting. Jose had placed his cup of coffee and a half-eaten donut on a table sitting next to the couch's left armrest.

Bruno sat at the right end of the couch, took a bite of his donut, a swig of his coffee, and said, "Jose?"

The man lowered the paper he was reading, looked at Bruno, and asked, "I'm sorry, senor, but do I know you?"

"No, you don't, but, if I'm not mistaken, you are an acquaintance of Hector Falano. Isn't that right?"

"Si. I mean, yes. I know Hector. But what is it you want, senor?"

"I represent a large hotel chain in Myrtle Beach and Hector is a person of interest to us."

"Okay, but how is this my business?"

"Our hotel chain is seeking to diversify our hotel staff."

"That's nice but…?"

"It seems Hector, being Hispanic and well-educated, comes very much recommended."

"Again, I ask you," said a puzzled Jose, "what are you asking of me?"

"Character references."

"Character references?"

"Yes. We need to know Hector's personal side. What are his hobbies? What does he do during his spare time? Who, besides yourself, are his associates? What type of people are they? Where does he go when he seeks entertainment? That kind of thing. We understand that you, being a good friend of Hector's, might provide us with some insight into Hector's character. Is he someone you would recommend to fill a high-profile job?"

"How did you come to me…, I'm sorry sir, but what was your name?"

"I'm sorry for not introducing myself. That was rude of me. My name is Gugino. Frank Gugino. Hector listed you as a reference."

"Funny, he never mentioned it to me."

"Maybe it slipped his mind. We've been a little behind in weeding out candidates. Maybe he thought he wasn't under consideration any longer."

"Well, I can tell you that Hector is a standup guy. He would do anything he could to help someone out."

"That's good to know," replied Bruno. Just as he was about to ask Jose another question, Jocko came sauntering over. He had a coffee in one hand and, based on the white powder stuck in the stubble of beard surrounding his mouth, he had eaten at least one powdered donut.

*Chances are,* thought Jose, *he had eaten many a donut in his lifetime.*

"This, Mr. Perez, is my driver, Ed Julio."

Perez nodded at Jocko and Jocko returned a smile, saying, "Good donuts."

"Yes, they are," said Perez, somewhat taken aback by the huge man with hands the size of a catcher's glove.

"Ed, why don't you wait for me in the car. I'll be just a few more minutes with Mr. Perez."

"Okay, Bruno."

They watched Jocko walk out the door.

"Why did he call you Bruno? I thought you said your name was Frank."

Thinking fast on his feet, Bruno replied, "We have known each other since we were kids growing up in the Bronx. Bruno was my nickname back then. Ed continues to call me by my childhood nickname. I don't mind though."

"He looks younger than you," stated Perez.

Perez's observation was not a mistake. Bruno was 12 years older than Jocko and neither of them grew up in the Bronx. In fact, Bruno had known Jocko for only three years.

"I don't age well. It's the job. Hey, we were talking about Hector. Do you know what he did with his free time?"

"We were in a bowling league together."

"Oh? Hector bowls? What kind of average did he have?"

"He was a good bowler. Carried about a 175 average. From what I understand from some mutual friends, he swung a mean golf stick too. I don't play golf but the other guys who played with him said he plays well."

"Where did you guys bowl?"

"In Surfside."

"Can you give me the names of the guys he played golf with? I'd like to talk with them too."

"Let me see," said Jose, his eyes finding the ceiling while he recovered the names from memory. A moment later he rattled off the names of Freddie Cruz, Chico Álvarez, and Mike Perez. "He is of no relation," said Jose, while waving his hands like he was calling a runner safe at the plate.

"Where can I find them?"

"They hang out at a bar called Greg's Cabana. It's in Garden City, right in front of the Wal-Mart."

"Are they there often? Would they be there today?" asked Bruno.

"After work, most likely."

"What time would that be, Jose?"

"I'd say around 5:00 or 5:30."

"What do they do?"

"They have a tree-trimming company."

"Is that so? What's the name of the company?"

"The Tree Amigos."

"Cute," said Bruno with a sly smile.

"They thought it was clever."

"Do you know where they played golf?"

"No, I can't help you there. I'm sure the others could tell you."

"I see. What else can you tell me about Hector?"

"He escaped from Cuba and came to America about 15 years ago."

"I knew he was from Cuba, but I didn't know about the escaping part," admitted Bruno.

"Oh, yes, senor. There are rumors about him being a legend in Cuba."

"That I hadn't heard. What was that all about?"

"He never talked about it, but some say he rescued some political prisoners, including his parents, from a prison and then sailed them to the safety of the states."

"Interesting," said Bruno.

"Oh, and he loves movies. He favors action movies, like the James Bond films, the Jason Bourne flicks, and almost anything that Clint Eastwood was in."

"Is that right?" said Bruno, feigning interest.

"Oh, yeah. I think he had a few hundred movies in his collection."

"That's nice, Jose, but were there any places he may have frequented that might be… oh, let's say… not family friendly?"

"You mean like strip joints?"

"That could be one, yes."

"Oh, no. Hector and Corrina are inseparable. He would do nothing to hurt her."

"Anything else, Jose?"

"There's one other thing he enjoyed doing, which I thought was crazy."

"Oh, and what might that be?"

"There's a rope course down on Business 17. I think it's around 20th Avenue. Hector went there once a week."

"A rope course! What's that?"

"Hector loved going there. They have these ropes strung between trees and people walk them. It's goes high into the trees. Hector said they range from easy to very difficult. There are multiple degrees of difficulty. Ziplines are available too. I've done zip-lining, but that rope climbing thing… it's not for me."

"Anything else you can tell me about your friend?"

"I think I've told you all I know, Mr. Gugino."

"Well, thanks for your time, Jose. Here, let me pay for your coffee and a donut," said Bruno as he placed a ten-dollar bill on the table.

"That's unnecessary, Mr. Gugino."

"Maybe, but take it, anyway."

Jose watch the man leave and then he returned to reading his paper.

Ten minutes later, the 8:00 local morning news came on and they began with a story about a man found murdered in an abandoned parking garage in Cherry Grove.

Jose, being curious, put down his paper and rising from his seat moved toward the television, stopping when he was standing a few feet away. He thought he heard the reporter state the victim's name, and he wanted to hear it again.

As he stood there listening, he felt a tap on his shoulder.

Turing around, he saw two men, one tall and large, the other much smaller and thinner.

The taller, larger man spoke.

"Mr. Jose Perez?"

Jose, looking bewildered, nodded.

"FBI, sir. We need to speak with you about Hector Falano."

Behind him, he heard the tv reporter say, *"They have identified the victim as Hector Falano."*

Jose whirled around to hear the reporter say, *"They have also reported his wife, Corrina Falano as missing."*

# CHAPTER 18

**While Ron and** Tim were interviewing Jose Perez at The Donut Man coffee shop, a plane left Miami, bound for Charlotte, North Carolina. Sitting in row 2, seat C, was a purveyor of death by the name of Isabella Sanchez. Her final destination would be Myrtle Beach.

Her connecting flight landed at the Myrtle Beach International Airport at 10:00am. Having traveled first class, she was the third person off the plane. She didn't stop at baggage pickup because she had no luggage.

A handsome, dark-haired, brown-eyed, six-foot physical specimen in his late 20s met her as she exited the airport and escorted her to a waiting limo. She climbed into the back seat and immediately made a phone call to someone in Miami saying she had landed. After ending the brief call she spoke, asking, "What's your name?"

"Michael," replied the driver.

"Take me to the Georgetown Police Department."

Sanchez's beauty was near indescribable. It began with her dark gleaming hair. Dark brown eyes, big and round, dominated a face that radiated with a soft glow of a well-tanned beach goer. She stood five-foot six and weighed only 120 pounds with not an ounce of fat. She was the epitome of Penelope Cruz, Salma Hayek, and Eva Longoria, all rolled into a picture perfect package.

Her physical beauty was beyond compare, but her intellect was equally admirable. She spoke fluent Spanish, English, and Portuguese, with nary a hint of an accent.

She was a Sicario by trade, which in English translates to: Assassin.

Employed by the Juarez Cartel, Isabella had elevated herself to the "Most Feared Flaka" in all Mexico.

She achieved this lofty title by stepping over the bodies of "Las Flakas" who had stood in her way.

After witnessing her beauty, it would be almost unthinkable to believe someone so stunning could also be an efficient and ruthless cold-blooded assassin.

The cartels had learned guile is often a better tool than brute force. Women, they learned, could keep a low profile and avoid the scrutiny and suspicions that men attracted. Thus "Las Flakas" or "Skinny Girls" came into being, and now, the ruling queen of "Las Flakas" had come to Myrtle Beach. She had a mission. She was to kill two people responsible for losing the Bongino brothers' operation. One was the Georgetown Chief of Police, and the other was an FBI agent named Ron Lee.

First on her list was Forest Lamb, the Georgetown Chief-of-Police. The cartel paid Lamb a great deal of money to keep them aware of what law enforcement might do that would jeopardize the cartel's businesses. Now, he was being held accountable for losing the Bongino operation the past November. He had failed to warn the brothers, both of whom died a violent death, of the FBI raid led by Special Agent Ron Lee.

The cartel not only lost two well-respected associates, but a profitable delivery route, accounting for 100 million dollars in revenue, was no longer operable.

For that, Forest Lamb would pay… with his life.

He would soon experience a visit from Isabella Sanchez.

Isabella's visit would not go well for Forest.

But seldom did visits from Isabella end well.

# CHAPTER 19

"**Okay, Jose, you've** told us about Hector's bowling, golf, ropes course, his love of movies, and a list of his friends. What else haven't you told us?" asked Ron.

They had been grilling Jose Perez for an hour.

"Well, like I told those other men…"

"Hold it!" shouted Ron. "What other men?"

"There were two guys here about ten minutes before you showed up. They asked me to give them character references for Hector."

"Character references? What the hell for?"

"They said he was being considered for a position in management for a big hotel chain."

"What hotel chain, Jose?"

"I… I didn't ask."

Tim, with pad and pen in hand, said, "Describe them for me, Jose."

"They were big guys. Their names were Frank Gugino and Ed Julio."

"Sure they were," muttered Ron.

"Mr. Gugino did all the talking. The other guy ate donuts. Gugino told him to wait in the car."

"Describe them for me, Jose," Tim repeated.

"Gugino, the guy who did all the talking, stood about six-two and went about 200 pounds. He had black hair, and a moustache. His eyes were dark brown, I think. His face was narrow and I think he had a broken nose."

"What about the other guy?" asked Tim.

"He was big! I'd say he was 300 pounds. Stood about five-ten. He had hands the size of a baseball glove. Mean looking eyes. They glared at you. He had a round face, like a pizza, and he had stubble. It looked like he hadn't shaved in days."

"That didn't set off any alarms, Jose? A guy asking for references and he looks like a bum and eating donuts?"

"What do you want from me? The guys I work with could be their twins. Have you checked out my physical resume? Do I look like a white-collar kind of guy?"

Ron and Tim, hearing that question, sat back and realized that Jose wouldn't be working in a bank in the immediate future. He too was scruffy.

"Okay, is there anything that you told them you haven't told us?"

"I can't think of a thing, Agent Lee."

"Okay, Jose. We'll get in touch if we have more questions," said Ron as they stood to exit the café. "If you think of anything, call us."

They were almost to the door when Jose called out, "Agent Lee! There is one other thing. Maybe it will help."

"What is it, Jose?"

"Hector loved to give clues to solve 'mysteries.'"

"Mysteries? Like what?"

"Well, one time at bowling, he hid my shoes. He said if I wanted to find them I'd have to solve three clues that he hid around our two lanes."

"Is that right? Did you tell the others about this?"

"No. I just remembered it. Sorry."

"Don't be sorry, Jose. Keep it between us. Okay?"

"You got it, Agent Lee."

As Ron and Tim made their way to their vehicle, Ron's phone rang. He looked at the caller ID and grunted.

"Who is it?" asked Tim.

"Baxter."

# CHAPTER 20

**Hours before Bruno** or Ron Lee talked with Jose Perez about Hector Falano, Sheriff Deputy Jack Clayton, having pulled the 11:00pm to 7:00am shift, decided it was time to eat.

His wife, Diana, had made him a roast beef sandwich and wrapped it, along with some pickle spears, and put them in a lunchbox with a thermos of coffee.

It was 3:00am when he turned left off of Forestbrook Road onto the curiously named, Whatuthink Road . His destination lay just a half-mile ahead. He always, when working the midnight shift, ate his sandwich in the Forestbrook Elementary School parking lot.

The school parking lot was his secret hideaway. The chance of a speeder distracting him from his meal, was next to nil. Seldom had he seen a vehicle on this road at this hour. He felt he could enjoy his meal with no distractions. Tonight, however, there would be "distractions."

Pulling into the school's lot, he made a U-turn so that the vehicle faced Whatuthink Road. It was a cold night with the temps in the upper 30s. Clayton kept his car running and the heat on low. He called in a 10-7 meal break to Becky, the night dispatcher.

"Have a nice meal, Jack," she radioed back. "10-4"

Reaching down to the passenger seat floor, he retrieved his lunch box and placed it on the console. His computer was lit up, providing all the light he would need. Removing the thermos, he unscrewed the top that served as a cup, and poured an ample amount of hot coffee into it. Taking a sip, he let its taste engulf his tongue and throat. Carefully he placed the cup on the dashboard before removing his sandwich from the lunchbox. After unwrapping the sandwich, he took a generous bite.

*Damn,* he thought, *Diana makes a good sandwich.*

Jack, his back turned to the side window, was about to wash down the sandwich bite with a swallow of coffee, when he heard the tap on the glass. A quick swiveling reaction resulted in the coffee spilling onto his lap, staining his uniform.

A burst of expletives escaped his lips, but the string of words ended with a somewhat mild, "What the hell!"

Looking through the window and seeing who it was, he placed the coffee cup on the dashboard. After lowering the window, he asked, "What are you doing here? It's 3:00 in the morning."

"Tidying up some loose strings," said the figure.

Sheriff Deputy Jack Clayton was staring at the wrong end of a .45, and before he could blink, the intruder blew his brains all over the interior of his cruiser.

"Well, now, there goes Mr. Lee's theory up in smoke," whispered the murderer.

A hundred yards away, hidden in the darkness against the school building, sat a black sedan. The killer scurried across the parking lot, entered the car and drove off the school property, making a right onto Whatuthink Road.

Smirking, the killer whispered, "Well, Agent Lee, I'll be wondering whatuthink of that?"

*************

While Bruno was talking with Jose Perez at The Donut Man coffee shop, a school bus load of kids was pulling into the Forestbrook Elementary School parking lot.

As the bus drove past Jack Clayton's cruiser, two young boys thought they saw a man slumped over in the car.

Yelling to the bus driver, one boy said, "Mr. Roberts. I think that policeman is sleeping in his car."

Glen Roberts, a 69-year-old retired factory worker, and now a school bus driver, acknowledged the young boy's observation, saying, "Maybe he's just catching a catnap, Billy."

"Maybe," replied Billy Sullivan, "but his window is open. Kinda cold to take a nap, don't you think?"

Roberts pondered Billy's words and decided that after the kids exited the bus, he would drive over to the patrol car and see if everything was all right.

And so he did.

And so it wasn't.

\*\*\*\*\*\*\*\*\*\*\*\*\*

Captain Baxter ordered that the school be closed for the day. Two state police cruisers blocked the entrance into the parking lot. There were cops everywhere. Forensic lab personnel were going over every inch of the vehicle.

The bus driver, Glen Roberts, upon seeing the carnage inside the car, almost lost the delicious pancake breakfast his wife had made for him that morning. He staggered back to his bus and using his cell phone called 9-1-1.

Baxter and his people were on the scene within minutes. They sent Glen home after he gave a brief statement.

Viewing the scene, Baxter reached into his pocket and extracting his phone, dialed Ron Lee.

"Hey, Bill. What's up?"

"Got us another dead cop, Ron. Killed in his car, just like the others."

"Where?"

"Forestbrook Elementary School parking lot. Do you know where it is?"

"Yeah, I do. We're at The Donut Man coffee shop on Business 17 right now. It will take a half-hour to get there."

"No hurry, Ron. This guy ain't going anywhere. Hey wait! Don't hang up!"

"Yeah, Bill. What is it?"

"Would you mine bringing me a chocolate-covered cream-filled donut? I haven't had breakfast yet. Oh, and a coffee, with sugar. Make it a large."

We're the FBI, Bill, not a food delivery service."

"Hey, Ron. Just this once. Okay?"

Bill, hearing nothing but silence, was about to hang up, when he heard Ron ask, "Did I hear you say you were buying, Bill?"

"Damn!" said Tim. "You're holding up another cop for a donut! Tell me, how low will you go for a donut?"

Ron shot Tim a glare and then speaking into the phone said, "You wanted a chocolate crème-filled donut, correct? That sounds mighty good. I'll get one of those for myself. We'll be there as fast as we can."

There was a short pause, and Ron hung up the phone after saying, "Don't you worry, Bill. I won't forget your coffee."

"You're disgusting," said Tim with a look of disdain.

"Maybe, but I'm still getting a free donut and coffee."

# CHAPTER 21

**When Bruno returned** to the car, he first chewed out Jocko for looking and acting like a slob.

"You almost blew it for us in there!" screamed Bruno, rebuking his sidekick. "Walking around in a pair of dirty jeans and a t-shirt covered in powdered-sugar. You're beyond disgusting!"

"Sorry, Bruno. I wasn't thinking."

"That's a fucking understatement. Besides, you don't get paid to think."

"Yeah, I know. I get paid to…"

"Yeah, well, get your game face on. You may have to do your job at our next stop. And get that damn powdered-sugar off your face!"

Bruno pulled out his phone and searched for the address of The Tree Amigos tree-trimming service.

"Garden City. Let's go."

"What's in Garden City, Bruno?"

"It seems Hector hung out with three guys who have a tree-trimming service. Their office is in Garden City. The Tree Amigos and I need to have a discussion."

As they were leaving, a black Yukon pulled into the lot and parked near the entrance to the cafe. Bruno immediately recognized the license plates.

"Damn! FBI."

"How do you know, Bruno?"

"The plates have U.S. government on them, and that SUV is a signature vehicle for the FBI."

"We better get out of here."

"No, go slow. I want to see these dudes. I'm sure they are here to talk to Jose."

Jocko had pulled out onto 2nd Avenue South at the rear of the property, and turning right, drove slowly toward Business 17.

Bruno watched as first Tim and then Ron emerged from the vehicle. Both wore dark suits.

"I know that guy," said Jocko, pointing at Ron. "Those two guys took down that serial killer who was leaving women's heads on golf courses."

"Yeah, and they were also responsible for the Bongino brothers," mouthed Bruno. "They're looking for the same thing we are, Jocko."

"The flash drive?"

"Yeah, the flash drive, but they are also looking for the people who killed their hidden spy. It looks like it will be necessary to leave nothing behind that can help them."

"We should have taken care of Jose."

"Yeah, we should have. It's too late now, but we will make it a point to meet up with Jose again."

"To leave a message, right?"

"It will be a warning to others that if they talk, bad things can happen. Let's go. Garden City. The Tree Amigos."

\*\*\*\*\*\*\*\*\*\*\*\*\*

"Turn left on Atlantic, Jocko, and watch for East Canal Street on the right. That's the location of their office."

Two minutes later, Jocko parked in a dirt driveway fronting a box-shaped building. A hand-painted sign, nailed against an outside wall to the left of the front door, identified the building as the office of The Tree Amigos.

"You wait here, Jocko. I'll come get you to clean up."

Bruno exited the car and strolled to the building's front door. He turned the doorknob, and the door swung open. He entered and closed the door behind him.

It was only 20x20 in size. Three very standard metal desks sat against the side and back walls. A doorway at the back wall led presumably to a bathroom. Occupying a fourth desk just inside the front doorway was a young

Hispanic-looking girl wearing a nametag that identified her as Maria.

"Yes, sir. May I help you?"

Bruno, seeing no one else in the building, asked, "Are the owners available?"

"Oh, no, sir. They are at a job site. They won't be back until tomorrow morning. Do you have trimming needs?"

Bruno, smiling at the girl's choice of words, said, "Yes, but I'd like to see their work before I hire them. Is there a chance I could watch them at their current job?"

"I'm sure they wouldn't mind, sir. I'll call Mike and see how much longer they will be at the job site."

"And where is the job site?"

"They are in Pawleys Island at the Precious Blood of Christ Church. That's on King's River Road. The church needed about 50 trees taken down or trimmed. They have been there for three days."

"I see. Don't bother calling them. I'll just drive by. You said the church was on King's River Road?"

"Yes, sir. If you pass the Waccamaw High School, you've gone too far."

"You've been very helpful,... Maria, is it?"

"Yes, Maria," replied the girl glancing proudly at her nametag.

Bruno smiled and left. He climbed into the car, looked over at Jocko, and said, "Make it quick, and don't make it messy."

Jocko left the vehicle, and with his blackjack in hand, entered the office. Moments later, he exited the office and climbed into the driver's seat.

"Where to, Bruno?"

"King's River Road in Pawleys Island."

# CHAPTER 22

"**He knew his** killer."

"What makes you say that, Ron?" asked Bill Baxter.

"Look at his holster. Still buttoned. The window is down, his coffee cup is sitting on the dashboard, his mic is still in its saddle, and, most telling, someone shot him square in the face."

"Put that together for me, please," said Tim, scratching his head, at what he believed to be his partner's thorough analysis.

"I'm thinking he's sitting here eating that sandwich and drinking his coffee."

"I got questions already," said Baxter.

"Hold them until I finish," commanded Ron, while holding up his hand in the typical 'stop' manner.

Baxter retaliated by giving Ron the single-finger salute.

"There are coffee stains on his trousers and jacket. That means he spilled them when whoever killed him approached the car unseen. They may have knocked on the window, made him jump, and spill his coffee."

"Sounds reasonable, Ron."

"I'm glad you approve, partner."

"So far. Don't get ahead of yourself," warned Tim with a smile.

"Not a chance. Okay, so he spills his coffee. He turns and sees someone standing outside his door. Now if it were a stranger, he would react by calling in a… what's the code for officer needs help, Bill?"

"He'd radio a 10-20 or a 10-30."

"But he didn't. Nor did he unbutton his holster. Knowing the person, he relaxes and places the coffee cup on the dashboard and lowers the window."

"Let me guess the last part, Ron," said Baxter.

"Go to it, Bill."

"He lowers the window, and because he knows this person, he gets a load of .45 lead planted in his face."

"Snap, crackle, pop!" said Ron, putting his hands together. "The question is, who knew his location?"

"He called in his location when he took his break."

"Standard procedure," said Tim.

"Who else?" asked Ron.

"I'm sure other officers in the area picked up on his 10-7."

"Yeah, but whoever did this was already here waiting for him. If someone did this after he gave his location, he would have seen them coming. Someone who knew his tendencies did this. Now who would that be?"

"His wife," said Tim.

"Do we have an alibi for her, Bill?"

"Her name is Diana. We sent someone over to pick her up."

"And?"

"She was home, but her sister from Ohio is visiting. Been here since last Thursday."

"Could she have snuck out?" asked Tim.

"She could have, but she would have needed to take her sister's van."

"Why is that?" asked Ron.

"Diana's car was in the garage. Her sister parked her van in front of the garage door. There was no way Diana could get her car out without moving the sister's van."

"I guess she could have switched the vehicles, but it seems someone would have heard garage doors being opened and vehicles being started. So," admitted Ron, "I guess her alibi is solid."

"I would say so," agreed Baxter.

"What do we know about their relationship, Bill? Was everybody happy around the home fires?"

"I'm not hearing anything at the moment, Ron. Maybe someone will offer some dirt, once things settle down," answered Baxter.

"Hey, maybe we got a cop killer on our hands," submitted Tim. "We could run some data and see if these three dead cops had a common perp."

"Waste of time, Tim," said Ron.

"How can you say that?"

"I'm convinced that this is personal."

"You're thinking the wives are in cahoots, aren't you, Ron?" asked Baxter.

"I'll admit, I am."

"Why?"

"It's the alibies. They are too pat. Peggy Patterson is at a Tupperware party with her mother! Sheila Bennington is playing cards with three other women. Both have tons of witnesses! Now this one has a sister staying with her. I'll bet you a dollar to a donut, those other two have good alibies for tonight. I still say it's a case of one hand washing the other."

"Can you prove it, Ron?" asked Baxter.

"Three women. Someone will make a mistake and then their makeup will fall off to expose them as killers."

"What do I need to do, Ron? I know you're involved with the murder of an FBI agent and can't give this your full support."

"For now, Bill, determine last night's whereabouts of Sheila Bennington and Peggy Patterson. If I'm right about this, one of them may have pulled the trigger. And try to find out where this guy's wife was when the other two cops were murdered."

"You said, one of them may have pulled the trigger, Ron. What's your thinking?" asked Tim.

"I'm thinking about my one hand washing the other theory, Tim."

"Yeah, so?"

"How many hands are there? That, my friend, is the question that needs answering."

"So you're thinking that the group is larger than three and maybe more cops are targets?"

"That's what I'm thinking, Tim, but I'm also thinking that the more links there are in the chain…"

"A chain is only as strong as its weakest link," said Tim, converting and finishing Ron's thought.

"I think the someone who planned and carried out these murders is also smart enough to know its limits."

"Do you think we've met the brains of this plot?"

"I'll let you know after Bill collects the remaining alibies, but…."

"But what?"

"Motive, Tim. Motive. What's the motive?"

"Infidelity?"

"Not for the person I suspect masterminded this."

"If it's not infidelity, Ron, then it has to be the old standby," surmised Tim.

"Money," nodded Ron. "Follow the money."

# CHAPTER 23

**"We got some** time, so tell me what the hell you're thinking, Ron."

After leaving the school parking lot, they headed out to find the three men associated with the tree-trimming business called, The Tree Amigos.

"About what?"

"Are you kidding me?" asked Tim, baffled by Ron's off-the-wall reply. "The cop killings! That's what!"

"Oh, that. It's formula, Tim. The killings are the same. Each guy gets blown away in a spot where he's comfortable. They are all shot as they sit in their vehicles. Each of them shot in the head. All shot with a .45."

"We know two of them are skirt chasers," interjected Tim.

"Yeah, and I'm betting this guy Clayton was too. The piece that has me convinced the most, however, is everyone's alibi. Each one is just too pat. Witnesses confirming each wife was somewhere and with someone that would make it impossible for her to have killed the husband."

"Ron, I've been giving thought to this, and one thing seems to cast a shadow over your theory."

"And what might that be, partner?"

"We talked to two of the wives. Both were very good-looking women."

"Agreed."

"But what struck me was their physical size. Both of them couldn't have weighed much over 110 pounds and neither were taller than five-two or five-three."

"Okay, but what's your point?"

"A .45 revolver is a hefty weapon and has a helluva kick to it."

"I see where you're going, Tim, and it's a valid point. The thing is, they killed these guys at close range. I'm guessing the range didn't exceed two feet. Now, if you're wanting to kill someone, there are two things you need covered."

"What might those be?"

"Glad you asked, partner."

"Oh, I'm dying to hear the obvious."

Sneering at his partner's wiseass remark, Ron said, "First, you need to be sure the weapon of choice will do the job."

"And the second?"

"A zero chance of missing the target."

"Well," said Tim, "there's little doubt a .45 would ensure the first requirement, and being almost in your target's face, takes care of the second requirement."

"That's right, Tim. The point being, you need not be a behemoth or a marksman to raise a .45 revolver and shoot someone two feet away."

"Do you think they are passing the weapon around?"

"They might be."

"We can check to see if any of them purchased a gun as of late."

"Waste of time. Whoever planned this, didn't overlook that mousetrap. I'm betting, with their husbands being cops, that all three women have a gun registered in their name. And I'll bet you a dollar to a donut... don't say it, Pond... that none of them own a .45. In fact, I'll bet they all have .22s."

"Interesting stuff, partner, but there's an important unanswered question here."

"What might that be, Sherlock?"

"Since when do you know the price of a donut?"

The question went unanswered as Ron pulled into the gravel driveway of the office of The Tree Amigos.

"It appears they could use a lot more business," expressed Tim, upon seeing the small rundown building.

"It ain't much to look at, that's for sure," concurred Ron. "Oh-oh!"

"What? What's the matter?" asked Tim in a hushed voice.

"The front door isn't closed."

"Geez, so what? Why are you so uptight, partner? Hell, I've left the door open at the house more than a few times. Wilma chews my ass out, and always says, 'You're letting all the flies in!'"

"Yeah, you're right. I used to hear the same complaint. Let's go talk with these fellas."

Tim was the first to reach the doorway and after stepping inside, muttered, "Damn!"

"Are they dead?" asked Ron, suspecting what Tim had found.

"No, but she is."

Ron stepped through the doorway and saw the girl lying in the middle of the floor. It was a bloodless scene.

Sprawled face-up on the floor, her brown eyes were wide open. A dark bruise ran from her left ear down across her broken neck. According to the nametag pinned to her blouse, her name was Maria. Ron made a silent guess that she was no more than sixteen years of age.

"Bastards!" said Ron in a whisper.

"They are after the three owners, Ron."

"Yeah, and I bet she sent them there. They killed her so she couldn't tell us."

"There's no computer, so they don't have a sophisticated way of scheduling their jobs," observed Tim. "I'll check the desks. Maybe they have a business card with a number we can call."

While Tim searched the other three desks, Ron called Baxter.

*"Yeah, Ron."*

"We just arrived at the office of The Tree Amigos tree-trimming company, Bill. We found the receptionist dead on the floor. Someone broke her neck. Looks like a heavy object did the job. I'm guessing a blackjack."

*"I'll have some of my guys there in five minutes."*

"How about the other two women, Bill? Got anything?"

*"Yes, we checked on the Bennington's whereabouts last night and all she could come up with is she was home, alone, in bed."*

"Really," said Ron, almost positive each of the women attached to these murders would have air-tight alibies.

*"Then there is Peggy Patterson,"* said Bill.

"What about Peggy Patterson?"

*"We went to her house, but there was no answer."*

"Did she leave a note on the outside door?" Ron asked with a noticeable hint of sarcasm.

Baxter, smiling at Ron's intentional dig, answered, *"No, but when we went to her mom's house, there was no one home there either."*

"What about Diana Clayton? Where was she the nights when Bennington and Patterson got waxed?"

*"She's in too much distress right now to answer questions. We may need to give her a few days."*

"I got a card, Ron!" shouted Tim, holding up a business card.

"Sorry, Bill. Gotta go," said Ron, ending the call.

"Ready?" said Tim."

"Read it out, partner."

As Tim called out the number, Ron dialed it on his cell. The phone rang once, twice, and a third time, before someone answered. After a few seconds of silence, Ron heard a gruff voice say, *"Too late, Mr. F-B-I."*

"Why you son-of-a-bitch!" screamed Ron.

*"Bye."*

*Click.*

"What was that all about!" said Tim.

"They're dead," answered Ron.

"Who?"

"The Tree Amigos."

# CHAPTER 24

**It took only** a half-hour for the FBI to discover the Tree Amigos' battered and bullet-riddled bodies in a wooded area behind the Precious Blood of Christ Church.

While Ron and Tim investigated that crime scene, another, in downtown Georgetown, was in progress.

It was approaching noon when a dark-haired woman entered the Georgetown Police Headquarters.

"Excuse me. I'd like to speak with the Chief-of-Police."

Looking up from his desk, Sgt. Max Dean, the on-duty desk sergeant, thought an angel had approached him. Although she was wearing a drab winter coat, the woman's Hispanic beauty lit up the station's surroundings like a Christmas tree. Taken aback by her soft complexion, her jet-black hair, and red strawberry lips, he fumbled for words. Then gathering himself, asked, "What would you be needing to see Captain Lamb about, miss?"

"I have information concerning the Tuesday night hit and run."

"Well, miss, I can take that information and pass it on to the captain."

"I would rather tell the captain, myself, if you don't mind."

Georgetown's Chief of Police, Captain Forest Lamb, sat in his office, pecking away on his computer while attempting to access his illegal off-shore account.

A buzzing intercom interrupted his searching.

"Yes, what is it, Sergeant?"

"Excuse me, sir, but there is someone here to see you."

"Who might that be, Sergeant?"

"Her name is Maria Gonzalez. She claims to have information involving that hit-and-run that occurred on 17 the other night."

Lamb's cartel contact had informed him a woman calling herself, Maria Gonzalez, would soon drop off a package detailing the new delivery routes and dates of cartel shipments.

"Send her in, Sergeant."

Dean, pointing toward the hallway, said, "His office is the last door on the left."

"Doesn't seem to be much activity in this police station… Sergeant. Why is that?"

"We have a small force, miss. Most are out on patrol."

"So, you're left behind all by yourself to guard the fort?"

"It looks like I'm it for the time being."

Smiling, she nodded, saying, "You said the second door on the right?"

"The left."

While awaiting the woman, Lamb closed the blinds in his office so they would have complete privacy.

Although the office door was void of blinds, a frosted window made it impossible to see inside.

As he closed the last blind, he heard a light knock on the door.

"Come in."

The door opened and Isabella Sanchez entered. Closing the door behind her, she turned to face Lamb. Her face held a slight smile that masked what was to come.

"My, my. I would have never imagined an emissary this beautiful. Please, have a seat."

"Thank you, but I won't be staying that long, Captain."

"They told me you had a package for me."

"Yes, but they lied."

"Lied? I don't understand."

"You failed to protect our investment, Senor."

Lamb, realizing what was happening, lunged toward his desk where he kept his revolver, but the woman opened her coat and exposed a hidden AK-47.

"Nice try, Captain," said Isabella as she raked the Captain with a burst of death. Then she turned and waited.

Rushing down the hallway, with his revolver in hand, Sgt. Dean burst through the doorway. His eyes had a split-second to witness the carnage before a fusillade of .39 caliber bullets made him a part of it.

Isabella walked over to where Lamb lay and fired another volley at the inert body.

Stepping over the sergeant's body, she made her way down the hallway and to a door where they stored the building's recording equipment. Opening the door, she stood silent for a moment, before bursting into laughter.

The system, covered in dust and cobwebs, had evidently been inoperable for years.

Still smiling, she closed her coat over the weapon, and left the building. A black limo pulled up, and she climbed into the back seat.

As the limo pulled away, she glanced at the building that just minutes earlier was a quiet police station. Now, however, it was as silent as a morgue.

# CHAPTER 25

**They watched as** the morgue guys wrapped the three men in body bags, lifted them onto gurneys, and wheeled them to a waiting vehicle.

"What now, Ron?"

"I've been thinking about what Jose Perez said about how Falano liked to play mystery games with his friends."

"You're thinking that maybe he left behind some clues to where he hid the flash drive?"

"Wouldn't you, Tim? Here you are, working undercover for the FBI in the biggest drug ring in the state, and you have the goods on them that could destroy their operation. Knowing there's always a chance your cover somehow gets blown; wouldn't you make sure that whatever it was you had, didn't fall into the hands of the enemy?"

"Yeah," agreed Tim, "but, if caught, you would want your side to find the goods."

"And what better way than to leave breadcrumbs, in the form of mysterious clues, along the trail."

"Where do you think he left them, Ron?"

"He'd have to leave them where people knew of his activities."

"That means his home, the bowling alley, the golf course, the ropes course. Anything else?"

"I don't know," said Ron. "Let's start at his house. I'm hoping the ransacking of the home didn't destroy whatever clues Hector may have left for us to find."

*************

As Ron and Tim headed toward the Falano home, Bruno was going over what he had uncovered with Cameron Driscoll.

"Removing those who might tell the FBI something of importance was a good move, Bruno."

"I wish we could have taken out that Perez fella at the donut shop, but there were too many people."

"So the FBI arrived just as you were leaving?"

"Yeah. I recognized that agent as the one who took out the Bongino brothers."

"What about Hector's house, Bruno? Have you been there yet?"

"We went through it when we were there..."

"Yeah, I know. Raping Corrina."

"Yeah."

"Well, get your ass over there, check it out again, and when you're done, burn it to the ground!"

"Okay, boss."

"When you're done with that deed, go find that donut shop guy..."

"Jose Perez."

"Yeah," said Cameron annoyed at Bruno's interruption, "and ask him what he told the FBI that he didn't tell you."

"What makes you think..."

"Because the FBI asks all the right questions, Bruno. I'm sure they jelled that guy's memory into remembering something – some small detail he didn't tell you. Find out what it was, and when you're done..."

"Yeah, I know. Discard."

"Well, get going, then. Time be a wasting, Bruno!"

∗∗∗∗∗∗∗∗∗∗∗∗∗

Arriving at Hector's home, the two agents find the doorway lined with the yellow crime scene tape but no one is watching the house.

"Call Baxter and have him send someone out here to watch this house 24/7, Tim. We can't let anyone else in here. As it is, it may be too late."

Entering the home, they began checking the house room by room.

"What are we looking for, Ron?"

"To tell you the truth, I don't know. Something unusual, I'm guessing."

"I'll start in the kitchen."

"Okay. I'll be in the master bedroom."

Five minutes passed when, from the kitchen, Ron heard Tim yell, "Hey, Ron, what do you make of this?"

Hustling toward the kitchen, Ron asked, "What do you have, partner?"

"They have a January calendar on the fridge. Look at the notations on the 15th and the 17th."

Ron walked over to the refrigerator and read the scribble in the block of the 15$^{th}$.

*"Three ahead of journey."*

"Now that's a weird notation if I have ever seen one!" exclaimed Ron. "That partner, has to be a clue. It has to be!"

He then read the note made on the 17$^{th}$.

*"Keeping it between the isolated feathers."*

"What the hell could that possibly mean, Tim?"

"God only knows. I haven't a clue."

"Who's handwriting is that, Tim?"

"Good question. It doesn't match with any of the notes on any other dates. My guess it is Hector's."

"Why do you say that?"

"Look at the other notes. Those are things that make sense. Look at the 7$^{th}$. It says 'dentist – 2:00pm'. Then there's the 11$^{th}$, 'pick up dry cleaning.' Sounds like things a woman would keep track of. Besides, the writing has a nice flair to it. That wouldn't be Hector. That's Corrina's handwriting."

"I'd have to agree, Tim. It won't be hard to prove. I'm sure we can find handwriting samples all over this house."

"So what do you think, Ron? Are those two of Hector's mystery clues?"

Before Ron could answer, the front doorbell rang. It was two of Baxter's patrolmen. Ron instructed them to sit out in front of the home and to not let anyone in under any circumstances.

"Getting back to your question, Tim. They could very well be clues. They are vague, but intriguing. And let us not leave out, mysterious. It's a good start, partner, but let's keep searching."

Ron returned to the master bedroom while Tim checked out the living room.

Finding nothing in the couples' dressers, Ron stripped the bed and flipped the mattress. Nothing. A thorough search of the closet, including searching every article of clothing, also turned up nothing.

Frustrated, Ron sat on the edge of the bed and perused the room. A small six-foot in diameter throw-rug covered the hardwood floor. Ron picked it up and checked the other side. Nothing.

Standing in the middle of the room, he swept it with his eyes and noticed the two night tables on either side of the bed.

*How in the hell did I miss those*, he thought. Five minutes later, he was disappointed to find nothing in either.

He entered the master bath. It was 16x20 in size. "Damn!" whispered Ron. "My damn bathroom isn't half this size."

One wall had a 12-foot long mirror above a triple sink.

*Who the hell needs a triple sink?* his mind asked.

A glass-enclosed shower stall, at least six-by-eight stood against the far wall. It had two shower heads at each end and what they called a 'rain shower head' in the ceiling's center.

"I bet they had some good times in there," said Ron with a sly smile.

There were three doors along the right side of the room. The first was a linen closet, the second a toilet, and the third opened into a six-by-six room that housed a desk-like table with a large mirror. It had a woman's touch all over it.

*This has to be Corrina's dressing table,* thought Ron. The table's contents included a vast array of women's lotions and creams, a bald wig mannequin, two mirror stands, makeup kits, and multiple brushes and combs.

The desk also had three regular drawers on each side. Built into the desk, just above the top drawer on either side, were two wooden knobs. Drawing out the knob on the right, exposed a writing board. The left-hand side had a slide-out tray, about two-inches deep, where Corrina kept an array of rings, watches, and necklaces.

Ron searched the six drawers and found nothing in the first five. Only when he opened the bottom drawer on the right side, did he find something of interest - Corrina Falano's journal.

It was black, decorated with an array of gold stars of various sizes, and bound by gold rings. Planted in the middle of the cover was a large solid gold colored 'C' which all but pronounced the journal was Corrina's.

Ron opened it to a random page and noticed the handwriting matched that of the notations on the calendar made on the 7th and 11th.

Turning the pages he found the last pages of writings. The handwriting was the same throughout.

Ron slammed the journal shut, muttering, "Hector didn't do any writing in this book."

They searched the rest of the house and found nothing that could have been a clue. Calling it a day, they took the calendar and Corrina's journal and left the house.

They gave a wave to the two police officers and drove away.

A half-block away, a black Mercedes parked along the street watched as the two FBI agents left Hector Falano's house. It did not go unnoticed by the vehicle's occupants that one agent was carrying a black-covered book.

Also, not going unnoticed, was the state police car sitting outside the home. There would be no burning of the Falano home tonight.

A call to Cameron Driscoll informed him of what they observed.

Upon hanging up with Bruno, Driscoll made a call. It was to the FBI.

*"Hello."*

"Listen to what I have to say."

*"Yes, sir."*

"Agent Lee uncovered something in the Falano home. You need to find out what it is he found."

*"Understood, sir. I'll do my best."*

"I don't think you understand, agent. So let me make myself understood. I expect much more than your best."

# CHAPTER 26

**The Ghost woke** at 8:30. He showered and shaved before eating a light breakfast. He had six hours to get done what needed doing before he had to report for work. Checking the weather, he saw it was a typical January day for the Grand Strand; sunny with temps in the mid-50s.

Sporting a dark t-shirt, a pair of jeans, a light jacket, and wearing a black pair of Nike running shoes, he left the house at 9:15. His destination would be the Grand Dunes area. His agenda had but one notation: killing a judge.

He had booked a tee time at the resort course under the name of Laverty. Upon arriving at the gate, the guard would ask him his business and he would reply, "Golf." The guard would then ask with whom and The Ghost would reply, "Laverty." Seeing the name "Laverty" on his list, the guard would raise the gate, and The Ghost would be free to do what needed doing; killing a judge.

Driving over the bridge, which was being renovated because of deteriorating conditions, he looked both ways down the intercoastal waterway and saw nary a boat on the water. *I'd rather be fishing right now than putting down some damn judge,* he thought. *But then again, I wouldn't be making ten grand, fishing, now would I?*

Passing the left-hand turn that would take him to the clubhouse, he instead continued straight ahead to La Costa Court where he made a right turn. Following La Costa for about a quarter mile, he made a left onto Bellasera Circle and looked for the first right-hand turn. Moments later, a sign stating Arignon Court appeared to his right. Turning, he passed the judge's house, which was the second home on the right. Only five homes occupied this street, and all were a good distance from one another.

The judge, the 72-year-old, Jeffrey Samuels, lived

alone in this huge home since his wife passed in 2009. The Ghost had appeared before the judge on multiple occasions, the latest being six months ago on a burglary case.

"I'm sure he will remember me," whispered The Ghost. "He claims to have a photographic memory. We'll see."

Thirty seconds after turning onto Bellasera, his right-hand turn appeared. Driving a little slower, he made his way around the semicircle street, checking the street for activity. There was, as expected, none. Most of the homes in this development were second or third homes for the rich and famous. After circumnavigating the street, The Ghost reentered Arignon Court and turning into the judge's driveway, pulled his car to the end of the drive.

Checking his weapon, he attached a silencer, tucked it behind his back, and made his way to the side door.

Ringing the doorbell, he heard a voice emanating from a speaker, asking, "Who is it?"

"Judge Samuels, it's Rudy."

"Rudy?"

"Yes, Your Honor. I work in the Member's Club Pro Shop."

"What is it, Rudy?"

"It's about your bag, Your Honor."

The judge, knowing he kept his bag at the club, asked, "What about my bag?"

"We damaged it, sir. I'm here to apologize and to present you with a new bag and clubs."

The door flew open, and the judge began to yell, "What happened..." but stopped upon seeing the man standing before him. He didn't appear to have dressed as a club pro would dress.

"You aren't a club pro! I know you from somewhere!"

"Yes, Your Honor, you do," said The Ghost as he pulled his weapon from the back of his pants.

"You're a cop! What the hell are you doing here!" he yelled.

"You know, Your Honor, I can't rightly say, but Mr. Driscoll said that I should call on you."

"Driscoll sent you to kill me?"

"That seems to be the case, Judge," said The Ghost, adding, "No pun intended."

Then, pointing the .22 pistol at the judge's heart, he said, "Sorry, Your Honor."

"Driscoll! That bastard!"

Those would be the judge's final words.

*************

While Judge Samuels was being tattooed by The Ghost's .22 assassin's weapon, Isabella Sanchez walked into FBI headquarters and asked to speak with Special Agent Ron Lee.

The receptionist asked, "What would be your business with Agent Lee, miss?"

"It involves the Driscoll cartel."

"Agent Lee isn't in today. It's his golfing day."

"Oh, I see. Where would he be playing?"

"I can't give out that information. Would you like to speak to one of our other agents?"

"No. I alone need to give this information to Special Agent Ron Lee."

"Well, he's in the office by 8:00 in the morning. He is working tomorrow."

"Thank you. I'll stop by in the morning."

Leaving the building, she walked to the black limo where Michael, the limo driver, held the door open for her. Closing the door, she pulled a folder from a briefcase sitting on the seat beside her. It was a dossier on Ron Lee.

She began reading aloud a specific section.

"Lives alone in an area known as Market Commons at 119 Willow Street. Sometimes plays golf on Tuesday with a group called 'Hagan's Hackers.' John Hagan is the leader of the group. He decides where and when the group will play."

Isabella put down the folder and picked up her cell phone. Searching the Myrtle Beach phone directory for a John Hagan, she found a half dozen of them. She began calling them on a burner phone. On the third try she had a bingo.

*"Hello."*

"Hello. My husband is playing in your husband's group today. I need to speak with him but he doesn't carry a cell phone, and he failed to tell me where they were playing."

*"Men,"* said Dorma, John Hagan's wife. *"They don't communicate very well, do they?"*

"No, they don't," replied Isabella, the woman's truthful remark coming through loud and clear.

*"Let's see,"* mumbled Dorma, as she made her way to a desk where John kept his golf information. *"John writes it on his desk calendar. Let me look. Ahh, here it is. They are playing at a course called Burning Ridge at 10:45. Do you know where that is?"*

"I have a GPS, so I'll be able to find it. Thank you for your troubles."

*"Oh, no trouble at…"* Dorma began to reply, but the woman had hung up.

"Michael, we need to go to the Burning Ridge golf course. Do you know where that is?"

"Yes, ma'am. It's about twenty minutes from here."

"Get me there. Now!"

It was approaching 10:35.

\*\*\*\*\*\*\*\*\*\*\*\*

Moments after Isabella had left FBI headquarters, the receptionist reported the request to speak with Agent Lee to his commander, Jim Braddock. Thinking anything to do with the cartel might be of importance, Jim attempted to contact Ron, but failed to reach him. Guessing that Ron had his phone turned off, he left a message stating what the woman had said and her description.

That message went unheard in the time it took Isabella Sanchez to arrive at the golf course.

Michael parked the limo near the rear of the parking lot and rolled down the window that separated the front seat from the back. It was 10:52.

"I know this place, ma'am. I suggest you enter and leave through that side door." said Michael, pointing to his right. "As you enter through that doorway, a snack bar will be on your left. Passing the snack bar, you'll enter the dining area. There will be two doors. One almost straight ahead of you will take you out the back of the clubhouse. That's the door golfers use when making the turn."

"Turn?"

"It's the halfway point of a round of golf. Golfers often grab something to eat or drink at that juncture of their round."

"I see. Go on."

"Door #2, to the left, leads to the Pro Shop. That's where you pay for the golf and where you'll find golf apparel and golf equipment for sale."

"I understand. It's like a department store."

"Pretty much," said Michael with a smile. "See those stairs that lead down to where they have parked the golf carts? That's the exit from the Pro Shop."

"The woman told me they would play at 10:45."

"That would be the first tee time. That means," said Michael, as he glanced at his watch and seeing it was 10:54, "that the second group is now on the tee."

"Take a walk over there, Michael, and find out Ron Lee's tee time."

Michael left the car and made his way to the bag drop area. He knew the guys loading the bags would have a list of the players. Mingling with the players, no one would notice he wasn't playing.

"Fourth Hagan group," yelled a bagman. Then reading from a list pinned on a wall, he spewed out the names of "Lowe, Durni, Daniels and McElrath!"

"Here we go," said a short but muscular older man. "I'm riding with McElrath. I'll drive."

Michael made his way to the list and scanned it looking for Lee. He found it. Lee was to go off at 11:22 in the sixth grouping.

Acting like he belonged, Michael asked a golfer standing nearby, "Have you seen Ron Lee?"

"Yeah, in fact I'm playing with him," answered Tim Pond. "He's out there on the practice green."

Michael glanced toward the practice green, and seeing about a dozen men, said, "Where?"

Pond, scanning the green, said, "That's him," as he pointed toward a man in the blue jacket and gray pants. "You can't miss him. He's the guy holding a putter in one hand and a donut in the other."

"Oh, okay. Got him. Thanks."

"What do you need him for?"

"Oh, he forgot his receipt."

"Oh," said Tim, losing interest.

Michael waited until the man who pointed out Lee had made his way to a golf cart, before he hurried back to the limo.

Settling into the seat, he turned to Isabella, saying, "He goes off in about 20 minutes. He's a big man, and he's wearing a blue jacket and gray pants. He's on the putting green right now."

"Where is this... putting green?"

"It's about 50 feet on the other side of that lineup of carts. You'll be able to see the whole area from the top of the stairs."

"Have the car parked at the end of that long walkway entrance."

"Yes, ma'am."

Checking her Glock, Isabella grabbed it and a sealed envelope and left the car. She walked up the long walk and entered the building. It was just as Michael had described it. She passed by the busy snack bar and entered the dining room, but not hesitating, headed left toward the doorway that led to the Pro Shop.

Entering the Pro Shop, she saw about a dozen men milling about. Some were talking, but others were examining the merchandise, which, by their sideways glances, she had become a part of.

She walked toward the door leading to the stairs that led to the bag drop area, but she had no intention of going that far.

Seeing a man about to exit, she asked, "Excuse me, do you know Ron Lee?"

"Yes, ma'am, I do," answered Rich Freeman.

"Would you give this to him for me? Please."

"I'd be more than happy to, miss."

"Thank you. That's very kind of you."

"Should I tell him who it's from?"

Hesitating for a moment, she smiled and said, "Tell him it is from Isabella."

"Consider it done," Richie said with a smile as he exited the Pro Shop.

Freeman was halfway down the stairs when he heard his name being called to load his bag. Spotting Ron Lee on the far side of the practice green, he hurried over to Ken Hall who was standing just a few feet away. Handing Ken the envelope, Freeman spoke a few words, and then rushed over to the bag drop area.

Isabella had waited until Freeman had reached ground level before walking out onto the top landing of the

113

stairs. She watched the man to whom she had given the envelope approach a man and hand it over.

*Michael needs to get his eyes checked,* she thought. *This guy is wearing a green jacket with gray pants.*

The target was only 40 feet away. Opening the left flap of her coat, she stood against the railing. She held the pistol, hidden from view by the open flap, waist high. She fired three muted shots. *Thump, thump, thump.* All found their mark.

She watched the man fall to the ground, twitch once, twice, and then no more. As men rushed over to the fallen man, Isabella entered the Pro Shop and retraced her steps back to the waiting limo.

Minutes later, Michael had the limo cruising east on Hwy 501. Isabella, her work complete, sat in quiet solitude in the back seat, and while sipping a glass of red wine, thought about her flight back home to Mexico.

# CHAPTER 27

**"Good morning, Heather**. What do our two famous FBI agents have you doing so early in the day?"

"Good morning, Fran."

The two women, both top-notch secretaries for their respective bosses, were standing in a small room that housed a copying machine.

"Where are your two bosses? I didn't see them this morning."

"Today is Tuesday and they are both playing golf. I expect they'll be in later this afternoon though. They came up with something important regarding the Falano case."

"Oh, really! What did they come up with?"

"They searched the Falano home yesterday and found a calendar with strange notations and the wife's journal. They were here until about 8:00 last night trying to decipher it. Ron wanted copies made of the calendar and specific journal pages."

"Mmm, a journal. That's always a grabber. Don't you think it reeks with mystery, Heather?"

"I must agree, Fran," answered Heather, nodding her head. "Heck, neither Ron nor Tim can make either heads or tails of it as yet, and those guys are brainiacs."

"I'm sure they will come up with something," said Fran. "Harry thinks those two get all the glamorous cases."

The Harry she was alluding to was Harry Albright, who also held, as did Ron Lee, the title of Special Agent.

"Harry, in all honesty, has a valid argument," remarked a grinning Heather. Then, as she completed making the copies, she asked, "Will I see you at lunch?"

"I'll be there, Heather. Have a good day."

Fran made copies of the documents she needed and then headed back to her office. As she returned to her desk, a few of the agents in the pool area stopped her to make small talk.

Knowing how much Fran liked to talk, two agents, both fond of Heather, stopped her as she made her way back to her desk. During their conversations, Fran let it slip about the calendar and journal. Anyone sitting nearby also heard the conversations.

By the time Fran returned to her desk, a dozen or more people in the pool area knew of what Ron and Tim had uncovered.

"Good morning, Mr. Albright," greeted Fran as she entered her boss's office. "Here are the copies you asked for, sir."

"Thank you, Fran. Anything happening that I should know about?"

"Not that I can say, sir. Oh, wait, there is one thing."

"What's that, Fran?" asked Albright as he sorted through his morning mail and memos.

"Special Agent Lee has found something important at the Falano home."

"Oh," replied Albright, stopping his sorting to look up at Fran. "And what did he find?"

"A calendar and Mrs. Falano's journal."

"Really. Well, that sounds interesting. I must talk with Ron."

"Oh, he is not working today, sir. He's playing golf."

"That's right. It's Tuesday, isn't it."

"Yes, sir," answered Fran.

"Could you get me some coffee, Fran? Oh, I didn't have time for breakfast this morning. I'm famished. Would you mind picking up a tasty pastry for me from the cafeteria? Something with chocolate, please."

"Be happy to do it, sir. Would you like for me to get your coffee, first?"

"No need for that. When you have the pastry, you can bring the coffee."

"I'll be back in a jiffy, Mr. Albright."

"No need to hurry, Fran. I won't starve to death."

Fran, closing the door behind her, headed to the cafeteria.

Albright took his cell phone from his jacket pocket and made a call.

Five minutes after Heather and Fran had used the copying machine, the door to the room was closed, and a sign hung on the door reading, "Out of Order."

Inside the locked room, someone was attempting to recover images of recently copied documents.

The recovery procedure was tricky, but with the right talents, it was doable.

By midday, Cameron Driscoll would have his own copy of the calendar and the journal pages.

Finding the flash drive would come down to those best equipped to solving a cunning puzzle.

Only one thing would slow the process: dead people.

# CHAPTER 28

**"What the hell** is going on, Tim?"

"It looks like someone has passed out, Ron."

"Who?"

"Let's go have a look-see."

Havoc was reigning around the fallen body of Ken Hall.

"Look at the blood!" yelled Joe Saffran. "It's everywhere!"

Ron and Tim, approaching the mob scene, heard Saffran's exclamation and immediately told those in front of them to "get the hell out of the way."

Having made their way through the crowd, Ron asked, "Who knows what the hell happened here?"

"Someone shot  him three times in the back, Ron," Tim said, after examining the wounds. "Two of the bullets went through. The third is still in there somewhere. He's dead."

Looking down, Ron noticed something in Ken's right hand. "Hey, Tim, what's that in his hand?"

Tim reached over and drew the envelope from Hall's dead hand.

"That's the envelope I gave to him, Ron," said Richie Freeman after making his way through the crowd.

"You gave him this envelope?"

"Yeah. She meant it for you, Ron."

"Me? She?"

"Yeah, the lady said to give it to you. Just as I started your way, they had called my name to load my bag. Since you were on the far side of the putting green, I asked Kenny to give it to you."

"Talk to me about this lady, Rich."

"She stopped me in the Pro Shop and asked if I would give you this envelope."

"Hold it a minute, Rich. Stay right here." Turning to face the crowd, Ron yelled, "This is a crime scene. I want everyone to get back at least ten yards. If any of you noticed a woman in the Pro Shop, we need to talk. If anyone saw someone they didn't recognize, we will need to talk. Until I say so, no one leaves!"

"I'll take care of calling Baxter, Ron," said Tim, pulling out his cell phone.

"Okay, Rich. Talk to me about this woman. What did she look like? How tall? How big? The color of her hair, eyes, anything you can remember. Did she say anything to you?"

"Yeah, she did."

"What? What did she say?"

"She told me her name."

"What! What did she say it was?"

"Isabella."

"Isabella? She told you that her name was Isabella?"

"Yeah, Ron, she said Isabella."

"What else did she say?"

"I was heading out the door, and she stopped me and asked if I knew you."

"She asked if you knew me. She said my name?"

"Yeah, she did."

"Then what, Rich."

"I walked out and, well, I told you the rest."

"Tell me what she looked like."

"She was about five-five, weighed... maybe 120. Her hair was jet black, she had dark brown eyes, and a perfect set of teeth. The lady was a looker, no doubt."

"Was she black or white?"

"Neither, I guess."

"What the hell is that supposed to mean, Richie!"

"I think she was from south of the border."

Which border would that be, Rich? Canada's or Mexico's?"

"Mexico's!"

"So she was Mexican?"

"Yes."

"I'm guessing," declared Ron, "that you know this because you may have eaten a fajita or two? Maybe even a taco, here or there?"

"I've eaten my share. Hey, what can I say. She looked... Mexican."

"Any other countries you might want to throw into the mix, Ricardo?"

"Perhaps. She may have come from Honduras, Columbia, El Salvador. I don't know."

"Have you ever thought about getting a job at the U.N."

"The United Nations?"

"Either that or Uncle Nick's store for hombres."

"Never heard of the place."

"I wasn't serious, Ri-car-do."

"Oh."

"Did she speak with an accent, Rich?"

"If she did, I didn't pick up on it."

"Hmm, no surprise there," murmured Ron.

"What's that supposed to mean?" asked Richie, a wounded look on his face. "What are you inferring?"

"I'm not inferring anything, Rich," replied Ron with a shit-eating grin. "Let me ask you something."

"What?" asked an indignant Richie.

"How did you target her as Mexican? Wait! Let me guess. She was wearing a sombrero, maybe?"

"No, she was a woman. They don't wear sombreros... do they?"

"Did you see her come out of the Pro Shop?"

"No, I..."

"I did," said a familiar voice.

"Fred?"

"Yeah, I saw her, Ron."

"What the hell, Fred, I can't deal with any of your bullshit, right now. You may as well tell me you saw Santa Claus fly over."

"Hey, Santa flew over about a month ago," replied Fred. Didn't you see him? Maybe you were in the house wrapping donuts."

"Get out of here, Fred."

"No, wait, Ron, I saw her. Honest."

"Honest? I thought that was a word they left out of your German vocabulary."

"Now don't be that way, Ron. I'm trying to help."

"Fred, if I were to put you on the stand to testify, they would laugh me out of court. Hell, the whole county knows you as 'Fibbing Fred.' Your testimony would be useless."

"I wouldn't mess around about something like this, Ron. I watched her come out of the Pro Shop. She stood on the upper deck for a moment and then she moved over and stood next to the railing. It looked like she was taking in the scenery."

"That's it? That's all you got for me, Fred? She stood next to the railing?"

"Yeah, well, she opened her coat and held out the left flap."

"Coat? You said nothing about a coat, Richie."

"I was getting to it."

"Getting to it? What? Do you think we got all goddamn day here, Rich?"

Then turning his attention back to Fred, Ron asked, "What else do you have for me?"

"That's it for me, Ron."

"You've been a great help, Fred."

"Really?"

"Ahh, no."

"Maybe I can help, Ron," said an approaching Al Lowe.

"And what revelations do you possess, Mr. Lowe?"

"I didn't see the guy…"

"Guy? What guy?"

"Give me a minute, Ron. Okay?"

"Sorry. Go ahead, tell me what you saw."

"As I was saying, I didn't see the guy approach the bag drop. I did, however, see him looking at the tee sheet posted on the shed's door."

"Are you sure he was looking at our tee sheet?"

"I'm damn sure, Ron, seeing it's the only fucking thing hanging on the door."

"No need to get testy, Al. I'll lock you up faster than Fred can tell a lie."

"Hmm, sorry, Ron, but you don't look that fast. In fact, I doubt anything living is that fast!"

"That's a good point, Al," said Tim.

Ignoring the verbal slaps directed his way, Ron asked, "How was he dressed, Al?"

"That's what caught my eye. He didn't dress to play golf. He wore black loafers and dress socks. Who the hell plays golf in loafers and dress socks? Huh? Tell me!"

"What else was he wearing?"

"He had on dress slacks. The kind you wear to church. He also was wearing a long-sleeve blue shirt and a dark blue vest. In my book, Ron, that's not golfing attire. Not around here, at least."

Tim, standing nearby, hearing Al's description of the man, blurted, "Hey, I talked to that guy!"

"You talked to him!" bellowed Ron. "What the hell did he say, Tim?"

"He asked if I knew you."

"Yeah, and then what?"

"Sorry to have to admit this, Ron, but I pointed you out to him," said Tim with a look of shame. "He said he was from the Pro Shop and you had forgotten your receipt. Hey, it sounded logical to me. Who knew?"

"It's obvious that you had no clue," answered Ron, before turning back to Al, saying, "Okay. You said you didn't see him approach. Did you see him leave?"

"I did! I bet you'd like to know where he went."

"Don't be a wiseass, Al. One of our buddies just got murdered."

Al's eyes flicked to where Ken Hall lay bleeding out on the edge of the practice green. Taking a deep breath, he answered, "He walked across the parking lot and got into a black limo parked at the far end of the lot."

"A stretch?"

"I wouldn't say it was a stretch limo. But it was a limo. A Cadillac if I'm not mistaken."

"Anything else you might have seen, Al?"

"That's about it, Ron. We drove by the limo on our way to the first tee. It had tinted windows all the way around, making it impossible to see inside."

As Ron was finishing up his interrogation of Al, the State Police arrived, along with a forensic team.

Robert Edge, the county coroner, wasn't far behind.

"Seems a fella can't even play a round of golf without worrying about being shot at these days, Ron."

"Thing is, Bob, I believe whoever did this meant for me to be the target."

"You don't say. Damn, what a waste."

"What do you mean, Robert?"

"Those bullets, hitting the wrong target. Real waste of good shooting if you ask me," replied Edge with a grin.

"Screw you, Robert."

"Never at a loss for crisp dialogue, are you, Ron?"

"Up yours, Bob."

"Yikes! There it is! Another of those Ron Lee snappy comebacks!"

"Oh, hell," said Tim, "he has a plethora of retorts."

"Wow!" remarked Edge. "Plethora and retorts! Those are some big words for a short FBI underling."

"Kiss my ass, Bob," replied Tim.

"Geez, Ron, you're rubbing off on your partner at a faster clip than I thought possible."

"I didn't realize how obnoxious you are, Bob," voiced Ron.

"In layman's terms," added Tim, "if case you couldn't decipher his true meaning, he's saying you're an asshole."

"I love working with you guys," laughed Edge as he made his way toward the body.

# CHAPTER 29

**It was nearing** 1:00 when Driscoll got the call.
*"I have what you need. Send someone to pick it up."*

An hour later Driscoll was sitting at his desk looking at the images his mole in the FBI had uncovered.

"Are you any good at solving puzzles, Tony?"

Tony Rabon, a Princeton University graduate and an otherwise brilliant individual, was not only Driscoll's accountant, but also his most trusted friend.

Knowing that the FBI was having difficulty in making anything out of the articles recovered, Driscoll called on the smartest man in his organization.

"Puzzles? I enjoy doing puzzles, but you're not talking about a puzzle in the truest sense of the word."

"No, I'm not. But all the same, this is…"

"Puzzling is the word you're searching for Mr. Driscoll. Make no mistake, Cameron, what we have here isn't a puzzle."

"Then what the hell is it?"

"It's a riddle."

"Okay, it's a riddle. I know I don't pay you to solve riddles, Tony, but I need your full attention on this. There's no certainty, but I believe what we are looking at is telling us where Falano hid that damn flash drive."

"Well, I'm thinking the calendar's scribblings have some meaning," remarked Tony. Then pointing at the dates of 15 and 17, he added, "Those two pique my interest. Read them to me, Cameron."

The one on the 15th reads, *"Three ahead of journey. The one on the 17th reads, Keeping it between the isolated feathers."*

"The other pages are from a journal. Correct?"

"Yeah," replied Cameron. "The wife's journal."

"Look again at the first notation, Cameron."

"Okay. What about it?"

"Three ahead of journey. Agreed?"

"Yeah, I'll go with that, Tony."

"Do you have a dictionary?"

Cameron, turned to a bookshelf behind his desk and extracted an Oxford Dictionary and Thesaurus.

"Hector was clever," acknowledged the accountant. "Look up the word, 'journey'."

"A few seconds later, Cameron excitedly said, "Got it!"

"Good. Now count backward from 'journey' three words and tell me the next word."

"Journal!" screamed Cameron.

"I'm more than convinced, Cameron, that Hector has coded the flash drive's location in his wife's journal."

"If that's true, Tony, I have what I need to find the flash drive. Damn, I knew I needed you for this. You're really smart, my friend!"

"I can't say the FBI has figured that out as yet, but it won't be long before they do. You had better find out the hidden message in that journal before they do."

"There are at least 20 pages here, Tony. Where do we begin?"

"When did you discover Hector had hacked your computers?"

"It was on a Thursday, the 17th. We overheard his phone call to his SLED supervisor."

"Hector made the notation on the calendar, two days prior. Therefore, we need to look at all the pages dated from Tuesday through Thursday."

"Tony, what's your take on the 'isolated feathers' notation?"

"That's where you'll find the flash drive, Cameron. Did Hector have birdhouses?"

"I don't know," answered Driscoll.

"How about pillows? Did your men check the pillows?"

"I doubt it. Hell, they lost the woman's damn finger! Why should I expect they checked the pillows? Do you think that's where it might be, Tony?"

"No, I don't. I'm sure the FBI searched the pillows and if they had found it, you'd be sitting in a cell by now."

"Good point, Tony. God, you're smart."

"Thanks but hold the applause until you have the flash drive in your hands."

"Let Linda make a copy of these pages for you," said Driscoll as he buzzed for his secretary. "You can work on this at home. You get this solved for me and I'll give you a real nice bonus."

At that moment Linda entered the office and Driscoll asked her to make Tony copies.

Once Linda left the room, Tony asked, "What's your definition of 'nice'?"

"How about fifty-grand?"

"I must admit, that sounds 'nice,'" said Tony with a huge smile. "But a hundred sounds better."

"I'll do a hundred if you solve it in the next 24 hours."

"Deal," said the accountant with a knowing smile.

Linda returned and handed Tony his copies in a folder and returned the originals to Driscoll.

"Listen, I need to get going, Cameron. I'm meeting my wife for a late luncheon at Sam Snead's."

"That's a nice place. Good food," commented Driscoll.

"I'll get in touch the moment I have something."

"You had better make it quick, Tony. Time is not on my side."

The threat was implicit, and Tony got the message.

*************

Knowing he was running at least 15 minutes late and hoping to save time, Tony took the Robert Edge Parkway where he merged onto Route 31 going south.

Traveling south on 31, the 2015 Mercedes was doing 77mph when it passed a Lowe's semi, loaded with appliances, destined for the company's store in Surfside Beach.

He had only moved past the big rig by less than 25 yards, when the car's right front tire blew. Tony might still be alive had he not been texting his wife that he was on his way. The distraction, however, impacted his reaction time, and the car swerved in front of the semi.

It was no contest.

Weighing over twenty tons and running at 73mph, the semi slammed the right-side of the Mercedes, smashing it into unrecognizable pieces of steel and plastic.

The impact of the collision threw Tony, having failed to attach his seatbelt, through the front window onto the highway. A split-second later, the truck's four rear wheels crushed his body like it was a ripe tomato.

When the coroner, taking the family's state of mind into account, released his report, he stated that Tony had died before being struck by the truck. How he could determine this, based on the condition of the body, went unquestioned.

The truck itself, while attempting to stop, jack-knifed, then flipped over, spraying, for a hundred yards or more along the highway, dozens of boxed refrigerators, stoves, and dishwashers.

It took almost six hours for clean-up crews to clear the area of debris, enough so that traffic could pass. State police arrived to investigate the accident, and to handle four lanes of southbound traffic that had backed up all the way to Route 9, twelve miles to the north.

Late that evening, long after darkness had fallen, an officer found the accountant's briefcase, still intact, under a guardrail. Inside was a folder and in the folder were papers, stamped, "Property of the FBI."

# CHAPTER 30

**It was half-past** two when Ron and Tim returned to their office. They had questioned everyone who saw either the man looking for Ron, or the mysterious woman seen in the Pro Shop. They had solid descriptions of both, and although both were suspects, no one saw either of them execute the shooting. There was, however, little doubt in Ron's mind, that it was the woman who fired the fatal shots.

Ron's beliefs were all but confirmed by Robert Edge, the Horry County coroner. Upon examining the entry wounds in Ken's back, Edge established that the bullets entered at a steep downward angle. To prove his findings, they took measurements from the railing where the woman had positioned herself, to where Ken had been standing. Ron was waiting for the results, but it was beyond doubt the shots came from the top landing of the stairway leading into and out of the Pro Shop.

The unenviable job of notifying Ken's wife, Irene, of her husband's death, fell to Bill Baxter. A contingent of Ken's golfing buddies and their wives went along for support.

"I was her damn target, Tim," Ron said, with a somber look covering his face. "If Richie had given this envelope to me instead of Kenny, he'd be alive, and I'd be lying buck naked on one of Robert Edge's tables."

"Now, Ron, that's an image my mind's eye could have done without. I'm sure it will haunt me for a few weeks, if not for a lifetime."

"Up yours, Pond."

Tim, putting the visual behind him, asked, "Who do you think she is, Ron? What are the chances her name really is, Isabella?"

"Just before I left the Air Force my buddies in the CIA, who were working on drug trafficking, told me that cartels are using women as sicarios."

"Female assassins, eh? Nice work if you can get it," said Tim.

"Yeah, they call them… 'Las Flakas', translated means Skinny Girl, which makes no sense to me."

"That is weird."

"Yeah. Anyway, they told me that there was one 'Flakas' who was more dangerous than most male sicarios. Her name: Isabella Sanchez."

"Damn, Ron, a Mexican cartel sent their best damn Flakas to Myrtle Beach to kill you! Why?"

"I'm not sure why, Tim. A good guess, however, would be our taking out the Bongino brothers."

At that moment their office door swung open and Jim Braddock rushed in.

"I just returned from a two-day closed meeting in DC. I was in flight when I heard the news. Are you two all right?"

After assuring Jim they were fine, they brought him up-to-date on their activities over the past two days. It started with the murder of Jack Clayton, the Horry County Sheriff. They spoke of their discussion with Jose Perez which led them to the murders of the Tree Amigos' receptionist, and of the Tree Amigos themselves. After grabbing a cup of coffee, they spent significant time on their findings at the Falano home. They ended with the murder of Ken Hall and of their suspect, Isabella Sanchez.

"You guys have been busy."

"Yeah, and today was our day off. How do you think that's going?" asked Tim with a hint of sarcasm.

Nodding that he understood where Tim was coming from, Braddock asked, "Are you convinced Sanchez is here in Myrtle Beach, Ron?"

"Am I sure? No. But there's some overwhelming evidence that she's here, including some eyewitnesses who talked with her. I've asked Heather to see if we have a file on her. Maybe there's a picture, but I wouldn't bet on it."

"There was a guy with her," added Tim. "One of our golfing buddies saw him getting into a black limo parked at the far end of the parking lot. I'm guessing he was her driver."

"We put a BOLO out on the limo," said Ron, "but I'm betting they have already switched vehicles."

"A black limo," said Jim. "Was it a Cadillac?"

"One witness thought it might be a Caddy. Why?" asked Ron.

"I received word that Georgetown Police found two police officers shot to death in the main station, including its Chief-of-Police, Forest Lamb. A passerby reports seeing a black Cadillac parked in front of the station."

"Isn't Lamb under investigation to having ties to one of the Mexican cartels?" asked Tim.

"Yeah, the Bureau is certain that he was responsible for keeping the coast clear when shipments came into the harbor down there," Jim responded.

"Hmm, if that's true," said Ron, "and I believe it is, then it appears the cartel wasn't too happy with their loss of the Bongino brothers. Someone had to pay and Captain Lamb paid the price for doing a bad job. May his soul rest in hell. Amen."

"That would cement your thoughts, Ron, on why this woman was looking to kill you," said Tim. "You orchestrated the Bongino raid. Some think that cost the cartel about 100 mil."

"Look," said Jim, changing the subject, "I want to talk with you about these cop killings. I know you're tied up with this Falano case, but we need to sort this out."

"I've been giving it some thought, Jim."

"And?"

"Let me talk with Baxter. He's checking on some alibies for me. I'd like to hear what he has to say. I also want to have the financial records of each couple checked, including all insurance policies on the husbands. Let's have the office pool work on that, Jim."

"Okay, Ron, I'll get that ball rolling. Today is Tuesday. Can you close this by Friday?"

"I won't make any promises, Jim, but we'll give it our best shot."

There was a knock at the door. Before Ron could extend an invitation, the door swung open and Heather stepped into the room.

"Heather!" cried both men. "We were just thinking about you," said Ron.

"Oh, was I wearing clothes in your thoughts?"

"Heather! What kind of talk is that? Are you implying that we are dirty old men?"

"Hey partner. Speak for yourself!" said Tim. "Heather, in case you hadn't noticed, I'm not old."

"Look, fellas, I've got some news for you."

"What do you have?" asked Ron leaning forward in his chair expecting something good coming his way.

"I have a report for Tim. It's the listing you wanted of all retail sales of white marble stone that exceeded 15 yards over the past two years."

"That's a lot of stone, partner."

"Yeah, it is, but I called the place on 501 that sells stones and asked how many yards it would take to cover a 100-foot driveway. They told me 15 yards."

"Why a hundred foot driveway?" asked Ron.

"That's the size driveway most builders are putting down nowadays."

"Hmm, I didn't know that," said Ron. "Why are you so sure that it's a driveway, anyway?"

"Remember the guy killed in the shootout at the garage where they found Hector's body?"

"Duh, yeah," said Ron going into his dumb-looking routine.

"Okay, okay, it was a stupid question. Anyway, I asked Baxter to have that guy's vehicle checked for marble stones in his tires."

"Let me guess," said Ron. "The lab found marble stone particles in the tread! Da-da!"

"Da-da. Yes they did!" replied Tim.

"Good job, Agent Pond. There's still a chance, albeit a slim one, that you might make a good FBI agent yet."

Ignoring Ron, Tim turned to Heather, asking, "How many in the list?"

"Twenty three. Here it is."

Opening the folder she had handed to him, he said, "It's more than I hoped for, but not as bad as I thought it could be. How many agents are available who can handle this job, Heather?"

"I think we can scrounge up three agents to do your dirty work."

"Okay, split the list up between them and have them meet me in the conference room first thing in the morning. I want to discuss what it is I'm looking for."

"What else do you have for us, Heather," asked Ron.

"I checked the files for Isabella Sanchez. We have photos but they aren't worth squat. There are, however, various descriptions of her made by some of our CIA contacts. They differ only in the color of her hair. Sometimes she's blond, sometimes a brunette,…"

"I get the picture," said Ron, reaching for the folder Heather was holding.

"Something happened this afternoon that may be of interest to you guys."

"What's that?" asked Ron.

"Tony Rabon," answered Heather.

"Driscoll's accountant? What about him?"

"Reports say he was just splattered all over Route 31 by a semi."

"Damn, it's 'accrual' world," remarked Tim.

"Talk about, depreciation," chimed in Ron.

"You two are callous," said Heather, as she left the office… smiling.

\*\*\*\*\*\*\*\*\*\*\*\*\*

It was nearing 9:00pm when Ron and Tim called it a day. They had been writing reports most of the afternoon, only taking a 30-minute break for dinner around 7:00.

They were about to leave the building when none other than Bill Baxter came walking through the front door.

"Glad I caught you guys."

"Oh, and why is that, Bill?"

"Did you hear about Tony Rabon?"

"We heard a semi ran over his sorry ass."

"I'll admit he was that all right, but no one should die like he did. Believe me, when I say, it was gruesome."

"That's not why you stopped by, is it, Bill?"

"No, Ron, it isn't," said Baxter, holding up a scuffed briefcase. "This was Tony Rabon's. One of my men found it at the scene of the accident."

"And?"

"And this was inside, Ron," answered Baxter as he opened the case and extracted a manila folder that he handed over.

Ron opened the folder and his eyes appeared to grow as big as saucers and his face turned almost as red as a radish.

"Son-of-a-bitch!" screamed Ron, his voice echoing through the almost deserted building.

"What is it, Ron?" asked Tim, shocked by Ron's outrage.

"Driscoll has Corrina Falano's journal pages!"

# CHAPTER 31

"**Tim, your three** agents are ready."

It was Heather reminding Tim of the meeting he had asked her to arrange. Attending the meeting were the agents Tim would assign to track down large deliveries of marble stone made over the past two years.

"Damn, Heather, I've only had one cup of coffee. How do you expect me to function?"

"You gotta up your game, Agent," chirped Ron, who was nibbling on a chocolate croissant.

"Is that right, Special Agent Donut? Oops, I meant Lee. When I get back, what's our action plan?"

"Corrina's journal. Although Driscoll has a copy, he lost the best person, in Tony Rabon, to help him solve it."

"Hey but aren't you lucky! You got me!"

"Yeah," said Ron with a look of feigned disgust, "I guess that makes Driscoll and me, almost even."

As the door closed, a clenched hand, showing a single finger extended, was the last thing Ron saw of Tim.

Ron grinned and then turned to Corrina Falano's journal.

As Tim and Heather walked toward the conference room, Tim asked, "Who do I have?"

"I volunteered Adams, Thompson, and Miller to do your bidding. All junior agents who are itching to get involved in whatever cases you and the Colonel are working."

"I'm guessing that this assignment might lower their standards regarding Ron and myself," said Tim, as he opened the conference room door.

"Morning, men. I guess you know who I am, but if you don't, I'm Agent Tim Pond, the brains and the backbone of the twosome of Agents Lee and Pond."

Smiles and grins broadened the faces of the three agents.

"Okay, fellas, let's get serious. As you know, someone murdered a fellow undercover FBI agent. During the autopsy, the coroner found traces of marble stone on his body. We also found that same stone in the tires of the man who tried to shoot it out with three Horry County sheriff deputies. I believe there is a driveway somewhere covered in white marble stone. I also believe that wherever this driveway may be, is the location where they tortured and murdered FBI Agent Hector Falano. We have a list of 23 addresses of people who have ordered large quantities of this stone in the past two years."

"You want us to find this driveway, I take it, Agent Pond," said Agent Paul Adams."

"Very deductive of you, Agent... Adams, is it?"

"Yes, sir."

"Let me give you some advice, Agent... Adams. From now on just sit and listen. This isn't a discussion we are having. You are being given a job assignment. Orders, if you will. This isn't a two-way conversation, Is that understood, Agent... Adams?"

"Sorry, sir."

"I'm not asking for an apology, Agent... Adams, I'm asking if you understood?"

"Understood, Agent Pond, sir."

"Good. Now here are your assignments. Heather has split up the addresses. I believe she has grouped them to minimize your travel. Is that correct, Heather?"

"That's correct, Agent Pond."

"Now, I suspect that you will find most of this stone used in flower beds, or maybe in walkways. But maybe, you'll be lucky enough to come across a driveway covered with white marble stones."

Agent Adams lifted his hand as if to ask a question. Tim shot him a look that said, "Do you want to die?" Adams, without saying a word, lowered his hand.

"If you come across a driveway of white marble stone, do nothing! Don't investigate, don't leave your vehicle, and don't drive back and forth in front of the property. All I want you to do is put a check-mark on your list next to that property's address. Complete the rest of your list – there may be more driveways out there with white marble stone. We need to know them all. Now maybe you're asking yourself, *'What do I do when I'm done?'*"

All three agents nodded their heads, although Adam's nod was briefer than those of the other two agents.

"When you're done, return to the office and locate the property owner's identification. Dig around. Find details about that owner. Simple, right?"

All three barked a simultaneous, "Yes, sir!"

"Okay, draw a car from the vehicle pool and get on your way. You have the entire day to complete this job. Have the results on my desk by 4:00pm. Thank you, and good luck."

Tim, without another word, left the room, leaving the three agents speechless.

Heather, seeing their faces, smiled, then said, "Here are your lists, gentlemen. One of you got lucky and drew the straw with only seven locations. The others have eight to check out. Happy hunting, fellas."

"Damn!" said Agent Adams, once Heather was clear. "I never realized what a hard-ass that guy is."

"You made quite an impression, Paul, but let me add, not a good one," said a grinning Sam Miller.

"You better hope you find the driveway, Paul," advised Agent Steve Thompson. "That may get you back in his good graces."

"Yeah, you're right, Steve. I had better, is right."

"Let's get going, guys," voiced Agent Miller.

While stopping at their desks to gather various items, someone curious, sitting in their vicinity, would ask, "What was that all about?"

Without giving it a moment's thought, they detailed their assignment to anyone who asked.

Before leaving the building, someone made a call.

Later that day, two of the agents returned by late afternoon and had their findings on Tim's desk by 4:00, as requested.

Paul Adams, however, didn't return. This went unrealized until 7:00 that evening.

By then, Paul couldn't have told you his own name.

# CHAPTER 32

**Police Lieutenant Thomas** Blake was a detective for the State Police. He was an intelligent and much decorated officer, but he was also heavily in debt to bookies. Tom, it seems, had a bad habit of picking losers.

Hindsight being 20-20, it was unfortunate that Tom walked into Greg's Cabana Bar on the night of June 10 in 2015. He drank a little too much and began telling his woes to a stranger who listened with way too much interest.

The stranger offered Tom a way out, and in a moment of weakness, fueled by desperation, Tom accepted the offer. He sealed his acceptance when he allowed the stranger to stuff $2000 into his jacket pocket.

It was a simple, but lucrative offer. All Tom had to do was 'share' any information the state police had about the Driscoll drug ring. Over the years, Tom only gave up information a half-dozen times. Most of it seemed meaningless, which to Tom's way of thinking, justified his deceit.

For those measly tidbits, Tom received a $1000 a week which he collected every Wednesday morning at 9:00am from a secure mailbox at the Surfside Beach Post Office.

************

The Ghost awakened early and after showering and having a light breakfast, selected a .22 revolver from his arsenal of weapons. Today's work required silence, and with a small silencer attached, the sound of a .22 was as quiet as it would get.

Before leaving the house, he made a call.

"I'm on my way. Should be there in about ten minutes."

*"You want me to turn it off at 8:50?"*

"I'd feel better if you turned them off at 8:45. Just to be on the safe side."

*"Okay, and I'll turn them back on once you have left the lot."*

"Perfect," replied The Ghost. "I'll leave your payment in the usual spot."

Hanging up the phone, he left his house at 8:35 and made his way to the Surfside Post Office, arriving at 8:48. Parking his vehicle in a space close to the post office door, he waited.

He didn't have to wait long.

It was 8:55 when Tom Blake's dark blue Chevy Malibu pulled into the lot. Like The Ghost, Blake parked as close to the front door as possible.

The Ghost watched Blake exit his vehicle and enter the post office. As he made his way toward the door, he searched through his key ring.

*No doubt he's searching for the key to the mailbox,* thought The Ghost as he scrutinized Blake's every move.

Waiting until Blake entered the building, The Ghost left his vehicle and strolled toward the post office door. He knew Blake's mailbox was in the corridor at the far left end of the building. Hoping no others would be in the corridor, The Ghost let go a sigh of relief when, after turning the corner, saw Blake as the corridor's lone occupant.

Blake was about to open his box when he looked up to see The Ghost, who he recognized from various police functions.

"Hey, fancy meeting you here," he said with a cheerful smile. "I'm guessing you have a mailbox in this section."

"No, I don't, Tom. I do, however, have a message from Mr. Driscoll."

From just ten feet away, The Ghost raised the .22 and fired twice. The two soft pops were no louder than a frog's fart. The first bullet penetrated Blake's brain just above the right eye while the second of the hollow-point slugs, shattered his nose, and broke off into dozens of fragments. More than one of those fragments breached his left eye and trachea. Blake fell to the floor, dead.

The Ghost, seeing a key sticking out of Blake's mailbox, decided he would open it and look inside. Stepping over Blake's body, he opened the box, and seeing the stack of cash, removed it and stuffed it into his jacket pocket.

"Just a small bonus for a job well done," he whispered as he walked up the empty corridor and out the building.

Inside, eyes watched as The Ghost's vehicle left the lot, and then a moment later, someone threw a switch that turned the security cameras back on.

The Ghost, as he drove north on Business 17, let his imagination soar to what he would do with the big windfall that would soon come his way. Those thoughts did not include Driscoll's $25,000.

*************

It was 6:00am when Isabella Sanchez awoke feeling fresh and alert after a full night's sleep. She showered and dressed, then called for room service.

"Would you send up a pot of coffee and some rye toast please? I'd like strawberry jelly on the side."

*"It will be there in ten minutes, Miss Gonzalez"*

She spent the night at the Hampton Inn on the Beach, registered as Maria Gonzalez.

Her breakfast arrived within ten minutes, as promised. After giving the waiter a generous tip, she waited a moment, and then checked the hallway for anything suspicious. Nothing seemed out of the ordinary. She had a habit of always siding with caution.

Isabella, savoring a hot cup of coffee, stepped out onto her balcony. She stood coatless in the chilly January air watching the blazing ball of fire rising out of the ocean. It would be a long-lingering memory of her abbreviated visit to Myrtle Beach. She was glad she chose this hotel. It had proven to be an excellent selection.

Michael, having ditched the limo, would pick her up at 7:45 to take her to the airport. While waiting, she flicked on the wide-screen television. She was walking into the bathroom to check her hair when she stopped dead in her tracks. The newscaster was reporting *that an unknown assailant had killed a man at the Burning Ridge Country Club. They have identified the murdered victim as Ken Hall, a resident of the Burning Ridge community.*

She whipped around and walked back toward the television. Standing with her face only a foot from the screen, she listened to the reporter give more detail to the story.

*According to reports, Mr. Hall was not the assassin's intended target. A witness said a Hispanic woman, calling herself Isabella, approached him. He said she asked about Ron Lee, a well-known FBI agent.*

"I should have shot that old geezer, too," Isabella hissed at the tv screen.

*Agent Lee, and the victim, were members of the same playing group. Officials now believe that Lee was the intended target of the assassin.*

"Well, pat yourselves on the back for putting that together," said a mocking Isabella.

*Police are searching for a black Cadillac limo parked nearby just prior to the shooting. The police have descriptions of its driver and the woman. A sketch artist has provided these images, now appearing on your television screen, of the two suspects. Officials ask that you call if you see or come in contact with either of these individuals. Authorities are quick to warn that you should not try to apprehend these suspects as they consider them armed and dangerous.*

Seeing her sketch, which captured the essence of her looks, Isabella's mind went into a frenzy. *Damn. I can't go back without finishing the job. If I do, I'll be dead five minutes after stepping off the plane. But I can't be too bold while I'm here either.*

Glancing back at the screen, she saw Michael's sketch. It was spot-on. *He has become a liability*, thought Isabella. She knew what to do with liabilities, but she also realized, she was also a liability. She had to finish the job before returning to Mexico, but now a huge obstacle stood in her way. Her best weapon, the element of surprise, was no longer available. They know she's here, and to make matters even worse, they have a dead-on description.

Calling Michael, she asked, "Have you seen the news?"

"Yes, I have. I've disguised myself as best I can. I'll pick you up at the front door in five minutes. The car is a silver BMW. Can you be ready?"

"I'm ready," she answered while glancing at her watch and seeing it was 7:30. "I'm heading toward the elevator as we speak!"

Arriving at the elevator bank, she pressed the down button and waited. She was wearing the same coat she wore yesterday when she killed the wrong person. Her right hand was in its pocket and she had a firm grip on her .22 pistol. She would kill anyone who might recognize her.

Her room was on the 12$^{th}$ floor and it made the wait for the elevator excruciating. But in fact, only seconds had passed since she had hailed it. It took another five seconds before she heard the arrival ding, and the elevator doors parted. There were two elderly people inside. They both smiled and said good morning. She nodded, and stepping into the cab, saw that the ground floor button was lit.

The ride down seemed interminable with the elevator stopping at floors 10, 8 and 4.

A passenger who boarded at the 8$^{th}$ floor had a local newspaper in her hand. While riding down, she opened it. To Isabella's horror, she saw her sketch on the front page. She wondered if the woman, after seeing the sketch, would realize she was on the elevator with the suspected killer. She clutched the gun and removed the safety. If recognized, she would kill all five passengers that now occupied the elevator.

But that wouldn't be necessary. The woman barely looked at the paper before folding it in half and tucking it under her arm. Isabella let go a sigh of relief. There would be no time to relax, however, for she knew an even larger gauntlet awaited her once the elevator reached the ground floor. She would need to navigate fifty or more yards of turf, in the form of plush carpeting, before reaching the front door. As the elevator reached the ground floor, she hoped, for her sake and for Michael's, that a silver BMW, parked at the door, awaited her arrival.

The elevator doors slid apart revealing the large expanse of the hotel's lobby. Although wanting to, Isabella refrained from her desire to rush from the elevator. Instead, she allowed all the others to exit ahead of her. While the others exited, she scanned the floor in search of a police force that might be in waiting with weapons drawn.

Not today. The lobby was relatively quiet. Isabella started to the front door. As she passed the front desk, the clerk called out, "Ms. Gonzalez!"

Isabelle came within a hair of whipping out her weapon and shooting anyone in sight, but somehow she held her composure. Glancing toward the young girl, she replied, with a calming voice, "Yes, miss?"

"We just want to say thank you for choosing the Hampton Inn at the Beach. You have a nice day now."

Isabella, her heart pounding like it never had before, smiled, nodded her head, and thanked the young girl who came within a whisker of taking her last breath.

Moments later, Isabella, with no further incidents, exited the front door. Neither a silver BMW nor Michael was anywhere in sight. A quick glance at her watch told her it was 7:33. Only three minutes had passed since she spoke to Michael. It seemed more like thirty. Then she recalled he said he would be here in five minutes. She had to wait an interminable two minutes. Trying not to look obvious, she sat in one of the rocking chairs that the hotel placed outside the door for those who waited for their rides to arrive.

"Good morning, miss," said a young valet. "May I get your vehicle for you?"

"No" she barked. Realizing how she reacted, she said, "I'm sorry. I didn't sleep well last night and I'm on edge this morning. What I meant to say is, I don't have a car. I'm waiting for a ride."

"I understand, miss. It is not a problem," replied the young man who walked away to talk with another valet.

She watched the two young men whispering among themselves while casting glances her way.

*They know,* she thought. *Damn it, Michael, why do you have to be so damn exact!*

She turned away from the gawking young men to see a silver BMW approaching. She rose from the chair and stepped toward the now stopped vehicle. Thank God, it was Michael. She opened the door without a moment's hesitation and climbed into the front passenger seat.

"The airport?" he asked.

She didn't answer Michael. She found herself breathing heavily. After taking a moment to gather her composure, she looked at him, saying, "No, Michael, not the airport. I need to kill the colonel before I dare leave."

"Where to then?"

"What time do the department stores open?"

"10:00."

Drive to a mall where we can wait until the stores open. I need a different look. And so do you."

"Okay, then what?"

"We must get rid of this vehicle. The valets at the hotel will eventually put things together and report this car."

"That won't be a problem, Isabella. I can get us another car in an hour's time."

"That's good. Get something not so ostentatious."

"Okay, but can you tell me why?"

"I'm thinking there is a funeral in our future."

\*\*\*\*\*\*\*\*\*\*\*\*

While Tim was in the conference room with the rookie agents, Ron was on the phone with trooper commander Bill Baxter.

"Bill, have you checked out the alibies I asked about?"

*"Yeah, I did Ron."*

"What did you find out?"

*"Well, the first thing I can report is that Mr. and Mrs. Clayton had no marital difficulties. They were both very much in love. I interviewed officers and friends, and they all swore that Clayton never even looked at another woman. His wife was just as loyal."*

"Interesting, Bill. That changes my thinking in a variety of ways. How about the other two women? Do their alibies stand up?"

*"Airtight, Ron."*

"Now, my friend, here comes the big money question. How about insurance policies?"

*"Yeah, Ron, you may have something there."*

"How so?"

*"Sheila Bennington has a half-million life insurance policy on her husband that pays double if his death is anything but natural."*

"What about the Patterson wife?"

*"She doesn't have an insurance policy, at least not one that pays much of anything, but get this Ron."*

"I'm listening."

*"Her hubby, Jimmy, comes from a wealthy family and by coincidence or maybe not, Jimmy is the sole beneficiary."*

"How much?"

*"Around $4 mil."*

"Yikes! That's a motive! Does the wife get that money now?"

*"All of it, Ron. Every single cent."*

"What about Jack Clayton?"

*"The only thing he had was the standard police policy."*

"That can't be worth spit."

*"I'm guessing she'll get enough to bury the poor bastard,"* suggested Baxter.

"Nothing at all there, Bill? There's no insurance, no hidden money, no inheritance? Nothing?"

*"Nothing, Ron."*

"Okay, here's what I'd like you to do. Check their phone records."

*"We did that. Remember?"*

"Yeah, I do. That check revealed that they hadn't been talking with each other. I'm now wondering if they may have talked to an accomplice. Check for a mutual number that appears only once or twice on both bills."

*"Both women? Not all three?"*

"No. I think the Clayton killing was a red herring to keep us looking in the wrong direction."

*"Are you suggesting those women had an innocent cop killed?"*

"It's possible, Bill."

*"Are you saying what I think you're saying, Ron?"*

"Murder for hire, Bill."

*"You think they hired a contract killer?"*

"That possibility is gaining ground."

*"I'm not sure I would know how to hire a killer, Ron. How in the hell would they know?"*

"That's a good question, Bill, but someone had the savvy."

*"So you're saying the killer murdered Clayton as a freelance thing, just so we would keep chasing our tails?"*

"I am, but that opens up another can of worms, doesn't it?"

*"Yeah,"* admitted Bill. *"It means someone knows how we're conducting the case."*

"Correct, and that means it has to be someone in law enforcement."

*"There's a mole?"*

"Yeah, and there's little doubt he or she is working for me."

# CHAPTER 33

**While Agent Tim** Pond was briefing the three agents on their assignment, Cameron Driscoll was receiving bad news.

"Damn! Damn! Damn!" screamed Driscoll when told of the auto accident that killed Tony Rabon.

"Sorry, boss," said Bruno, who had delivered the bad news. "I'm told he swerved in front of a big semi."

"I don't give a rat's ass about how he died," shouted Driscoll. "Accountants, even good ones, are a dime a dozen. The problem I'm having is he had something that, if found, and I'm sure it was, will reveal a dirty little secret. Something I've had hidden in my repertoire of dirty secrets for some time now. It getting out will jeopardize an asset far more valuable than Tony Rabon."

"Is there anything we can do, Mr. Driscoll?" asked Jocko.

"I don't know, Jocko. Can you read?" asked Driscoll, in a demeaning tone.

"Not too good," replied the 300-pounder.

"Then no, you can't help."

"Okay," said Jocko, backing away from Driscoll's desk.

Turning his attention toward Bruno, Driscoll asked, "What have you done about Jose Perez?"

Before Bruno could answer, the phone rang. Calling was Driscoll's "dirty little secret."

Driscoll listened with great intensity for over two minutes. As he listened, he jotted something down on a piece of paper. Laying the pen down, he said, "You had better watch yourself. I'm sure they found copies of the journal in Tony Rabon's wreckage. They'll know they must have a spy in their midst. As for this current situation, I have an idea. Go to the house. Wait there for Bruno. I'll call you and tell you what to do."

Hanging up the phone, Driscoll let go a hissing, "Damn!"

"What is it, boss?" asked Bruno.

"The cartel, it appears, has sent an assassin to kill, amongst others, Ron Lee, the FBI's so-called, Super-Agent."

"They didn't tell you?" asked Bruno.

"No, Bruno, it's obvious they didn't," responded Driscoll, while becoming more enraged by the second.

"You said, 'amongst others, boss. Who else did the assassin kill?" asked Jocko.

"She killed that cop down in Georgetown we were paying."

"She?" asked a surprised Bruno.

"Yeah, my source said it was a woman, who goes by the name of Isabella. She tried to kill Lee yesterday at a golf course but she killed the wrong man."

"Boss, I don't mean to upset you, but if they didn't inform you that she was coming, then it's possible…"

"Yeah, I know what you're thinking, Bruno. Maybe I'm on her list."

"I'm guessing losing the Bongino brothers has pissed them off," offered Bruno. "They're taking out anyone who had something to do with their being taken down." Then he added, "We're the ones responsible for Forest Lamb."

"Thanks, Bruno, but I know the score," snarled Driscoll.

Brushing aside for a moment his thoughts about the cartel's assassin, Driscoll said, "There's something I need you guys to do, right now."

"What's that, boss?"

"The FBI is sending agents out to find driveways covered in white marble stones."

"We got a driveway like that, Bruno," said Jocko.

"That's very good, Jocko," said Driscoll with a sneer. Then extending his arm toward Bruno, he said, "Here's a list of addresses that one of their agents is checking out. Supposedly he is checking them in order. Our place is fifth on the list. Intercept him before he gets there. Take him to the house. Our man will be there, waiting. Give him the list. There's a small, but important, task you must do for him. He'll tell you what that is."

"Okay, boss."

"Interrogate the agent and find out what he knows before you..."

"I got it, boss. Don't worry. We'll take care of it."

"When you get back, we need to discuss this cartel assassin. I don't want to be looking over my shoulder."

"We'll take care of her too, Mr. Driscoll," said Jocko.

"Yeah, okay, now get going. I need to work on this puzzle."

"Puzzle? I love puzzles, Mr. Driscoll," said Jocko with a big grin that exposed a few missing front teeth.

"Do you, Jocko? Well, that's a shame because you can't read and you need to read to solve this puzzle!"

"Someone could read it to me," replied Jocko.

Driscoll, losing his patience with the semi-retarded henchman, shot Jocko a look that would have stopped a train. Then, with his face contorted with hate, and a voice spitting venom, he growled, "Out! Get the hell out of my office! Do what I pay you to do! Now!"

Leaving Driscoll's office, the two henchmen left the building and as they got into Bruno's Mercedes, Jocko said, "He's not a nice guy, Bruno."

"No, he's not. We aren't nice either, Jocko, but that man... that man is the devil."

# CHAPTER 34

**The Coastal Grand** Mall was only a short ride from the hotel. They had been sitting in its parking lot for over an hour and still had an hour and a half to wait before the mall opened at 10:00am.

"Maybe we should use this time to switch cars, Isabella."

"No, Michael. Not a good idea."

"Why not?"

Isabella, having far more experience than Michael, explained.

"There's always a chance someone inside may recognize us. Then, they will use the outside security cameras to identify our vehicle. It's best to wait until after we leave, before we switch."

Michael, seeing the wisdom of her words, nodded agreement.

He had parked near the entrance to the Belk store.

"Do they carry wigs, Michael?"

"I wouldn't know, Isabella, never having a need for one."

"No, I guess you wouldn't," Isabella replied with a smile. Although she liked her driver, she knew, when she completed the job, Michael too, would have to die.

"I just checked on my phone, and Belk's has a hair and beauty salon," reported Michael. "They must carry wigs, but then again, it's just my assumption."

"I, too, would assume as much. We'll see."

An hour later the mall's doors opened.

Michael went in first, and after doing a quick scan of the immediate area, texted Isabella that all was clear.

Isabella walked into the mall wearing a scarf over her head, hiding much of her jet black hair. She had removed all of her makeup in the car, and although looking far from haggard, she appeared older than her 29 years. She headed straight to the clothing department where she selected an unusual dress. While checking out, the salesclerk held up the dress, then gave Isabella a questioning glance.

Isabella, seeing the look, laughed while saying, "Oh, it's not for me. It's for a friend."

Minutes later she was roaming around in the hair and beauty parlor department.

An older woman, wearing a nametag that identified her as Helen, approached, asking, "May I help you?"

"Yes, I'm looking for a wig. Something short, in light brown, or even dark blond."

"We may have a few selections that you might like. Please sit here at this dressing table. I'll be back in a moment."

Waiting until the woman had passed through a curtained doorway, Isabella, always leaning on the side of caution, left her chair and rushed over to the curtain.

When she peeked through the doorway, she saw Helen talking with a woman who she assumed was also a salesperson. She couldn't hear what was being said, but the other woman nodded her head as if she understood whatever it was Helen was saying. A moment later, the second woman bent down and sliding open two drawers, removed two wig mannequins and handed them to Helen.

Having returned to her chair, Isabella smiled as Helen approached.

"Here are two wigs that you might find to your liking, miss."

Isabella immediately knew that both would fit the bill.

"I'll take them," she announced.

"But... don't you want to try them on first?" asked the startled saleswoman.

"I'm sure they will be fine. Wrap them up."

"Yes, miss. They are on sale today."

"That's nice," said Isabella, never concerned about cost. "How much?"

"They are $300 each but they both have a $75 discount."

"So it's $450 then?"

"Plus tax, brings it to... $482."

"Do you take American Express?"

"Yes, we do, Miss... Gonzalez," answered Helen after reading the name on the credit card. "All I need is a photo ID, please."

"No problem," answered Isabella, handing the woman a Texas driving license.

"Oh, you're from Texas. My husband was a Texan."

"I'm sorry, Helen, but you stand corrected," voiced Isabella. "There's a saying: 'Once a Texan, always a Texan.'"

"Oh, you're so right. That boy has got cowboy blood running through his veins."

The chit-chat continued until Helen handed Isabella her receipt.

"Thank you. You have made my day," beamed a joyful Helen.

As Isabella was paying for her purchase at the cashier's counter, Sally, the woman she had seen in the back room, stepped from behind the curtain. Upon seeing Isabella, she stopped in her tracks and caught her breath.

While drinking her morning coffee she had read the local paper. She recognized Isabella from the sketch on the paper's front page.

"Holy shit," she whispered. "That's the woman who shot a golfer yesterday."

Rushing back into the curtained room, she found a phone and dialed 9-1-1.

*"9-1-1. What is your emergency?"*

"Hang up the phone, lady."

Turning, the woman saw Isabella with a gun pressed up against Helen's head.

*"9-1-1. Do you have an emergency to report?"*

"Hang up the phone. Now!"

Sally did as told.

Isabella, whose eyes see all, witnessed Sally emerging from the back room, and saw her reaction. She knew immediately that the woman had recognized her. Pulling her pistol from her coat pocket, she told Helen to move to the back room. They got there just as Sally was making the phone call.

"Is that what they call a silencer?" asked Sally pointing at Isabella's gun.

"Yes, it is… Sally," answered Isabella, seeing the woman's nametag. "It keeps things quiet. I wonder why they don't call them a quieter?"

Sally somehow smiled, but even at its best, it was one of weakness.

As Sally watched, Isabella turned to Helen, saying, "You know that nice commission you just made, Helen?"

Helen, with frightened tears running down both cheeks, nodded.

"Well dear, you won't be spending it."

The gun popped and Helen's head exploded.

Sally emitted a small portion of a scream before Isabella planted a .22 slug in her forehead.

"Sometimes, I just hate this job," mumbled Isabella, as she left the curtained room carrying bags holding her two wigs and the dress.

She made one more stop at the bedding department. Seeing what she needed, she made the purchase, and then exited the mall the same way she entered. Minutes later she opened the car door where Michael, wearing a pair of fancy sunglasses and a brimmed fedora, sat waiting.

"Gosh, Michael. Is that you?" asked Isabella, feigning seriousness. "I thought for a moment it was Tom Cruise."

"How'd it go?" he asked, ignoring her sarcasm.

"I'm guessing that it could have gone better. Let's switch cars and then find a hotel."

An hour later, they were driving a 2018 white GMC Yukon with Mississippi plates.

"Where would you like to camp out tonight, Isabella?"

She was wearing the light brown wig but hadn't changed into the dress she had purchased.

"I was hoping to find a crowded hotel where we wouldn't stand out, Michael."

"There's a Hampton Inn down in Murrells Inlet that stays busy because of the hospital. Friends and family of those in the hospital keep it crowded year-round."

"Let's try it," she replied.

"Should we get one room or two?"

"What do you have in mind, Michael?"

Michael, 27 years-old, stood at an even six-foot. His body was lean and muscular. He had blue eyes and dark brown hair, and a smile that had swooned many a damsel between the sheets.

"I never asked. Are you married?"

"Would it matter?" she asked.

"Yeah, it would. I wouldn't want to be looking over my shoulder for an angry husband."

"So you think if we were to… fool around, shall we say, that I would rush home to my husband and confess?"

"Some women have a guilty conscience."

"Do I look or act like I have a guilty conscience?"

Letting out a small laugh, Michael replied, "You got me there, Isabella."

"I think I would prefer… one room, with a king-sized bed."

A bigger than life smile crested Michael's face. He glanced at the time on the vehicle's dashboard and saw it was 12:40.

"I'm now praying there's a vacancy."

Isabella gazed at the young man and while desiring him, she thought about the upcoming consequences.

Years earlier, her colleagues had given her a well-deserved nickname. It wasn't flattering, by no means, since it spoke of a spider who, after mating, killed her partner.

Having mirrored that spider on multiple occasions, she became known as The Black Widow.

# CHAPTER 35

**Just about the** time Isabella and Mike were buying disguises at Belk's, Agent Paul Adams was checking out the second on his list of eight addresses.

Heather had broken up the list of 23 addresses into two groups of eight and one of seven. She separated the addresses by north, east, west, and south. Adams drew the northern quadrant, while Miller, although drawing only seven addresses, drew both the east and west quadrants. Thompson drew the eight addresses in the southern portion of the Grand Strand.

Miller offered to trade quadrants with Adams, but Paul declined, saying, "My mom lives up on Route 9. I told her I'd stop by for lunch."

Adams' first address resulted in the stones being used in a rose garden. He had better luck with the second address, a brick ranch style home off Route 51 in Little River. Here, the stones covered a circular drive fronting the home. Adams entered a check-mark next to the address and was about to drive away when he disobeyed orders and decided to recon the residence.

It was a bad decision and it would be his last.

Parking alongside the road, he advanced to the front door and rang the doorbell. Moments later the door opened and a man pushing 80 answered.

"Good morning, young man. What can I do for you?"

Adams had his answer prepared.

"I was admiring your driveway, sir. May I ask who did the work?"

"Me! I did the work, sonny. I had the stones delivered, and I did the spreading."

"Congratulations, sir. That's a lot of work for someone of your age," commented Adams.

Having meant it as a compliment, Adams didn't realize the old man considered it derogatory until he heard, "Are you saying I'm too old to work!"

"Ahh, no, sir. I didn't mean it I that way. Please, accept my apology."

"I can still do the job, young fella, however," said the old man, while pointing his index finger of his right hand, "I'm not for hire."

Adams, realizing this wasn't the address they were looking for, thanked the man for his time and made his way to his car.

He was about to open the car door when he heard a voice calling his name.

"Agent Adams?"

Turning, he saw two men, one of better than normal size, the other gigantic.

"Yes. Do I know you?"

"No, but we know who you are," growled Bruno, pulling a gun from his jacket. "We need you to come with us, agent. Give my friend the keys to your car. Where is your list?"

Adams, shook by the man's knowledge, stuttered his answer.

"It…it's… on the front passenger seat."

A minute later, Adams, his hands and feet shackled, was sitting in the backseat of the Mercedes.

"How did you find me?"

"We have friends, Agent Adams."

"Are you telling me you have a mole in the FBI?"

"Yes, we do, and in just a few minutes, you'll be meeting him."

Adams' blood ran cold. Hearing Bruno's declaration, meant only one thing. He was a dead man.

It took less than five minutes to get to the destination where Adams knew his life would end. The white marble stone covering the driveway confirmed his worst fears. Parked in the driveway was the Buick Regal he always drew from the carpool, and a white Toyota Camry he thought he recognized. As the Mercedes pulled in, the Regal was backing out. Adams glanced over at the driver as the two cars passed. He couldn't believe it. It was Samuel Miller! The man he sat next to at the morning briefing. The man he shared office space with ever since they both arrived at the field office six months ago.

When Miller's eyes met those of Adams, he gave Adams a knowing grin.

"You bastard!" screamed Adams.

"You'll get no argument from me," said Bruno, while pulling Adams from the car. "There's nothing worse than a traitor. It may not make you feel any better, but I promise to kill him for you when he's outlived his usefulness."

"You're right. It doesn't make me feel any better."

"C'mon, agent, let me show you where you'll be… let's say, hanging out for the next few hours."

# CHAPTER 36

**"Listen to this** entry, Tim."

"Damn, Ron, do I have to? It's almost 11:00. We've been at it for only two hours but it feels like two days."

"I'm feeling your pain, partner, but this is our only hope of finding that drive."

Their minds were weary. It had been two mind-boggling hours of trying to determine if entries in Corrina Falano's journal were clues. Clues left by her husband, Hector, that would lead to the whereabouts of the hidden flash drive.

During those two hours, The Ghost had already killed Detective Tom Blake, Isabella Sanchez was executing two Belk's clerks at the Coastal Grand Mall, and Agent Paul Adams' abduction was in progress.

"Let's hear it," said Tim, already weary from listening to one unfathomable entry after another.

Ron went on to read: *"Hector was helping me hang clothes, that I had just washed, on the clothesline in the backyard. I was about to hang my unmentionables when Hector said, 'you'd best hang them up real high, Corrina. There's always a chance that the guy down the street who thinks he's a girl, might borrow them.'"*

"Doesn't sound like a clue to me, Ron. What are your thoughts?"

"It's so odd, it's hard to believe it could be anything but a clue. But I haven't the foggiest idea of its meaning, if, in fact, there even is a meaning."

"I wonder if there is a guy down their street who thinks he's a girl?"

"Shit, Tim, are you kidding me? I'd be willing to bet there's someone like that on every damn street in town. In fact, I sometimes wonder about you."

Tim, ignoring Ron's attempt at humor, asked, "What about that word, 'unmentionables'?"

"I thought about it being in her underwear drawer, but someone went through it with a fine-toothed comb, as did we. It's obvious they found nothing. We found less."

"That earlier one you read seemed a bit weird."

"You must be much more specific, Tim. As far as I'm concerned, they all appear to be a bit weird."

"The one that read, 'I like to watch the sunset, but Hector likes to watch it rise."

"What's so strange about that?"

"Maybe he's saying the drive is somewhere east?"

"East of what?" asked Ron.

Tim was about to voice an assumption, when Heather came in and announced, "Chief Baxter is on line one, Ron. He sounds distraught."

"Oh-oh, that doesn't bode well," said Ron, picking up the phone.

"Bill? What's happening?"

Ron listened for a moment, then with a sense of urgency, said, "We'll be at the mall in five minutes."

"What's going on?" asked Tim, grabbing his coat off the back of his chair.

"A detective got killed."

"At the mall?"

"No, at the Surfside Post Office."

"Why then, are we going to the mall?"

"Because that's where Isabella Sanchez just murdered two women."

# CHAPTER 37

**"What happened here,** Bill?"

"Near as I can make out, Ron, one, maybe both, of these women recognized Sanchez from the artist sketch that was in the morning paper."

"How did you come to that conclusion?"

"There's a coffee cup over there," said Bill, pointing to a small table where the employees sat while having a meal. "The newspaper, under the cup, is open to the sketch."

"It appears this woman... whose name, according to her nametag, is Helen, took a bullet at pointblank range," announced Tim, who was examining the bodies. "She has powder burns on the side of her head."

"Yeah, that's Helen Hastings," nodded Baxter. "The other woman is Sally Fisher. She got it between the eyes. I'm guessing from five or six feet away."

"Well, I guess we know why Isabella was here," Ron said, as he left the back room and stepped out onto the sales floor.

"Buying a wig," said Tim, realizing the obvious.

"Yeah, maybe more than one," suggested Ron. "Is there a manager around?"

"Yeah, Ron," answered Baxter. "His name is Sam Lucas. He's waiting outside."

"Take me to him, please."

A moment later, a sorrowful-looking man stood before Ron. He was an emotional wreck.

"Mr. Lucas, I'm Special Agent Ron Lee of the FBI. I'm sorry for what happened to your two employees, sir."

"Wonder... wonder.. wonderful ladies," he cried.

"I'm sure they were, sir, but I need you to pull yourself together."

"What do you need, officer?"

Ron, seeing the man's state of mind, didn't correct the man's mislabeling of his title.

"Can you tell me, sir, if someone made a purchase this morning? I need to know the items purchased and anything else you can tell me about the transaction. Can you do that for me, Mr. Lucas?"

"Yes, sir. I'll need access to the B.P. computer."

"B-P?"

"Beauty Parlor."

"Oh, okay. Is it that one over there?" asked Ron, pointing toward the only visible computer in the room.

"Yes, sir."

"Go to it, Mr. Lucas. It's all yours."

Less than a minute later, Lucas, after accessing the computer, said, "There was a purchase of two items by a Maria Gonzalez at 10:28am."

"What were the items, Mr. Lucas?"

"I'll check the stock numbers to be sure," replied Lucas, "but based on the payment, I think it is safe to say it was two wigs."

"What color are those wigs, Mr. Lucas?"

"Give me a moment and I'll have that information for you, officer. I'm opening the inventory files now."

Only a moment or two passed before Lucas announced, "Just as I thought, it was wigs she purchased. One was light brown, the other dark blond. Both were medium cut double monofilament wigs."

"What the hell does that mean, Mr. Lucas?" asked Tim.

"Don't bother telling us, Mr. Lucas. Show us the same wigs she bought. Can you do that?"

"I can. We have the identical wigs in the stockroom."

"Maybe you had better wait until our people are through with their investigation, Mr. Lucas," suggested Ron, not wanting the manager to see the carnage in the back room.

"I see you have security cameras, Mr. Lucas. Are they operational?" asked Tim.

"Yes, they are operational 24 hours a day."

"Could you show me the video for this department, sir?"

"The video center is in the basement. I could take you there."

"Lead the way, sir."

While Tim and the manager were heading for the video room, Ron began a conversation with Baxter.

"Okay, tell me about this detective, Bill."

"His name was Thomas Blake. He was one of my top guys. A very smart and crafty detective. Cracked cases as easily as a safecracker robbing a piggybank. A much-decorated officer. Everyone who knew him liked him."

"That seems not to be so, Bill. It appears as if at least one someone wasn't all that fond of him. Is he married?"

"Divorced."

"So his wife didn't care for him all that much."

"It's a long story, Ron."

"How long?"

"He gambled… and lost, a lot."

"Is that why he's divorced?"

"Yeah, he lost their house a few years back. I guess it was the last straw."

"Okay, tell me about the murder."

"It happened in the Surfside Post Office at 9:00 this morning. Blake had a box there. When our men got there, his box was open, but empty."

"Maybe they killed him for whatever was in his box," Ron surmised.

"Maybe so," agreed Baxter.

"Where does Blake live?"

"Somewhere in Deerfield Plantation."

"Would he have a home mailbox?"

"Yeah, I suppose he would."

"Then why a post office box, I wonder?"

"Another good question, Ron."

"What about security cameras? I'm sure the post office has them."

"That's the thing, Ron. Someone turned the cameras off."

"When?"

"They were off from 8:45am to 9:10am."

"How convenient. Maybe the killer works for the post office?"

"No, I don't think that's the case, Ron."

"Why not?"

"Well, there are only four employees working the morning shift. All claimed the others were on the job when the murder occurred."

"How is the security system activated?"

"A flip of a switch."

"So one of the four flipped the switch. Which one?"

"That's what we're trying to figure out."

"I just had a thought, Bill."

"I'm listening."

"Blake was here at 9:00am. Correct?"

"Yeah. That's when the post office opens."

"I think it's safe to assume that he was expecting something to be in the box."

"Good assumption, I'd say," agreed Baxter.

"Someone had to put whatever it was he was expecting, in the box. The question is: when?"

"I see where you're going, Ron. The security tapes from yesterday might show us who dropped off whatever was in Blake's box."

"You're beginning to read my mind, Bill."

"Damn, that's scary!"

"We'll go over there with you as soon as we finish up here."

"That would be good, Ron. I know you guys are juggling about a half-dozen balls, so I appreciate whatever time you can spare."

"We'll do what we can, Bill. Hey, I've been meaning to ask you. Have you uncovered anything regarding the wives making calls to the same number?"

"Now that you mention it, yes."

"Now that I mention it! When were you going to tell me?"

"Hey, take it easy, Ron. Things have been a wee bit hectic lately. I got this mess, the murder at the post office, two murdered cops, and a murdered judge."

"A murdered judge? Why wasn't I told about a murdered judge? What's the judge's name?"

"Your boss, Jim Braddock, didn't want me burdening you. The judge's name was Jeffrey Samuels."

"Well, when we finish up at the post office, I want you to send me the case file on the murdered judge. Now tell me what you have regarding the widowed wives."

"Someone made three calls to a burner phone prior to the killings."

"Three? Are you telling me that all three women called the burner phone?"

"No. Someone made the calls from just one phone."

"Whose?"

"Peggy Patterson's."

"Isn't she about to collect a four-million dollar inheritance?"

"Yep!"

"Are you tracking the burner?"

"We are, but as you know it's tough to do."

"Give me the number. I have a few ideas."

"Oh? What sort of ideas?"

Before Ron could reply, Robert Edge walked by, saying, "We're all done in there, fellas. We're taking the bodies to the morgue."

"Okay, Robert," nodded Ron. "Send me a report."

"Will do."

"Ron!"

It was Tim, returning with the manager from viewing the security footage of the parlor.

"What did you find, Tim?"

"We have Miss Sanchez in living black and white, Ron. We also have her driver and the car they are using."

"Great! Anything else?"

"Oh, yeah!"

"What?"

"It seems, before she left, she stopped in two other departments to make purchases."

"What did she buy, Tim?"

"A dress and a pillow."

"Let me guess. The dress was purchased in the maternity department."

"That, my friend, is a bingo!" replied Tim.

"Clever girl," said Ron with an appreciative smile.

"Do you think she'll use those items as a disguise to sneak out of the country?"

"No, Tim, I don't. I think she has bigger fish to fry."

# CHAPTER 38

"**Heather, this is** Ron. Tim and I are on our way to the Surfside Post Office to investigate the murder of a detective. How are things at the office? Anything we need to know?"

There was a pause for a moment, followed by Ron saying, "That's great news, Heather. We need no more distractions. Listen, I need a favor. Ask the staff to do some research on the following."

Ron gave Heather a list of three names.

"Have whatever you find on my desk when I get back."

A pause while Heather spoke.

"I don't know what friggin' time we'll be back, Heather! Today it seems, although inconvenient for us, is a good day for some people to die. Goodbye."

"You were a wee bit rough on our girl Heather, don't you think, partner?"

"Yeah, I guess I was. I'll make it up to her."

"I don't think splitting a donut will get the job done, Ron."

"Screw you and the donut jokes, Pond. How much longer before we get to the post office?"

"That depends."

"Depends? Depends on what?"

"Whether or not we stop for donuts."

"I take it back."

"Take what back?" asked Tim.

"My saying you aren't an asshole."

"You never said that."

"I know I didn't, but I still take it back."

"You're taking back something you never said?"

"Yes."

"And I'm the asshole?"

They arrived at 1:10. The post office had been cordoned off from all but police traffic. Tim parked near the front door, close to the dead detective's car.

As Ron exited the car, he surveyed the local establishments. To the left of the post office was an H&R Block and a furniture store. Neither had outside security cameras.

To the right of the post office was Tomlinson's clothing store, and a store labeled, Consignment @ 5$^{th}$. They too, had no outside security cameras.

The Conway National Bank, located on a diagonal from the post office, had security cameras, but they came with a caveat.

Between the post office and the bank was a frontage road, a grass divide, the southbound lane of Business 17, another grass divide, and the northbound lane of Business 17. To make matters even worse, the post office sat back from the frontage road 75 yards or more.

Ron had estimated the distance between the two buildings at 200 yards. If the bank's security cameras captured images in the post office parking lot, those images would lack clarity from such a distance.

Seeing all he had to see outside, they entered the post office, where an officer directed them to the far corridor on their left.

Turning the corner, they saw the sheet-covered body of Detective Tom Blake. Above his head, was the open door to a mailbox. Bill Baxter was standing next to

Deputy Coroner Patty Bellamy, Robert Edge's long-time and highly qualified assistant.

As they stood surveying the scene, Tim said, "I'll have a talk with the employees."

As Tim walked away, Ron asked, "What was the weapon of choice, Patty?"

"The guy used a .22, with hollow-point shells. It was also the weapon that put Judge Samuels to sleep yesterday."

"The weapon of a pro. A silencer, no doubt?"

"Without a doubt," agreed Patty.

"Made it as quiet as a wink," commented Ron.

"The guy made a small mistake, Ron."

"Oh, and what was that?"

"Do you see the blood puddling around this guy's head?"

"Yeah, what about it?"

"The killer didn't step in the blood. But he stood here for a moment. See this roundness in the puddle. That's where the blood ran into the guy's shoe and stopped."

"So his shoe has blood on it?"

"I'd say that's a good assumption. Not a lot, but some. Look for it on the edge of the shoe's right sole."

"That's good, Patty. Thanks."

"Why, I wonder, is a paid assassin killing a judge and a cop, Ron?"

"I can think of a reason, Bill, but you may not want to hear it."

"Go ahead, say it. You've piqued my interest."

"Someone thought they would crack."

"Come again, Ron?"

"Our dead FBI agent made a copy of Driscoll's computer files. On it, amongst other things, are the names of people Driscoll pays for protection and information."

"You're not implying that Blake…"

"Tell me, Bill. Has Blake been in financial straits as of late? Say, the past two years."

"No, I don't think so. I assumed he had learned his lesson."

"Check his bank accounts, Bill. Tell me what you find and then I'll answer your question."

"Are you telling me that one of my best men was on Driscoll's payroll, Ron?"

"I don't know that for certain, and I'll apologize right now if it's not true. That's why I asked that you check Blake's bank accounts. Do the same for the judge. Maybe I'm wrong."

Bill, upset at Ron's assertion, suggested, "Maybe there's a connection between Blake's murder and the other murdered officers."

"I don't think so, Bill, but anything is possible."

Ron looked up to see Tim returning from his talks with the employees. He looked somewhat chagrined.

"I was thinking about looking at yesterday's tapes, Ron, to see if we could identify whoever may have left something in Blake's box."

"You thought of that too?" asked Ron.

"Yeah, I did. What? I'm guessing, by that shocked look on your face, that you think you're the only one who can walk and chew gum at the same time?"

"Okay, Tim. Did you look at the tapes?"

"There aren't any. Seems they got erased sometime last night. A glitch in the system, they're saying."

"What about last week's tapes, Tim?"

"They keep them for 48 hours, then they're recycled."

"This was a hit," voiced Ron. "It's way too clean to be just your everyday killing."

"Not much doubt with that assessment," replied Baxter.

"When we arrived, Bill, I scanned the outside businesses for security cameras. I didn't see any in the immediate businesses, but the Conway Bank will have them. Problem is, they are 200 yards away, across the street."

"I'll have someone go over there and check it out," replied Bill.

"Tim, why don't you go too. See if it's worth taking them back to the office."

"I can't believe Tom Blake was taking bribes from Driscoll."

"Desperate people do things they would never contemplate doing under normal circumstances, Bill."

"Bastard," snarled Baxter as he stared down at the white blood-stained sheet. Then looking at Patty, he snapped, "Get him out of my sight."

Baxter, without definitive proof, had become the judge, jury, and although a bit late, the executioner of Tom Blake, who, only hours earlier, was a favorite son.

# CHAPTER 39

**"See that car** sitting in front of that furniture store, Ron?"

"Yeah, is it a Chevy Malibu?"

Tim didn't answer, but he smiled a sneaky smile.

They were looking at the security camera footage taken by the Conway National Bank from 8:00am through 9:15am.

After returning to the office at 2:30, Tim spent the next hour reviewing the tape before showing it to Ron. They had watched a half-dozen cars park and their drivers enter and exit the building. The building was now empty.

"That car pulled in at 8:48," said Tim. "The driver stayed in the car."

"The post office doesn't open until 9:00."

"True, Ron, but watch."

Tim fast-forwarded the tape to 8:58. A car pulled in, the driver exited, walked to the door, and entered.

"Is that Blake?" asked Ron.

"It is. Now watch the other car."

They both saw a figure emerge from the car and walk into the post office.

"Okay, it's 9:00, and the guy goes into the post office. So what?"

"That's true, Ron, the post office doesn't open until 9:00. The outside doors, however, open at 6:00am for anyone who wants to mail a letter, or self-mail a package, or... visit their mailbox."

"Okay, so what's your point?" asked Ron.

"Let me back this tape up about 30 seconds. Now watch the guy again, Ron. What do you see?"

179

"He gets out of his car, walks to the door and walks in. What am I supposed to be seeing, Tim-o-thy?"

"He turned to the left, Ron."

"Yeah, so?"

"The part of the post office which requires human intervention, is to the right. If that guy was waiting for the post office to open, he would have gone right. He wasn't though. He was waiting for Blake to arrive."

"How many people entered the building between the time he parked until he went into the building?"

"Five."

"When he walked in, who remained inside?"

"Blake and a guy buying postage stamps."

"Then that's our killer."

"That's our killer," agreed Tim.

"He's just a blur."

"True, but…"

"But what?"

"He's tall and well-built."

"That narrows our list of suspects down to everyone but you, me, and some women."

"He isn't driving a Malibu, Ron."

"What's he driving?"

"Watch and learn."

At 9:04, the figure exited the post office and entered his car. He made a left turn onto the frontage road . He drove the short hundred yards to the 5th Street intersection where he makes a right turn and gets caught by the light.

Being a hundred yards closer made it possible to identify the car as a Lexus. Because the cameras recorded in black and white, they couldn't determine the car's color, although both men thought it looked black or blue.

"You can see his face!" Ron shouted.

"Yeah, but he's wearing sunglasses, and he has pulled his hat down. Not the best of looks, unfortunately. He'll make a left turn onto 17 north."

"Maybe we can catch his plate number when he makes the turn," suggested Ron.

"That's what I also thought, partner, but this guy is crafty. He waits until the car on the opposite side makes a right before he pulls out. This maneuver blocks the camera from picking up the plate number, and in seconds he's out of the frame."

"What about earlier when he arrived? Couldn't the cameras have picked up his plate then?"

"He used the Frontage Road and pulled in at the consignment shop, hugging the building all the way to where he parked. He knew the bank's cameras couldn't record with any clarity at that distance."

"Damn!" shouted Ron. "Wait! How about cameras further on down 17?"

"I checked, but no luck. Wells Fargo had cameras, but they caught nothing we could use."

"Okay. Our hit man who goes about six-foot two, drives a dark-colored Lexus."

"Let's do a cross check with the DMV on the car against registered .22 pistols, Ron. I'm thinking the list won't be all that long."

"That's a good idea, Tim, but I doubt you'll come up with anything."

"Why is that?"

"I doubt he's using a registered firearm."

"True, but I'll ask Heather to do it, anyway. It can't hurt."

"Agreed," said Ron.

No sooner had they mentioned her name, did Heather enter the office.

"Here are two reports on the assignment you handed out this morning, Tim. Paul Adams hasn't returned as yet."

"It's 4:00, Heather. Where is he?"

"I haven't a clue, Tim," answered the secretary while giving Ron a cold stare.

Seeing her look, Ron said, "Look, Heather, I'm sorry I was so…"

"Nasty?"

"Yeah, I guess I was. Wasn't I?"

"Yes, you were."

"Please accept my apology. We just got hit with so much, I guess I was just stressed out. It's no excuse to act the way I did, though. Sorry about that."

"I accept your apology, Colonel, on one condition."

"Name it!"

"Might you have a donut?"

"Sure, have a whole one," said Ron, smiling like a Cheshire cat.

Tim just shook his head in disgust.

Ten minutes after giving Heather a new assignment for a staff member, the two agents went to work on solving the mystery of the journal.

"What about this entry where she says, '*I asked Hector to take a walk in the woods with me but he said, just one is enough.*'"

"What are your thoughts, Tim?"

"Is he saying that just one walk is all he wants to do?"

"He's saying one, which indicates singular. The only word construed as a plural in the whole sentence is woods. But in the context used, even it is singular."

"A single walk. Does that bring anything to mind, Ron?"

"Maybe he's not talking about taking a walk, but a walkway. A path? Aren't all walkways or paths singular though?"

"Okay, next entry. We'll come back to that one," said a frustrated Tim.

"Okay. How about this one? She says, *'I asked Hector for a new car but he said we need to cut expenses and save a few more dollars. But not in that exact order.'*"

"That almost sounds like a normal conversation."

"Almost?"

"That last part 'not in that order' seems strange."

"Yeah, it does. There's nothing really odd about the reply until he says that. Is there?"

"Maybe he's giving us pieces of an anagram."

"That's a strong possibility, Tim."

They were dissecting the latest clue when Heather's sudden barging into the room interrupted their discussion.

"I'm sorry, Colonel. But this is important. Bill Baxter just called saying they found one of our pool cars on fire behind the stores in Fantasy Harbor."

"Tell me that's the worst of it, Heather."

"I'm sorry, Colonel, but they said there was a body inside, burned beyond recognition."

"Who checked out the car, Heather?" asked Tim.

"Paul Adams."

# CHAPTER 40

**They had gone** to the scene of the burned-out Toyota Camry. They watched as firemen, under the supervision of Horry County Coroner, Robert Edge, extracted, from the still smoldering wreckage, the charred remains of who they assumed to be Paul Adams. Edge took the body to the morgue to certify the identity of the victim. It was 6:00pm when they returned to the office. Heather was there, awaiting their return.

"Was it…?" she began to ask, her voice quivering.

"We can't be positive, Heather, but his badge was in the car," explained Ron. "So, yeah, we believe it was Paul."

She left the room, in tears.

"I need her," said Tim. "There are things I need done."

"Give her a little while, Tim. This is the first time we've lost an agent. She's having trouble accepting it."

"What do you think happened, Ron?"

"The mole told someone that we had sent agents out to locate white marble driveways. They sent someone to keep Adams from discovering it."

"That makes no sense, Ron. They have to know that we'll send a force out to check the same locations that Adams was checking."

"You're right, partner. Something doesn't add up, unless…"

"Unless what?"

"Unless Adams was the mole, and they decided he was too hot, and, if caught, would spill the beans."

"Adams? The mole? Damn, Ron, I don't want to disparage a guy who just got lit up, literally, but Adams wasn't the brightest light in the room. Again, no pun intended. Wouldn't you think their mole has to be clever to remain undetected all this time?"

"I can't argue with that logic, Tim, but we're not the people who put him in place. I'm sure their thinking was along different lines. Maybe to them, he was a liability who they needed removed before he did them harm."

Quiet gathered in the room as both agents went into seclusion with their own thoughts.

Sitting on Tim's desk were the two reports the other two agents had compiled. He flicked through them and saw that Thompson, who covered the southern portion of the county, found no driveways of white marble stone.

Sam Miller's report, covering the northern section of the county, noted he had found one driveway, which was the second address on his list. He attached the information about the property.

Tim noted that Miller had recorded a check-mark next to the address and had put an X next to all the other properties, except for the first.

*I wonder why he didn't X-out the first property,* thought Tim. He also noticed that he had noted the checked property in pencil while he noted all the X-out properties in ink.

A few minutes later, Heather, somewhat composed, walked in.

"I know it's late and you guys have been at it since early this morning. Would you like some coffee?"

If you're up to it, Heather," said Ron. "You could go home, if you'd rather."

"I'm fine, Colonel. As long as you guys are here, I'll stay."

"Heather, I hate to ask," said Tim, "but could you get me the list of addresses you gave to Paul."

"I'll put the coffee on and bring you the list, Tim."

"Sounds good to me."

Two minutes later Heather walked in carrying the list Tim had requested.

Ron, like Tim, had gone into his own dark space. While there, he began perusing the documents Heather had left on his desk regarding the names he had given her earlier that day.

The top document was for the late Judge Jeffrey Samuels. It had everything Ron could have asked for, especially the judge's bank account history.

*Just as I thought,* said Ron's inner voice. *He was taking bribes.*

The next folder was for Detective Tom Blake, also deceased. Although he had asked Baxter to get his hands on Blake's bank account, Ron knew the FBI could access it faster and with far more secrecy.

There it was, just like clockwork. A thousand dollar deposit made to a Wells Fargo savings account every Wednesday, going back as far as October 2016.

It was while reading the contents of the third folder did Ron bolt up in his chair.

Heather was walking into the office carrying two cups of hot coffee, when Ron, not seeing her approaching, yelled out, "HEATHER!"

"Damn, Colonel! You almost made me spill these coffees. What the hell are you screaming about?"

"Sorry, Heather, I didn't see you come in. Here, let me take the coffee off your hands."

After taking the coffee from the shaken secretary, Ron grabbed a notepad and tearing off the top sheet where he had jotted down instructions, handed it to Heather saying, "I would like you to do the following for me. Have someone on the night staff get to work on this ASAP."

Heather was heading out of the office when Tim perked up with, "Heather, I know you're under duress, but you gave me the wrong list for Paul Adams."

"I did? That's queer. I could swear I gave you the north quadrant list."

"You did, but Paul was doing the east-west quadrant."

"No, he wasn't Agent Pond," answered Heather, resorting to formality when questioned about her abilities.

"I think you may be mistaken, Heather."

"Agent Miller drew the east-west quadrant, Agent Pond. The south quadrant went to Agent Thompson, and the north to Agent Adams. I was there when they selected their quadrants."

"Then how come Agent Miller filed a report for the north quadrant?"

"I couldn't say, Agent Pond."

"First, call me Tim. Second, contact the carpool and find out who drew the Toyota Camry."

"Heather, I need that stuff I gave you pronto," reminded Ron in a soothing voice.

"On my way, Colonel," replied Heather as she took a step toward the door. But before she took a second step, she halted, whirled around, and with both men staring at her, she unleashed a torrent of profanity-laced suggestions.

"Why don't you two pricks give some of this bullshit workload to others in this goddamn department.

Those assholes can also do this shitass job. But no, you two dickheads have an unquenchable need for bullshit glory."

She turned around and walked out.

"Girl has a mouth on her I didn't know she had," said Ron.

"I should have asked," said Tim, "if she ate with that mouth?"

"Hey, it's late, and she's been through a lot and we are throwing stuff at her left and right. She has a right to be pissed."

"I'm fine with it, Ron. She'll get no crap from me. She's a great asset. Let her blow off some steam."

"Amen, partner. What's going on over there?"

"Something is fishy about the assignments I handed out this morning."

"What means that?" asked Ron.

"Miller, who Heather said drew the east-west quadrant, turned in a report for the north quadrant."

"Maybe they switched. You can ask Miller when he comes in tomorrow morning."

"I plan on doing that. The question remains, why would they switch? There's another thing bugging me."

"Talk to me."

"There's a peculiarity about Miller's report."

"What's peculiar?"

"It isn't consistent."

"Such as?"

"He used a pencil for part of it, and ink for the rest."

"Maybe the pencil broke."

"That's a plausible answer," said Tim, not believing it for a moment.

"What else is… peculiar, Tim-o-thy."

"He checked off every address except for the first."

"Hmm, I guess he just wasn't into a rhythm until later."

"Don't you think that's strange, Ron?"

"Somewhat, I guess."

Heather, looking meek, reentered the room, unannounced.

"I'm sorry about what I said. If you want me to leave or if you want to fire me, I won't blame you."

"I'm sorry, Heather, but what the hell are you talking about?" asked Ron.

"Before… what I said… I was way out…"

"Sorry to interrupt your blathering, Heather, but I need to know if our Transportation Department has sent any information our way?" Tim asked.

"I… yeah… I… here it is… Tim, and thank you, both."

"I don't know what you're thanking us for, but I sure could use another cup of coffee."

"Sure thing, Colonel. Oh, and I'll have that autopsy report for you in about ten minutes."

"Thanks, Heather."

"Damn!"

Ron, hearing Tim's cuss, asked, "What's the problem?"

"That's the problem, Ron. There is no problem."

"How about running that by me again, Tim, but this time try it in English."

"Adams checked out the Toyota."

"Well, since his charcoaled body was in it, that makes sense."

"Yeah, I guess so."

"Unless…"

"Unless what, Ron?"

"That's a log from a computer. Correct?"

"Yeah, it is."

"Could someone with hacking capabilities, go into the file and change information?"

Tim pressed the intercom button and hearing Heather's voice, he asked, "Heather do our systems keep track of all updates made to a file?"

"Yes. They do that in case we need to reconstruct a history."

"Can you check the carpool file and get me a record of all transactions made on this Toyota Camry?"

"I'll have it for you in five minutes, Tim."

"Can't wait! Thank you!"

"While you're waiting, Tim, let me run some… theories by you."

"Sounds good, partner. Fire away."

"Do you remember Vivian Hanson?"

"Yeah. She was the mother of Peggy Patterson. I remember for being 54 years of age, she looked better than most women half her age. Why?"

"She's a widow."

"Okay."

"Her husband was an alcoholic. New York City cops arrested him dozens of times for brawling in public. Bars, restaurants, department stores, you name it."

"I know you have a point you're heading toward."

"In 2011, Mr. Hanson fell in front of a subway car as it was pulling into the station. Splat! He be as dead as Julius Caesar."

"Hmm, did he have any last words akin to those of Julie?" asked Tim. "Like, pour me a stiffy!"

"I couldn't say, for sure, Tim, but he may have said, 'Et Tu, Vivian!'"

"What! You're thinking he may have had an assist falling in front of that car?"

"I am. Do you know why?"

"No, but I have a feeling you're about to tell me."

"Vivian Hanson, from 1992 through 2010, was in various New York hospitals 14 times."

"Accident prone, wouldn't you say?" said Tim. "What happened to her all those times?"

"Well for starters, she fell in the kitchen, she fell in the bedroom, and she fell in the bathtub, three times! She has had numerous solo car accidents, and various other misfortunes, some of which involved the removal or breakage of teeth."

"Hubby beat her?"

"That's my guess."

"So where is this leading you?"

"Heather is contacting doctors who may have treated either Sheila Bennington or Peggy Patterson."

"You might have better luck with hospitals, Ron."

"I'm way ahead of you, partner. She's also contacting local hospitals to determine if either lady has been a patient in the past three years."

"So you're thinking their husbands were beating them too?"

"I am," Ron admitted.

"You know that their doctors will not give you any information ."

"I know. Doctor-patient confidentiality. Now, I may not see why they went to their doctor, but maybe I'll be able to see how many times they went."

"Okay, so let's say they have had multiple visits to hospitals and doctors," suggested Tim.

"Okay, let's say they have. What are your questions?"

"Are you thinking Vivian arranged for the husbands murders?"

"I am. Vivian, having lived through 18 years of beatings, didn't want her daughter to end up dead."

"Okay, that's logical for her daughter's husband, but why the Bennington woman's husband?"

"Sheila and Peggy were high school friends. I'm sure they confided in each other. I'm guessing Peggy shared Sheila's situation with her mother. Vivian, hating wife beaters, saw the opportunity to make it look like there was a serial cop killer on the loose. She had Bennington's husband killed first to divert suspicion away from her daughter when she had Patterson put down."

"Smart move."

"Very smart move, Tim. When someone killed Peggy's husband, no real suspicions fell on Peggy. She was just another new widow."

"So Vivian planned it all?"

"That's my thinking. She made sure the girls' alibies were solid. I can't prove it... yet, but a little white lie planted here and there might do the trick."

"Was she responsible for the Clayton killing?"

"Negatory, partner."

"Who's responsible for Clayton?"

"The same killer, but I haven't figured out why. I'm afraid if we don't solve this soon, another cop will go down."

"Who do you think is pulling the trigger, Ron?"

"I hate saying it, Tim, but I believe it's a cop."

The intercom's buzzing interrupted Ron's revealing discussion.

Ron hit the talk button, saying, "What is it, Heather?"

"Tim, someone altered the records of the Toyota Camry."

"When?"

"Today, at 4:10pm."

"When did Miller and Thompson return?"

"Thompson checked his car in at 4:17. Miller checked his in at 4:03."

"Thank you, Heather."

"Miller is the goddam mole," said Ron.

"He's also a murderer," added Tim, his mouth filled with venom.

# CHAPTER 41

**As soon as** the FBI traitor had returned from his assignment, he called Cameron Driscoll to inform him that there was a small oversight in the plan to intercept Agent Adams.

"What's the problem, Agent?" asked Driscoll, annoyed that Miller had contacted him.

"I shouldn't have taken the car Adams was driving. We each had to sign out for our vehicle. I brought the wrong car back."

"That doesn't sound good."

"No, sir, it does not."

"What can you do about it?"

"I'll hack into the file and change the cars."

"You can do that?"

"Yeah, I can, but Thompson, the other agent involved in the assignment, knows that Adams had the Buick and I had the Toyota."

"Well, you best take care of that problem. Wouldn't you agree?"

"What! We're here in the office. I can't…"

"You seem to have a dilemma Agent Miller."

"A dilemma? What do you mean?"

"You either take care of Thompson, or else I won't be needing your services any longer."

Miller blanched at Driscoll's not-so veiled threat.

"I'll see what I can do."

"It's best that you do, Agent Miller. Keep me informed."

*Click.*

A shaken Miller took care of swapping vehicles in the computer files to make it look like he had the Buick and Adams had taken the Toyota. He knew that if anyone was worth their salt, they would soon uncover the switch. His time in the FBI was coming to a rapid ending.

Giving thought to Driscoll's suggestion that he kill Thompson, he wondered if he had whatever it takes to kill another human being. Knowing Adams would soon die, if he wasn't dead already, he told himself that he wasn't responsible. That's what he told himself, but he knew it wasn't the truth.

Returning to the office pool area, he wandered over to Thompson's desk, and seeing the agent pecking away at his computer, asked, "Doing your report, Steve?"

"Yeah, I was lucky. None of my eight addresses had a stone driveway."

"That is lucky. No complaints here. I had but one."

"Where's Paul?" asked Steve as he glanced around the open office area.

"I'll bet he's still out there looking for that elusive driveway," suggested Miller.

"No, Sam, he's not. When I checked my car in, I saw his Buick Regal being taken for clean-up. I reckon he's here someplace."

It was nearing 5:00 when Sam noticed a flurry of activity at the far end of the room. He watched as Ron Lee and Tim Pond rushed from their offices and headed toward the elevator. His gut told him Paul Adams was dead.

After saying goodbye to Steve, Miller decided he would leave town as soon as he could pack his bags. As it would turn out, packing wasn't a good idea.

＊＊＊＊＊＊＊＊＊＊＊＊＊

As soon as Driscoll had hung up with Agent Miller, he placed another call.

*"Mr. Driscoll, nice of you to call. It provides me the opportunity to inform you all three accounts have been closed. I expect the full payment to be in my account in the morning."*

"It will be there."

"Why the call?"

"I have a very important job I need you to do now!"

"Now? I was just sitting down to my dinner."

"I need you to kill an FBI agent."

"That, my friend, is a job for someone who is crazy. Killing an FBI agent is suicidal. They will never quit looking until they find the killer. Never!"

"I'll pay you a hundred thousand."

There was a pause of some length, before The Ghost replied, "Who's the target?"

*************

She was more beautiful naked than he thought possible. But, alas, there was more! She was also an expert in satisfying a man in ways he could never have imagined.

He was more lover than she had ever experienced, as he brought her to fulfillment on every occasion.

As lovers, they were the most perfect of matches.

They had spent the entire day enjoying each other's charms in room 303 of the Hampton Inn in Murrells Inlet.

"I'm famished," Isabella declared, as she sat up in the bed and stretched her arms.

"I could use a break," replied Michael with a boyish grin crossing his face.

"It looks like we wore out this guy," said Isabella as she fondled his flaccid manhood.

"Well, he just had the greatest workout of his life. He has asked me to thank you for all that you contributed."

"I must admit, Michael, he's a stand-up guy," said Isabella while chuckling at her pun.

"Yes, he is. Perhaps after a good meal, and a glass of wine, he might rise to the occasion again."

"I'm looking forward to it," replied Isabella.

"What? The meal or him?"

Laughing at his sense of humor, she answered, "Don't make me make a choice. I might disappoint you."

"There's a Japanese Steak House across the street or there's a nearby Italian restaurant. What's your fancy?"

"Pizza and a beer sounds great!"

"Pizza, the lady shall have," rejoiced Michael as he put on his pants.

Isabella, without putting on underwear, placed the pillow she bought on her stomach and secured it using the tie string from the robe hanging in the closet. She then slipped the maternity dress over her head.

"How does it look?"

Michael stepped back, saying, "Am I the father?"

"I want to test it out at the restaurant."

"Good idea, but being pregnant, you shouldn't order any alcoholic drinks."

"Hmm, good point, Michael. Damn! I was looking forward to a Corona."

"I'll buy a six-pack after dinner. You can enjoy a beer or two when we return."

"Is it possible to make love while drinking beer?"

"I believe you can, if you're the one in the saddle."

"Ahh, yes, my favorite position," she said as they walked out the door.

# CHAPTER 42

"**Bob, can I** make a phone call from my cell with the person receiving the call seeing a different number?"

"It's not legal, so the answer is, no."

Answering Ron's question was Bob Truitt, head of the FBI's technology department.

"Listen to me, Bob. This could save a cop's life."

Hearing that, Bob's reluctance vanished into the wind.

"What kind of phone is it you want to imitate?"

"It's a burner."

"Do you have this phone?"

"No. All we have is the number."

"How many hidden pieces are there to this puzzle, Ron? I'm expecting a fastball and you throw me a curve."

"Sorry, Bob. I guess I'm a bit anxious about this whole deal."

"Okay, here comes another question. What kind of phone is receiving the call?"

"A landline," responded Ron.

"Okay, let me get this straight. You want a landline to receive a call from a cell phone using the number of a burner phone that exists but you don't have. You want to use a phone that you have but has a different number that you want to replace with the number of the burner phone you don't have. Is that about it?"

"You make it sound complicated, Bob, but yes, I think you have a handle on it."

"I think we can do this, Ron, if we use a burner phone to make the call, instead of your personal cell."

"I'll get you a burner."

"Don't bother, we have plenty in the lab."

"You do? How come?"

"We use them," Bob replied with a wicked grin, "to set off bombs."

"Funny, Bob, but stick to your day job."

"When do you need this phone?"

"Yesterday."

"That figures."

Glancing at his watch, Bob reached back behind his ear, and while scratching his head, said, "It's 8:15 now. I'll have it ready at noon. Will that do?"

"What! Are you guys on strike in that lab?" Ron asked with a huge smile. "Just kidding, Bob. Noon would be great. Thanks."

"Give me the number of the phone you don't have."

Taking the number Ron had written on a piece of paper, Bob, said, "This is illegal."

"I know, but if I'm caught, I promise I'll never give you up."

"Bullshit! From what I hear, you'd sell your soul for a half-dozen Krispy Kreme donuts."

"Maybe for a dozen, Bob. But a half-dozen? Never!"

\*\*\*\*\*\*\*\*\*\*\*\*\*

Ten hours earlier, Ron and Tim had set out to arrest Sam Miller. Miller lived in the Ridgewood Plantation apartment complex off Garner Lacy Road.

"What's the address, Tim?"

"110 Tibwin Avenue, apartment 4E. It's 10:15. Maybe we'll catch him asleep."

"Wouldn't that be nice?" Ron mumbled.

It took 15 minutes to make the jaunt from the office to Miller's apartment.

"Park here at the end, Tim. I don't want him seeing us coming."

Exiting their SUV, they made their way to Unit 4.

"He's here," remarked Tim.

"How do you know?" asked Ron.

"That's his Mustang," replied Tim, pointing at the car parked just a few spots away from where they were standing.

"Each level has three apartments, Ron. Apartment E is on the second level."

"Wouldn't you know it, the son-of-a-bitch has to live on the second floor."

"There's an elevator, Ron."

"Thank the Lord for small favors."

As the doors were closing on the elevator, they both saw a Horry County cruiser heading toward the exit.

"Wonder what he was doing here?" asked Ron.

"Doing what he's supposed to do. Patrolling the area. These places have a lot of car break-ins."

The elevator took 30 seconds to go up one floor.

"That's the slowest damn elevator I've ever been on, Tim. No wonder Miller's late so often."

"I didn't know he was late a lot."

"That's because you're even more late!"

"Yeah, with your friggin' donuts and coffee."

"Poor excuse, Tim-o-thy."

"Apartment E is down at the end," said Tim, leading the way.

They both drew their weapons as they approached the door.

"It's open!" said Tim in a loud whisper.

Seeing the door cracked about an inch, they stepped to either side of the door with their backs against the wall.

"Miller! This is Special Agent Ron Lee! Come out with your hands in the air!"

Nothing.

"Miller! We know you're in there. Come out with your hands raised!"

Tim stood to the door's right. Ron stood to its left.

They would breach the doorway, known in the military as the Fatal Funnel, using the classic military maneuver called Close Quarter Battle.

Tim communicated to Ron he was ready with a nod of his head.

Placing his hand on the left edge of the door, Ron pushed it until it was almost wide open. Tim, with both hands on his weapon, swung his body around where it faced the open doorway. He rushed through the door swiveling back and forth. Ron followed right behind. The first door to their right was Miller's bedroom. There was no need to look further.

Miller's body was lying across a half-packed suitcase. There were at least three bullet holes in his skull. The bedspread, once all baby blue, was now half crimson red.

"Driscoll covering his tracks?"

"I imagine so, Tim. Call it in."

It was 11:00 when Robert Edge arrived and seeing Ron and Tim sitting in the living room, said, "Do you guys ever sleep?"

"We took a short nap waiting for your sorry-ass to get here," answered Ron.

"Damn, Ron, you are a crusty old bastard."

"Lot of dead people of late, Bob."

"Gee, Ron. Welcome to my world!"

"Yeah, how do you keep so jolly, Bob?"

"I look down at each body I come across and if it's not me lying there, I tell myself, 'be jolly!'"

"I need not ask, but I will, just to make it official. What killed this prick?"

"A .22 did the damage. But, hey, what's up with the nastiness, Ron?"

"This guy is one of ours. He was Driscoll's mole. There's no doubt he was responsible for Adams' death."

"I see," replied Edge. "Listen, I sent you a report, but since we're all here, I'll break the news in person. They beat Adams to death with a blackjack."

"So he was dead before the fire got to him?"

"Yeah, I suppose that falls under," Edge offered in a soothing tone, "that old cliché, 'at least he didn't suffer.'"

"The people who killed Falano, also killed Adams?"

"That's correct, Tim, and," added Edge, "the young receptionist and at least one of the Tree Amigos."

"I'll kill that son-of-a-bitch with my bare hands."

"Don't be too hasty, Ron. He might be the guy who lifted Falano by the neck with one hand. I recommend you, shoot first, then ask questions whenever you get the chance."

"I hear you, Bob. I hear you."

\*\*\*\*\*\*\*\*\*\*\*\*

While Ron and Bob Truitt sat talking about imitating phones, Bruno and Jocko sat outside The Donut Man restaurant, awaiting Jose Perez.

Jose didn't disappoint.

As soon as they saw Jose pull into the parking lot, Bruno dispatched Jocko to get him and bring him to the car.

Bruno watched as Jocko waited for Jose's small pickup truck's door to open. When it did, Jocko stuck a pistol in Jose's ribs. Twenty seconds later, Jose was sitting in the back seat of Bruno's Mercedes. Bruno, with a silver pistol pointed at Jose's chest, sat beside him. Jocko occupied the driver's seat and within seconds the car was cruising south on Business 17.

"So Jose, tell me something."

Jose, fearing for his life, asked, "What do you want with me? I told you all I know."

"We think not, Jose. We believe you told the FBI more than you told me. Now I want you to tell me."

"Senor, I swear, everything I told you, I told them."

"I'm sure that's true, Jose, but let's turn that around, shall we?"

"What do you mean, senor?"

"I want you to tell me... everything you told the FBI."

"Senor, I told them about his golf, his bowling, his rope course, his love of western and mystery movies. All the things I told you."

"You left something out, Jose."

"I did? What?"

"That's what I want to know. Think, Jose. What did you tell the FBI that you didn't tell me?"

Jose, shaking like a leaf, closed his eyes and thought about the conversation he had with the heavyset FBI agent. Just when it seemed he had nothing more to share, his eyes popped open!

"Oh, yes, now I remember! There was this one thing I told them that I may not have told you, senor."

"What was that, Jose?"

"Hector loved riddles."

"Riddles?"

"Yes. He would hide something. To find it, we had to solve riddles or clues he gave us. He would buy a beer for whoever solved the riddle. Hector was very clever."

"I wondered why the FBI took the journal. You've answered that question, Jose. I thank you," said Bruno with a reassuring pat on Jose's knee. "I only wish you had shared it during our previous talk. It would have made this meeting unnecessary."

"It just slipped my mind, senor."

"I understand, Jose. Are we there yet, Jocko?"

"One minute out, boss."

"Where are you taking me, senor?"

"Do you like dinosaurs, Jose?"

"Dinosaurs? Yes, I guess so."

"Good, because you will love this place."

A moment later Jocko pulled into a driveway that ran alongside a putt-putt golf course. The course, closed for the season, had a dinosaur theme where plastic replicas of dinosaurs populated the property. Although closed, the course was a front for the Driscoll drug ring, and the keys were always available.

"Get out of the car, Jose."

Jocko, after parking the car, opened the back door and Jose exited.

Bruno exited on the other side.

"Follow us, Jose."

With a gun in his ribs, Jose followed Jocko into the course. They traveled down a putting surface until they reached a cave, which they entered.

"Please, senor. Don't kill me. I have three small children and a wife."

Bruno asked, "How old are your children, Jose?"

"Nine, seven and three. Two girls and a son."

Softened by Jose's revelation of having children, Bruno got in Jose's face and with spittle flying, said, "Tell anyone who knew Hector, that they are never to say a word to the FBI. Understood, Jose?"

"Si, Senor. Si."

"If I hear of anyone talking to the FBI, I'll make your children orphans, Jose."

Jose shook his head both yes and no.

Bruno gave Jocko a slight nod and Jocko gave Jose a slight smack on the head that knocked him out cold.

After returning to the car, Jocko remarked, "Jose seems like a nice guy."

"He is a nice guy," agreed Bruno. "It's unfortunate his memory failed him."

"I gotta tell you, boss, I'm surprised you didn't kill him."

"We can't kill everyone, Jocko," answered Bruno. Then in a murmur, he added, "Especially someone with three young kids."

Jose would awaken three hours later. He would stumble out of the cave and hail a taxi back to the Donut Man restaurant where his truck sat waiting.

Jose wasted no time driving home. Gathering his family, and as much of his belongings a trailer he rented could hold, he left Myrtle Beach, never to be seen again.

# CHAPTER 43

**"Ron, I'm taking** Steve Thompson to find that house with the marble stone driveway. It has to be on the route Heather gave to Adams."

"He marked the second address on his list."

"Yeah, he did, but that's not the house. If it were, Miller would have erased the check mark. It has to be one of the last six addresses on his list."

"Sounds logical, Tim. What's your plan when you find it?"

"I'll return to get you and a small army."

"That won't be necessary. They know we discovered Miller as the mole and they know we'll be going over that list again. I'm sure they have left that house high and dry."

"True, but we can still establish that's where they tortured Hector and Adams."

"Yeah, there is that," admitted Ron.

"What are you working on?"

"I asked Bob Truitt to do some phone work for me. He said he'd have it ready by noon."

"What are you going to do?"

"I will call Vivian to ask for my payment for dastardly deeds done!"

"Think it will work?" asked Tim.

"A multitude of results may arise from this venture. Only one would be a failure."

"She hangs up."

"That's the one, partner."

"We should be back by early afternoon, Ron. Wait for me before you make the call."

"I will record the whole conversation."

"Let's hope there is a conversation," added Tim.

"Yeah, let's hope. While I wait, I'll take time to work on the journal. Catch ya later."

************

They found the elusive driveway within an hour of leaving the office.

"No cars in sight, Agent Pond," noted Thompson.

"I see that, Steve. And please, call me Tim."

"What do you want to do... Tim?"

"Well, Ron thought there wouldn't be anyone home. Let's see if that's true. Get the shotguns out of the trunk. We're going in."

After calling in a request for backup, Tim and Steve breached the front door and entered the old plantation home.

As they made their way through each room, they couldn't help but notice the lack of furniture in the house.

"No furniture to speak of, Tim. What do you make of that?"

"I don't. There's a door off the kitchen. Let's check it out."

Opening the door brought a draft of wind that reeked of death.

"Damn! What is that smell?" asked Thompson.

"God knows I'm in no hurry to go down there to find out, but I'm afraid we must. Got your flashlight?"

"Yeah," responded Steve.

"Let's go."

A minute later they were standing in the old wine cellar where the torture and killing of Hector Falano, Paul Adams, Horace Simpson, and countless others had taken place.

"Look, Tim," said Steve, pointing at the ceiling. "A hook."

"This is where they strung people upside-down and beat them to a pulp," commented Tim. There was an unfamiliar growl in his voice that would belie Loretta Small's assertion that his voice was more high-pitched than usual.

"There's blood that appears to be recent Tim. It's still sticky."

"I'd be guessing that it's Adams' blood."

Forensics would find that the dried blood found on the cellar floor, under the hook, would measure almost an inch in thickness. They estimated that more than two dozen victims had bled out under the hook. Further lab results would increase the count closer to three dozen.

When Forensics arrived, Tim and Steve returned to the office. It was half-past one when Tim stepped into his office and saw Ron and Bill Baxter talking.

"What's going on, fellas?"

"We were trying to make heads or tails out of these journal entries."

"It's tough, isn't it, Bill."

"Yes, it is, Tim. There is, however, something I'm hearing that has tickled my mind. I just can't place my finger on it, as yet."

Turning to Ron, Tim asked, "How did the call go?"

"Bob Truitt called me about an hour ago, saying they had run into a glitch trying to imitate the phone number I gave him. He said it might take him another hour or so. We're into the 'so' portion now."

"Good! I'll be here when you make the call."

Interrupting their conversation, Baxter asked, "Would you read me that third clue again, Ron?"

"Okay, here goes. *I saw Hector talking with someone I didn't recognize. I asked who it was and Hector said the guy had no name, but that a mortician friend referred to him as, Joe.*"

"Damn, that's strange!" announced Bill in a raspy voice. "What makes it strange is the mortician reference."

"Hey, Tim, listen to this one, Ron said as he read, *Two guys came to the house today. They arrived in a black car. The driver was ugly and smelled bad. The other guy, the rider, although he looked pale, seemed like a good dude.*"

"What do you make of that?"

"You know, Ron, that seems like it could be a legitimate entry. Maybe some of Driscoll's guys stopped by to talk with Hector about business."

"That's a good point, Tim, except for these strange adds," said Ron.

"What adds?"

"She writes, *the other guy* and then adds, *the rider.* She's already told us the driver was ugly and smelly, so why add *the other guy* or *the rider* when either would have sufficed? Then there's this *looked pale* addition."

Before Tim could comment, Bob Truitt knocked on the door, and, not waiting for an invitation, let himself in.

"Got it, Ron. It should do the trick. We tested it in the lab and it was a home run."

"Great, Bob. Thanks. I'll let you know how it turns out. Hey, before you go, I have a question."

"What would that be?"

"If someone calls this number, what happens?"

"That number will ring."

"Does that mean this phone will ring and the real phone that has this number will also ring?"

"Yes."

"Will I be able to hear their conversation?"

"Yes, although you know it's against the law."

Ron, ignoring Bob's warning, proclaimed, "Hot damn, Bob. That is fairly fucking fantastic!"

"You have a flair for alliteration, Ron. That tongue qualifies for writing poor pre-pubescent poetry." said Bob as he walked out the door.

"Wise-ass!" yelled Ron, but too late for Bob to hear.

"All right, guys, here goes nothing," as Ron began dialing the landline number of Vivian Hanson.

It rang three times before being answered.

She answered as if asking a question.

*"Hello?"*

Ron, muffling his voice with a hanky, said, "Bring my money, tomorrow, at noon, at the Books-a-Million store in the Inlet Square Mall. Don't be late, Vivian, because I have a bullet with your name on it."

*"I thought we agreed we'd wait until the insurance..."*

"Tomorrow, noon, Books-a-Million, Inlet Square Mall. Bring my money. No more questions."

Click.

"What did she say, Ron?"

"Well, first off, based on how she answered, I believe she recognized the number."

"How did she answer?" asked Bill.

"It was like a question rather than a statement. Like, a puzzled 'Hello?', not a blunt-like 'Hello.'"

"That's not solid, Ron," said Tim. "We get calls at home from numbers we don't recognize and answer those somewhat like you described."

"That's true, Tim, but what she said next convinces me she knew who she was talking to."

"What'd she say?" asked Baxter.

"She said, *'I thought we agreed to wait until the insurance'*…" then I cut her off.

"Let's listen to the recording," suggested Tim.

After listening to the taped recording, both agreed with Ron on his assessment.

"What now?" asked Tim.

"We have two options. If she knows the hitman, then we have to go in as we are and arrest her. If she doesn't know him, then we can send someone who we wire up, and get a full confession."

"Okay, so which way do we go?"

"Bill? Would you like to be our hitman?"

"It would be my honor, Ron."

"Good, then we go with option two."

There was a knock on the door.

Ron called out, "Come on in."

It was Heather.

"Thought you guys would like to know they have set your friend's funeral for noon on Saturday morning."

"There will be a wake from 5:00 to 8:00 Friday night at Goldfinches Funeral Home in Conway.

"Thanks, Heather," said Tim.

"Irene asked if I would give a eulogy at the funeral service," Ron commented. "I said I would."

"Neither Friday evening nor Saturday will be fun days," said Tim.

Tim had no idea how prophetic his words would be when the weekend was over.

# CHAPTER 44

**After a marathon** day of sex, both Michael and Isabella slept in late, not awakening until almost 9:00.

"Good morning, Isabella," said Michael, sliding over to her warm body and wrapping his right arm around her until he cradled her left breast in his hand. He kissed her on the neck, ear, and shoulder as he pressed his body against hers.

"Hmm," she said. "Based on what I'm feeling pressed against my butt, I think someone else had a good night's sleep and appears to be ready for some morning exercise. What do you have in mind, Superman?"

"A replay of yesterday wouldn't be a bad idea," replied Michael as he let his hand slide down her stomach and beyond.

"That sounds good to me, Michael, but first I need a shower, followed by breakfast."

"That's first and second," said Michael. "I'm coming in third?"

"I suspect you'll be coming in third, fourth, fifth, and maybe even sixth!" she said with a soft giggle.

Leaving the bed, she found the remote, and turned on the television. She searched for a local station and finding it, turned up the volume and made her way to the bathroom. Isabella didn't bother closing the bathroom door while relieving herself, for fear of missing the news she was anxious to hear.

After flushing the toilet, she reached into the shower and turned on the water. She was about to step in but stopped when she overheard the newscaster mention a funeral. Stepping to the bathroom doorway, she listened to the reporter's story about the upcoming Ken Hall funeral.

*"Mr. Ken Hall, killed at the Burning Ridge Country Club on Tuesday, will have his remains laid to rest at noon on Saturday at the Hillcrest Cemetery and Chapel with full military honors."*

*There will be a wake on Friday for family and friends, from 5:00pm to 8:00pm, at The Goldfinch Funeral Home, located in Conway.*

*Mr. Hall, mistakenly gunned down while waiting to play golf, was a retired New Yorker who made Conway his home.*

*The suspected killer, Isabella Sanchez, identified as a Mexican cartel assassin, is still on the loose. The identity of her male accomplice is still unknown.*

*Some local officials believe she has returned to Mexico, but there are others who doubt that theory."*

Stepping into the main room, Isabella announced, "Sorry, Michael, but playtime is over for the time being. We need to check out the gravesite and that funeral home today."

"I understand Isabella. I don't like it, but I understand."

Smiling at his honesty, she said, "Let's get showered, dressed, and grab some breakfast. After we eat, we'll take a ride out to the funeral parlor and the cemetery."

Ninety minutes later, Michael was driving the recently gained white Yukon past the Goldfinch Funeral Home. He made two passes before pulling into the parking lot.

Isabella, wearing the maternity outfit and the light brown wig, said, "We'll both go in together. You check to see if there are any details about the wake and the funeral.

I'll scout out the interior of the building. Let's find the room where they plan on holding the wake. I'll want to scrutinize it and everything around it."

They both entered and immediately broke off in different directions with Michael heading toward the Home's offices. Isabella just wandered along the halls until someone stopped and asked, "May I be of help, ma'am? I'm Josh Campbell. I've been with the company 27 years."

"Maybe so," answered Isabella. "A good friend has passed away. His wake is being held here on Friday. My father is nearing the end, and I wanted to see if I might..."

"No need to explain, ma'am. I understand. Come, let me show you our facilities. We have a nice Celebration of Life Center that we are proud to offer our customers. It is a place where family and friends can gather for comfort and remembrance."

"That sounds appealing," said an insincere Isabella.

"Our rooms are of different sizes to best fit the needs of the family. We also offer flower arrangements, help with obituaries, stones for the gravesite, grief counseling, and so much more."

"I must admit, this place has the definite feel of warmth and comfort. Where will they hold Mr. Hall's wake?"

"Oh, that was a terrible tragedy, wasn't it? Imagine just standing waiting for your tee time and..."

"A terrible waste of life," I agree, said Isabella without an iota of compassion in her heart.

"They will hold Mr. Hall's wake in room 1C at the end of the main hall. Come, I'll show it to you. When are you due if you don't mind my asking?"

"What?"

"Your baby."

"Oh, I'm sorry, I was thinking of Ken. The baby is due in April."

"Well, congratulations. Will this be your first child?"

"Yes, it will."

A moment later they entered the room 1C. It was nothing more than a big rectangular room with chairs bordering the walls on the longer sides. There were two double-doors, one at each end; one for entering, the other for exiting.

"Good size," commented Isabella. "May I see the Celebration Center, please?"

"I would be most happy to show it to you. This way, please. You're not getting tired are you?" asked Campbell, remembering pregnant women get tired standing on their feet for prolonged periods, even more so in the third trimester. "Might you like to sit a spell?"

"I'm fine," replied Isabella, not having to lie for a change.

As they stepped into the Celebration Center, the immaculate hardwood floors first caught her eye. Her first thought was, *"very nice."*

They had furnished the room with ten identical round tables. Five comfortable-looking chairs surrounded each table. There was also a full kitchen, including cupboards, a sink, and all necessary appliances.

"Is Ken's wife planning on using this room?"

"Yes, ma'am, she is. She's having a small meal with tea, soft drinks, and coffee."

"Well, thank you for your time Mr...."

"Campbell. Josh Campbell, ma'am. Glad to be of service."

"Oh, there you are!" It was Michael.

"I've been searching everywhere for you. Have you seen everything you needed to see?"

"Yes, Mr. Campbell, gave me a very nice tour. Mr. Campbell this is my husband, James."

"Nice to meet you, James, and congratulations on your first child."

"Well, thank you, sir. Should we be going, dear? You shouldn't be on your feet for long spells."

"That's what I told her, James, but she insisted on seeing everything."

"She's bull-headed like that, Mr. Campbell. I've grown accustomed to it."

"Well, it's been nice meeting you both. I'll see you on Saturday."

"You may, sir. It all depends on how junior is acting come evening," said Isabella, patting her pillow.

"Oh, it's a boy then!"

"Yes, it's a boy. Does a lot of kicking."

"Sounds like a rowdy guy!"

"Goodbye, sir, and thank you for the tour."

Back in the car, Isabella turned to Michael, saying, "Damn! I thought when you showed up we would get tripped up, since we didn't prepare corroborating stories."

"I realized that, so I didn't offer any information."

"What did you uncover concerning the funeral?"

"Well, Isabella, in baseball parlance, we have hit a home run!"

"What is it? Tell me!"

"Guess who is going to give a eulogy?"

"You're kidding, right?"

"Nope. It's right here in the printed program."

Taking it from his hand, she opened and saw the list of speakers. There, listed as the fourth of six, was the name of Ron Lee.

"Take me to the cemetery gravesite. I think I know how I will kill FBI Special Agent, Ron Lee."

*************

At the same time Isabella was showering, Cameron Driscoll was sorting through the pages of the journal that Miller had extracted from the FBI Xerox copier. He was making no headway. He cursed Tony Rabon for being dead.

Bruno and Jocko were sitting in the room with him, waiting for his next order.

"Can we help, Mr. Driscoll?" asked Bruno. "We know how important it is to find the flash drive."

Driscoll, seething at the very thought that these two goons could find something that he couldn't, decided he would shut them up by giving them each a page. It would keep them out of his hair.

"Sure, here you go," said Driscoll, handing two pages to Bruno. "Give one to Jocko. You know he can't read, so you'll have to read it for him."

"I know, boss. It won't be a problem."

"Okay but go in the other room. I need quiet. I can't concentrate if I hear you reading aloud."

"Okay, boss. We'll let you know what we come up with."

"You do that, Bruno."

The two left Cameron's office and closed the door behind them.

"Let's go to the kitchen, Bruno. I saw some cold-cuts in the fridge and some cold beers."

"Sounds like a plan, Jocko."

Ten minutes later, both men were sucking down a cold Heineken and eating a salami and cheese sandwich.

"Read me a clue, Bruno."

"Okay, Jocko, here you go."

Bruno started reading.

*Hector had something clenched in one of his fists. I asked him what it was, and he answered, 'money'.*

"That doesn't make a whole lotta sense, does it, Bruno?"

"Couldn't agree with you more, Jocko."

"Read another one, Bruno."

"Okay, let's try this one."

*I asked Hector for a new car, but he said we need to cut expenses and save a few more dollars. But not in that exact order."*

"That's two that says something about money, Bruno. Anything else along that line?"

"Not that I can see, Jocko. Here's a strange one. *We watched the sun set in the west, but Hector said he'd rather watch the sun rise in the east."*

"Now that's a mind-twister if I ever heard one, Bruno. It sounds like he prefers east over west."

"Listen to this, Jocko."

*I asked Hector to take a walk in the woods with me, but he said, just one is enough."*

"Hmm, sure enough is a stumper, ain't it, Bruno?" asked Jocko as he washed down the last of his sandwich with a swig of beer.

"It sure is, Jocko."

The two men sat silent for a few minutes, drinking a beer and thinking.

"Son-of-a-bitch!" howled Jocko.

"What? What is it?"

"I can't tell you where the disk is, Bruno, but I got a good idea."

"Well, tell me, so I can tell Driscoll."

"I know you think I'm a big dumbass, Bruno, but I got me some smarts."

"Well then, show me how smart you are, and tell me what you think you know."

"Bruno, let me ask you a question. How much do you think that bastard would pay to know what I know?"

"Are you going to blackmail Driscoll? He'll have us both hanging from some damn hook while he beats our brains in with your fucking blackjack!"

"Not if we know where the disk is, he won't."

Bruno stood and contemplated what Jocko, a man with the intelligence of a retarded goat, was saying. There was no doubt in Bruno's mind that somehow Jocko, who despised Driscoll, had figured something out.

"All right, Jocko, I'll be with you on this, but first you have to show me what makes you think you solved this puzzle."

"I'm good at riddles, Bruno. I'll give you a tidbit, but if you tell Driscoll, I'll tear you apart with my bare hands."

"You have my word, Jocko. Tell me something that will make me believe you know what you're talking about."

"That Perez guy told us, Bruno, but we didn't listen."

"What? What the hell did he tell us?"

Jocko leaned forward and whispered into Bruno's ear.

Bruno sat still for a moment, digesting the two words Jocko had whispered. Two words, that by themselves meant nothing, but combined with the clues, all fell into place. The lights came on. It was revelation time!

"Damn it, Jocko! You're right!" screamed Bruno, his face getting as wide as a kid who finds a new bicycle under the tree on Christmas morning.

"Now, the question is," asked Jocko, "how do we get rewarded?"

"Let me work on that, Jocko. We'll make that bastard pay big for this."

# CHAPTER 45

**The Books-a-Million bookstore** had no more than a dozen customers floating up and down its many aisles, perusing books.

Seeing no more than three employees, Ron, hidden near the rear of the establishment, wondered how shoplifters hadn't robbed the store blind by now.

*Damn,* he thought, *I swear I could walk out of this place with an entire set of encyclopedias and no one would be the wiser.*

Tim, disguised so well that even Ron had a hard time recognizing him, was behind the checkout counter, posing as an employee.

Sprinkled around the store were groupings of comfortable chairs and couches. Bill Baxter, playing the part of the hitman that Vivian Hanson allegedly hired to kill two police officers, was planted in one of them. He had a full view of the store's entrance.

Pretending to read a magazine, Bill would lower it every few seconds, hoping to glimpse Vivian's arrival. It was approaching noon, and she was nowhere in sight.

Each man was wearing a wire that kept them in constant communication with one another.

Bill, in addition to the wire, also had his cell phone poised to record his conversation with Vivian.

\*\*\*\*\*\*\*\*\*\*\*\*

After receiving the call from the man she thought was her hired killer, Vivian went into a full panic.

His demand for payment was unexpected. They had agreed he would be paid once her daughter received the insurance payment.

She could pay what she owed him out of her own savings, but it would drain her of everything she had. So now she was between the proverbial "rock and a hard place." Pay and be broke for an extended period, or don't pay and get a bullet in the head.

"I will not pay, but I will not let him kill me either," she mumbled as she paced around the house in panic mode.

Making her way upstairs, she entered a seldom used bedroom. Entering its walk-in closet, she opened a door that led to a crawlspace. This is where she had stored things she thought she would never have a need for ever again.

But she was wrong. There was something Vivian needed. Her dead husband's .38 revolver. It had been in its case and placed in a trunk that now occupied a space near the rear of the crawlspace.

Flicking on a light switch shed an eerie glow along the entire length of the crawlspace. Somewhat disconcerted by spookiness, she nevertheless made her way back to the trunk through a myriad of dusty cobwebs. Reaching the trunk, she opened it and extracted the case. It had been eight years since she last held it. Back then, she thought the instrument inside the case would be what would eventually put her in the ground. If she had let her abusive husband live any longer, that scenario was a strong possibility.

Leaving the crawlspace, she returned to the guest bedroom and placed the case on the bed. Opening it, she extracted the snub-nosed silver-plated handgun with a black rubber grip and held it in her hand. She had fired the revolver before, but it was ten years ago. Checking the chambers, she found them empty, as expected. Needing bullets, she reopened the case, and saw three rows of four .38 caliber shells placed in a depository built into the gun case. She removed the first row of shells.

After inserting the four shells, leaving one chamber empty, she closed the cylinder and spun it. The clicking sounds it made as it spun, sent a shiver up her spine and raised gooseflesh on her arms. Her mind questioned whether it was a turn-on or a reaction to what she was about to do.

She didn't bother trying to figure it out. Vivian had decided. If he was unreasonable, she would kill him.

*************

If Big Ben had been in the vicinity, anyone around would have heard it chiming high noon.

But Big Ben wasn't in sight and neither was Vivian.

"Nothing, Ron," whispered Bill into his left cuff where they had attached his mic.

"Show some patience, boys. Remember, fellas, we're dealing with a woman."

"So true, partner," whispered Tim. "My wife was late for our wedding."

"We have a bogey heading this way at 10:00," reported Bill.

"Okay, Bill, it's your show. Good luck," said Ron with crossed fingers.

"10-4," answered Bill.

Vivian passed through the main entrance and walked another ten feet before stopping to pan the room. She was holding a large paper shopping bag emblazoned with the Belk's insignia.

"She's giving the room the once over, Ron, like she's looking for someone she recognizes," reported Bill. "What do you want me to do?"

"Can she see you?" asked Ron.

"No, I have the magazine in front of my face."

"Drop it and let's see her reaction."

Bill lowered the magazine and stared at Vivian.

It took a few moments before their eyes met. Bill gave her an ever so slight nod.

She saw it! She nodded in return.

Bill stood, turning ever so slightly as he did, and spoke into his mic, "We're a go."

As planned, Bill walked toward the exit, stopping just inside the door.

Vivian followed.

Bill continued outside and sat on a bench which the store had placed, for its customers, along the outside wall. It sat just three or four steps from the doorway.

A moment later, Vivian took a seat next to his.

"Ron, they are outside," Tim reported, as he made his way to the exit.

Ron, hearing Tim's report, made his way toward the front door. As he did so, he heard Bill ask, "Do you have the money?"

"I have some of it. I need to wait until they pay the insurance claim. That's what we agreed to. Why have you changed the deal?"

"I need the money now, Vivian. All of it."

"I can't give you all of it!"

"How many people have you asked me to kill, Vivian? Have I ever let you down?"

"No, you haven't, but can't you see…?"

"Haven't I always done what you have asked?"

"Yes, but this is all I have."

"What did we agree on?"

"We agreed to $200,000. I paid you $50,000 up front. I have $75 with me now."

"How long have we been in business, Vivian?"

"Since 2011. Why?"

"Ever since I helped your husband have that accident. Right?"

"Yes, and I paid you well for your efforts."

"Yes, you did. You paid me on time too, I recall."

"That was the same situation. You waited until I got the insurance money."

"Yeah, you collected a cool half-million and what did you pay me. Peanuts!"

"Peanuts? You think $75 grand is peanuts?"

"You had me kill your husband because he was beating you. Ain't that right, Vivian?"

"Yes, I told you that."

"Is that the same reason I killed those two cops?"

"They were both wife-beaters. They needed killing before they killed those two girls."

"Well, I did my job and now I want my money… in full!"

"You won't take this partial payment then?"

"No, Vivian, I want it all or else."

"Yeah, that was my thinking too, you bastard!"

Bolting out of her seat, Vivian reached into the bag and pulled out the revolver and pointed it at Bill's head.

Bill's eyes, horrified by this unexpected turn of events, grew as big as saucers. He realized, as he had often remarked, that he never saw this coming.

"No, Vivian, don't do it. I'm a…"

Vivian pulled the trigger… once, twice and a third time.

It had been over ten years since Vivian had handled a gun and this moment highlighted that fact. Each time she pulled on the trigger, nothing happened.

Vivian had forgotten to remove the safety.

# CHAPTER 46

**While Bill Baxter** and Vivian were exchanging pleasantries, Isabella and Michael were preparing to scope out the Hillcrest Cemetery and Chapel.

After leaving the funeral parlor, they had stopped at a florist to buy a graveside flower arrangement. Based on their request, the florist said it wouldn't be ready until 5:00 at the earliest. Isabella hastened the project by offering triple the cost if finished by 2:30. The woman assured her it would be done.

And it was.

The information Michael had collected at the funeral home included the gravesite's general location.

The cemetery had multiple roads that weaved their way through the quiet grounds. Not knowing how to get to the gravesite, they turned off Route 544 at the south gate entrance and stopped at the office to get directions.

Michael went inside and was met by a woman who asked, "May I help you?"

"We feel somewhat foolish but would it be appropriate to leave flowers at an open grave site?" asked Michael. "We won't be able to attend the funeral but we had a very nice arrangement made to show our condolences for our good friend."

"And who is this friend, sir?" asked the woman.

"Mr. Ken Hall is being interred in quadrant F."

"Yes, I know of that funeral," she said as she handed Michael a map of the grounds.

"Follow this road. Bear to your left at the second right turn," she said, using her finger as a pointer. "Stay on this road. It loops around at the very back of the property.

Keep going until you see a gravel service road on your left. There will be a white tent erected on your right. That's the Hall gravesite. Leave your flowers under the tent. Someone will place them as part of the burial's preparation."

"Thank you, ma'am," said Michael as he headed out the door. "I appreciate your time."

Minutes later, they were standing beside their vehicle, viewing the gravesite. The distance from the road to the grave was only fifty steps.

As they stood there eyeing the grounds, Isabella, from out of the blue, screamed, "Wait!"

"What is it, Isabella?" asked Michael with a look of deep concern.

"That news report we listened to this morning."

"What about it?"

"The reporter mentioned something that slipped past me until this very moment."

"What was it that she said?"

"She reported that Ken Hall's burial service would include… full military honors."

Michael understood immediately.

"A 21-gun salute," he said almost in a whisper.

"Exactly, Michael. That's when I'll kill Special Agent Ron Lee."

************

"Vivian, sit your ass down on that bench," said Ron Lee, mortified that Bill Baxter had come within a gaff of having his head blown off.

Neither Ron nor Tim had given thought to the possibility of Vivian having a weapon. This would result in a well-deserved condemnation on both their records.

Tim, seeing Vivian taking the gun out of the bag, reacted with lightning speed. Rushing out the door, he tackled the woman just as she realized her mistake of leaving the safety on. If given another moment, she would have turned the safety off and bullets would have flown.

Ron's thought was, if it had been him, and having nowhere near the quickness Tim displayed, he would have shot her dead.

Baxter was off losing his breakfast somewhere. No one was blaming him.

Turning to Vivian, Ron held court right there on the bench where moments earlier, Vivian had confessed to having her husband and two cops murdered.

"It's obvious, Vivian, that you never met the man you hired to kill your husband and those two police officers, one of whom was your daughter's husband."

Vivian, shaking like a leaf, mumbled, "True."

"Do you know his name, Vivian?"

"I wouldn't have pulled the trigger if I had known that fella was a cop, Agent Lee. Never. I thought he was…"

"Okay, Vivian, we believe you," said Ron in a soothing voice. "You were about to say something. You thought he was…who?"

"The Ghost."

"What! Who?"

"He told me to call him, The Ghost."

"The Ghost? Why?"

"I don't know. I suppose it's because no one has ever seen him."

"How would you know that?"

"I don't for sure. The person who put me on to him in New York, told me they never saw him either."

Thinking about what Vivian had just said, Ron asked, "Did you pay him $50K upfront?"

"Yes, I did."

"How did that occur?"

"What do you mean?"

"Did you leave it somewhere? Mail it to him? Meet him? How did he get his money?"

"Well, I didn't meet him. If I had, I would have known what he looked like. Wouldn't I?"

"I agree," said Ron, hoping to trip her up.

"I left it in a trash can."

"You left $50,000 in a trash can! Where?"

"At a restaurant."

"What restaurant?"

"Manny's Deli."

Ron, knocked back by her answer, composed himself, then asked, "What time did you do that, Vivian?"

"It was right after Manny closed up. He told me to wait until Manny left and then put the package – the money – in the trashcan sitting outside the restaurant."

"How did you request his services? Wasn't he in New York?"

"I guess he was. I don't know. About a year after I moved down here, I received a note in the mail. It said that if I ever needed his services again to call the number written on the note."

"So you called him to get rid of your son-in-law."

"Yeah, I did."

"How much time passed between when you called him until you put the upfront payment in the trashcan?"

"I called him at 5:00pm that day. I told him what I needed. He told me the cost, what he needed upfront, and I dropped the money in the trashcan that night."

Tim, standing nearby and jotting down notes, blurted, "That means he…"

"Quiet, Tim!" barked Ron.

"Vivian, I want you to do me a favor. A big favor. I can't promise you anything for your cooperation, but I'll put in a good word, if your help pays off."

"Let me guess. You want me to call The Ghost."

"I do," said Ron. "I'll take you home. I want you to call him and tell him you have his money. All I want you to do is to agree to anything he tells you."

"And for doing this I get nothing?"

"That's the best I can offer, Vivian. You had two cops killed. There ain't much forgiveness for that. Too bad it wasn't two or three politicians. The public is somewhat more forgiving when they are weeded out."

"Or lawyers," chimed in Tim.

"That too," agreed Ron.

"Do you think these circumstances will affect my daughter's inheritance?" asked Vivian.

"No, I don't," answered Ron, "but Sheila Bennington may have a problem."

"She wasn't aware of what I was doing!"

"She might be okay. If not, since she and your daughter are as tight as ticks, maybe Peggy will throw her a bone or two."

"There was a third cop killed. Just to be straight, Mr. FBI, I had nothing to do with that."

"We thought as much, Vivian, but the guy you hired, did. This son-of-a-bitch needs to be off the streets."

"Well, take me home and let's have it."

# CHAPTER 47

**They were sitting** at Vivian's dining room table. Ron, instructing Vivian, had placed her landline phone on the table in front of her.

"This is what I want you to say, Vivian, and nothing more. Tell him you have his money and you'll leave it wherever he says. Suggest nothing. Let him dictate. I'm guessing he'll want to do this tonight."

"What if he says tomorrow during the day?"

"If he says tomorrow, suggest late afternoon. If he asks why, tell him you have a funeral to attend that will require your time from 10:00 until 2:00. He may give you an argument but be firm. He'll cave because of the money."

"I think I'm ready."

"Let's call him."

Ron dialed the number and once it began ringing, he put it on speaker and sat the device in front of Vivian. It rang four times before a gruff voice said, *"Why are you calling me? What do you want?"*

"I have your money," answered Vivian.

They could hear traffic sounds in the background. Ron surmised that The Ghost was in a car with the window open.

*"You've already received the insurance payment?"*

"Yes, it arrived this morning."

*"It was my impression that the payment would take two weeks or more."*

"Well, it didn't. What can I say? Where do you want me to leave it?"

*"How large is the package?"*

"About the size of a shoe box, I'd say," answered Vivian, manufacturing the dimension on her own.

*"I would have thought that $150,000 would be bigger than that."*

"Think size 16 wide. It's all in hundreds. Fifteen packs of $10,000. Just as you requested. It's in a shopping bag sitting here on my dining room table."

*"Get a black duffel bag and put the money in it. Do you know where the Surfside United Methodist Church is?"*

"Yes. It's about a mile from here," answered Vivian.

*"There is a covered vestibule at the church's rear entrance. If there are no cars remaining in the parking lot, park under the vestibule. Leave your car and place the bag against the door at exactly 9:30 tonight."*

"What should I do if there are cars in the lot?"

*"Return every 15 minutes until the lot is clear."*

"Can I ask you a question?"

Hearing her getting off the script, Ron wagged his finger at her and shook his head.

*"It depends."*

"I will never need your services again…"

*"You can never be too sure about that,"* interrupted The Ghost.

"It's all but guaranteed that I won't," she insisted, knowing her fate was going to be life in prison.

*"So what's your question?"*

"I've never seen you and I never will, but I'd like to know, why are you are called The Ghost? Is it because no one has ever seen you?"

*"I got that name courtesy of my college buddies many years ago. I didn't like it then, but I thought it would be a good business name."*

"You still haven't told me why you have that name," said Vivian.

*"I guess it won't hurt to tell you, Vivian. It's because my hair went prematurely snow-white when I was in my early twenties."*

Ron and Tim both flashed each other a knowing look with Ron jotting something down and handing it to Tim.

Tim, taking the note, glimpsed it and then left the room and made a call on his cell. Ron then turned to Vivian and gave her the "keep it going gesture" indicating he wanted her to continue the conversation for a few more minutes.

"I see," said Vivian. "My brother had that problem as well. His hair turned all white when he was only 29. He's bald now."

*"That's nice, Vivian. How about you telling me your plans for tonight? I want to make sure we have all our ducks in a row."*

"Really? I may be old, but I'm not senile."

*"Let me hear it, Vivian."*

Vivian, playing the role to the hilt, replied, "Okay. If I must. You ready?"

*"Yeah, I'm ready. Get on with it."*

"I'll leave the money in a black duffel bag at the church at 9:30, assuming the parking lot is empty of cars."

*"It's been nice doing business with you, Vivian."*

Then in the background, Ron heard, *"Officer…"*

There was an audible *click,* and the conversation was over.

"Damn!" Ron barked.

"What's the matter?" asked Vivian, afraid that she had done something wrong.

Tim entered the room, asking, "Did you hear it?"

Ron responded, "All I heard was *'Officer'* and then he hung up. I can't be positive it was the call we put out."

"I'm sorry, Vivian. I'm not pissed at you. You did a hell of a job!" exclaimed Ron. "You had me worried there when you asked him that question, but I'm glad you did."

"I ain't the smartest broad around but I'm guessing that you guys think this Ghost guy is a cop. Is that right?"

"No comment, Vivian, but you ain't no dummy."

"What now, Mr. FBI?"

"Tim and I need to make some arrangements with the church, but as for you, you get to enjoy a few more hours of freedom."

"We need a black duffel bag," voiced Vivian. "Are you going to trust me to go buy one?"

"Negatory, Viv," said Ron, shaking his head. "The Ghost, however, may be watching to see that you're not hooked up."

"Hooked up?"

"Working with the law."

"I guess it's official, then. I'm hooked up."

"If he is watching you, then we should make everything look normal. I guess that will require that you purchase the bag."

"My last shopping venture," Vivian said with a touch of remorse.

"Someone will follow you, from a distance, no doubt. You will drive to the Garden City Wal-Mart. We'll have someone inside to keep track of your activities. Buy the duffel bag and drive back home. You'll be under surveillance the entire time."

"Is there anything I can do without being watched like a hawk?" asked Vivian.

"Sorry, Viv, but you can't even go pee without someone being with you."

"You're kidding."

"Vivian, you seem to forget. You had two policemen killed. Your life, as you know it, is over."

\*\*\*\*\*\*\*\*\*\*\*\*\*

Isabella, using her cell phone's camera, began taking reconnaissance photos of the immediate area in and around the gravesite.

Preparation for the funeral had already begun. The tent, fully erected, was at least 40x40, and sitting under it was an estimated six dozen folding chairs. Podium steps were in place at the northern portion of the tent, but not the podium itself.

Michael had witnessed two military funerals, and he had a reasonable idea of what was to transpire. Isabella, listening to what Michael was saying, laid out in her mind how she would execute the first portion of her plan to kill the FBI agent. The second portion was the escape route.

An hour later, they headed back to the hotel.

"Are you going to attend the wake, Isabella?" asked Michael.

"No," she answered with no hesitation. "It would be foolish to attempt anything at the funeral home."

"Why do you say that?"

"Two reasons, Michael."

"And they are?"

"The first is the opportunities at the gravesite far outnumber those at the funeral home. More spots to take the shot from, better cover, and plenty of time. The second reason is the escape will be easier at the cemetery than it would at the funeral home."

"What role will I play?" asked Michael.

"You will be the key to the escape. In fact, I want you to plan our escape route once we are off the cemetery grounds. Can you do that?"

"Not a problem, Isabella. So, tomorrow, we will have nothing to do for most of the day?"

Knowing to what he was alluding, she smiled at him, saying, "We may have some free time to fill in. Might you have any ideas?"

"It might be hard, but I might come up with something," he answered with a slight emphasis on the words 'hard' and 'up.'

"Oh, I'm sure you will, Michael, and please, keep me abreast of what's going on."

"Worry not, Isabella. I'll keep filling you in, as much as possible."

She laughed at his boyish enthusiasm.

*Perhaps,* she thought, *I won't discard him when this is over.*

# CHAPTER 48

**The church had** been empty since 8:00PM when the Men's Golf Group Committee adjourned. The parking lot was void of any vehicles.

Arriving at 9:30 sharp, Vivian parked under the vestibule, and while leaving her vehicle running, exited her car with the duffel bag in tow. She walked to the rear-entrance and placed it against the door, after which, she returned to her car and drove off. Hidden in her back seat was Agent Steve Thompson. He was to escort her back to her home where they would wait until they heard that they had captured the elusive Ghost. Thompson would then escort Vivian to FBI headquarters where they would hold her until Monday morning when they would file formal charges.

Earlier that day, Ron had men discreetly positioned in and around the church where they would wait until The Ghost appeared to pick up the duffel bag.

The bag contained the $150,000 payoff The Ghost expected, but it also contained a dye pack. Whoever opened the bag would set off an explosion of red dye. Ron also had a tracker imbedded in one of the $10,000 packets. He didn't expect The Ghost to elude the contingent of FBI agents hidden in the immediate vicinity, but stranger things have happened and he wanted backup. The tracker would provide that.

Ron and Tim were in the home of Mr. and Mrs. Bailey who lived on the corner of 13th Avenue and North Poplar Drive. They had called the Bailey's and explained the situation. The couple was excited to help. The two agents, to avoid detection, entered the couple's home through the back door after making their way through various yards between North Cherry and North Poplar.

Ron, using infra-red binoculars, was standing in the Bailey's front room, which was darker than Hitler's soul.

The countdown began just moments after Vivian had exited the lot.

"What time is it, Tim?"

"It's 9:32, Ron. It's a bit early to ask me that, don't you think?"

"Maybe, but for every minute he's late, it makes me think he's on to us."

\*\*\*\*\*\*\*\*\*\*\*\*\*

After Vivian had exited the lot, she made her way east on 13th Avenue North for two blocks where she made a right turn onto Cedar Drive. She continued on Cedar until stopping at the 10th Avenue intersection where she made a left turn. She had traveled no more than 100 yards when flashing blue lights appeared in her rearview mirror.

"It's a police car," she said to the hidden FBI agent.

"Pull over, Vivian. I'll take care of this," said Steve Thompson.

Vivian parked alongside the road and rolled down both her window and the rear driver side window.

In her side mirror, she watched the officer exit his car and approach hers.

As he came to the rolled down rear window, Agent Thompson said, "Officer, this is an FBI…"

"I know what it is," said the white-haired police officer as he shot Thompson in the face three times.

"Vivian, I'm very disappointed in you. We had a nice thing going."

You're The Ghost. You're going to kill me, aren't you."

"Did you leave the money where I told you?"

"Yes."

"I am going to kill you, Vivian, but because you're a woman, I won't shoot you in the face."

Three soft pops later, Vivian was lying across the seat with three holes in her chest.

\*\*\*\*\*\*\*\*\*\*\*\*

The call came in at 9:45.

Tim, listening to the message, turned to Ron and reported in a solemn voice "There's a report of a shooting just a few blocks from here, Ron."

"Yeah, so what?"

"They found Vivian's car pulled over on the side of the road. Local cops report there are two victims: Vivian and Agent Thompson. Both fatal."

Ron, his face turning a crimson red, snorted, "Damn, he was on to us. Get everyone over there! That mother…"

"Everyone?" asked Tim.

"Everyone!" roared Ron.

Turning his head toward the lapel of his jacket where he had attached his mic, Tim, with a sense of urgency, announced, "All agents are to leave their current positions and proceed to Cedar and 10th."

Tim took off backtracking his earlier journey to the Bailey's back door. It wasn't until he got to their vehicle did he realize that Ron wasn't with him.

"Son-of-a-bitch!" Tim yelled. Then, speaking into his mic, he said, "Ron. What are you doing?"

*"Waiting,"* came the terse reply.

"Waiting for what?"

*"The Ghost, Tim. He still wants his money."*

"I'm coming back," said Tim.

*"NO!"* Ron responded vehemently.

"What do you want me to do?"

*"Go to the scene. If he sees you, then he may think we are both there and he'll come here to get his money."*

"What makes you think he's at the scene, Ron?"

*"Oh, he'll be there. In an official capacity, but he'll stay in the shadows, so he can disappear."*

"What will you do if he shows, Ron?"

*"Arrest him, or…"*

"Or what?"

*"Make him dead."*

"I'll get back to you after I get over there."

*"Don't be too conspicuous, Tim."*

"This ain't my first rodeo, partner."

Ten minutes later, Ron heard Tim's voice in his earpiece.

*"He may be here somewhere, Ron, but I don't see him."*

"I told you he'd be hiding in the shadows."

*"Yeah, but maybe we got this wrong."*

"We don't have it wrong, partner."

*"How can you be sure?"*

"Because he's pulling into the parking lot as we speak."

*"Hot Damn!"* yelled Tim. *"I'm on my way!"*

The car turned off of 17 Bypass onto 13<sup>th</sup> Avenue North. Its blue lights were flashing but there was no siren. It slowed as it approached the church's parking lot entrance and made the left turn. It crept to a stop under the vestibule. The driver remained in the car.

Ron, who left the Bailey's home via the front door, ambled across the street and into the unlit parking lot.

The driver opened the door and began making his way toward the church's back door.

Ron waited until the man had incriminated himself.

The dark figure went to the door and lifting the duffel bag from its position, made his way back to the patrol car.

"Officer Garrett, what brings you here?" Ron called out, his gun at the ready.

Clyde Garrett, a professional hitman, stayed calm.

"Special Agent Lee. I guess I could ask you the same question."

They were only 20 feet apart. Ron stood on one side of the police cruiser; Garrett stood on the other.

"I've got a good answer, Clyde. I was waiting to see who would pick up that duffel bag. What's your excuse?"

"A caller reported having seen someone lurking around the rear of the church. I responded to the call. Seeing this bag sitting by the door, I collected it to take to the station."

"They put a call out, you say?"

"Yeah, dispatch sent out an 11-54. That's code for a suspicious vehicle."

"I know what a 11-54 is, officer. I want you to drop the bag, Clyde, and get on the ground."

"What's this all about?"

"Do what I say, Clyde, or maybe I should call you, The Ghost."

"What the hell are you talking about, Agent Lee?"

"I have suspected you for quite a long time, Clyde. I wasn't positive I had the right man, however, until you told Vivian how you got that nickname."

"Who's Vivian?"

Ron was about to answer, when in his earpiece he heard the voice of his partner.

*"Ron, be careful. That guy may also be Driscoll's hitman! The coroner says that a .22 killed Vivian and Thompson."*

Taken aback by Tim's disclosure, Ron, losing his concentration for just a split-second, took his eye off Garrett. It gave The Ghost all the time he would need.

Drawing his pistol from his holster as fast as a top-notch old west gunslinger, and aiming it at Ron's head, he shouted, "Drop the gun, Agent Lee."

"Son-of-a-bitch!" growled Ron. "So, Clyde, besides killing three cops, you're also responsible for the murders of a judge and a detective."

"I'm afraid I must plead guilty to those charges, Agent Lee, but there's not much you can do about it, is there? Now drop the gun and kick it away or I'll drop you right where you stand."

"You're working for Driscoll," Ron declared as he placed his gun on the ground and kicked it ten feet to his left.

"Once again, guilty as charged."

"Anything else I should know?"

"Well, Agent Lee, if you really need to know, I also killed that mole you had in your office. Driscoll was desperate to have him dead. He paid me $100K. I'm guessing you weren't all that upset with his death, being he was a traitor to the F-B-I."

"To be honest with you, I wasn't," Ron admitted.

"I thought that might be the case."

"Was that you who drove by as we approached his apartment?"

"Yes, it was. A few minutes earlier and you might have had me, although I doubt it."

"Anyone else you want to add to your ever-growing scorecard?"

"Well, there's a cop down in a Hilton Head swamp called Last End Point, who won't be doing any evidence checking any longer."

"What about Officer Clayton? Why did you kill him? Vivian didn't pay you to do that."

"Well, thanks to that mole, I knew where you were going with the case and I wanted you to stay on point."

"So why Vivian?"

"I got a little suspicious earlier when while talking to Vivian, a call came over my radio asking my 10-20. That's a call we seldom ever get. So just to be cautious, I did a drive-by of Vivian's house and to my surprise, someone, not to smart, parked an FBI vehicle outside on the street."

"You're lying. We would have seen you drive past her house."

"You're right, you would have, Agent Lee, if I had been driving a black-and-white, but today I was driving an unmarked car."

"So why a black-and-white now?"

"Oh, I asked for some overtime."

"So why kill Vivian and another FBI agent?"

"I figured that if you were staking out the church, which you were, then I needed you to get out of here. You know what's hilarious, Ron?"

"Can't imagine."

"I called in the 'shots fired' call."

"You wanna hear something equally as funny, Clyde?"

"What would that be?"

"That bag you're holding?"

"What about it?"

"It's filled with cut-up newspaper."

"Damn, you say!"

"Hey, we're planning to capture The Ghost. Why would we need real money?"

The Ghost, never taking his eyes off Ron, took three steps forward and placed the duffel bag on the hood of the cruiser.

"If what you say is true, Agent Lee, then you are taking your final breaths."

With his right hand aiming his service revolver at Ron, his left hand unzipped the bag and pulled the two sides apart.

There was a soft 'pop' and the red dye exploded in The Ghost's face. Blinded, Garrett began firing instinctively toward Ron's position.

Ron, seeing the dye pack explode, immediately fell to the ground, and while bullets whizzed overhead, he collected his weapon from where he had kicked it. Staying down to avoid Garrett's wild shots, he moved to a position behind the cruiser's passenger door. He was about to come up firing when he heard the distinctive sound of an FBI issued Glock .22. He heard three rounds fired – *bam, bam, bam.*

It was dead quiet for a few seconds before Ron heard Tim's familiar voice ask, "Partner, are you all right?"

"Yeah, Tim. I'm okay."

He next heard Tim say, "We have a suspect down behind the Surfside United Methodist Church on 13th Avenue North."

Ron walked around the vehicle to where The Ghost lay dead. Tim had hit him with all three shots.

"Nice shooting, partner."

"I go to a lot of carnivals and fairs. I win a teddy bear almost every time."

"Almost?"

"I miss on purpose once in a while just so folks know I'm human."

"In a way, it's too bad you killed him, although I was about to do the same."

"Why is it too bad?"

"He confessed that Driscoll hired him to kill the judge, the detective, and Miller."

"Damn! We could have nailed Driscoll to the cross if…"

"Yeah, if."

"What's next, Ron?"

"I don't know about you, Tim, but I plan on getting some much needed sleep. I'm flat worn out. Tomorrow morning, however, I'll get up and write Ken's eulogy. Somewhat lost in all this excitement is the fact that tomorrow at noon we'll bury a good friend."

"I'm not looking forward to that, Ron."

"I'm with you on that, partner."

Someone, however, didn't share their solemn outlook. In fact, if the truth be known, Isabella was looking forward to it.

# CHAPTER 49

**Waking at 5:30,** Ron showered and ate a breakfast of cereal and toast. Before the clock chimed 7:00am, he had completed the eulogy outline for Ken Hall's funeral. Scheduled to be the fourth of six eulogy speakers, it was something he didn't relish doing. It wasn't because of the situation, but because he hated being in front of a large audience. Public speaking was never his strong suit.

He spent the next 30 minutes watching the news, but boredom got the best of him. He dressed in the suit he would wear to the funeral. Tucking the eulogy paper into his jacket pocket he turned off the lights and although it was Saturday, he headed for the office.

It was 8:00am when he arrived. Pouring himself a cup of coffee, he searched, with no luck, for a donut, before trudging to his office.

The previous night's encounter with The Ghost was already behind him as he looked to solve the mystery of where Hector Falano had hidden a valuable flash drive.

Convinced the answer was in the cryptic entries of Corrina's journal, Ron read and reread each page of her daily experiences. When finished, he was no closer to solving the riddle than he had been a week earlier.

It was 8:15 when the office door opened and Bill Baxter walked in.

"Morning, Bill. Dare I ask what brings you here?"

"Just want to say thanks for closing a half-dozen open murders, Ron."

"Did you contact Hilton Head about the cop who worked in their evidence department?"

"Yeah, I did. They say he's been missing since Sunday. They're sending out a search unit to…"

"Last End Point?"

"Yeah, that's the one."

"Did you happen to bring a donut with you?"

"Sure, Ron, got it right here in my pocket."

"Screw you, Bill."

"Now that's the Colonel Ron Lee I know!"

"Bill, having read these journal pages, do you have any idea what some of these screwy entries might mean?"

"I was thinking about some of them, Ron."

"Which ones?"

"She asked Hector what time he wanted to have dinner, and he replied, *'ten after three.'*"

"A little early for dinner, don't you think, Bill?"

"I do. They didn't have any children, did they?"

"No. Why do you ask?"

"Well, after the dinner comment, she wrote that Hector said to her, 'Hey Corrina, I'm pa, you ma.'"

"How about this one, Bill? She writes, 'After Hector watches a movie he wants spaghetti for dinner.'"

"Movies and spaghetti," noted Baxter. "Does he watch Italian movies?"

"How the hell would I… hey, wait a minute!" exclaimed Ron.

"What is it, Colonel?"

"That Perez guy told us that Hector loved to watch action movies… and westerns! Spaghetti westerns, Bill!"

"Damn, Ron. Now those two clues make sense!"

"Which two, Bill?"

"The walking in the woods and he'd rather watch the sun rise in the east. Wood, east. Eastwood! Clint Eastwood!"

"Damn it, Bill. You're right!"

Ron picked up the page they had just discussed. He repeated parts of the writing.

"Ten after three is 3:10. I'm pa, you ma. Yuma! The 3:10 to Yuma. All these clues refer to westerns, Bill."

"Hang her undies high. Hang em High!" screamed Bill.

"The three guys who visited him in the black car. The Good, the Bad and the Ugly!" shouted Ron.

"He has hidden that damn flash drive amongst his western DVD's, Ron!"

"Where's that calendar?" asked Ron, scrambling through his desk. "Here it is. Listen to this clue."

"I'm listening."

Ron read the notation written on the 17th.

"Keeping it between the isolated feathers."

As they sat there, mumbling that phrase over and over to themselves, Tim, carrying a box of donuts, walked in, looking like the cat who had swallowed the canary.

"Why the grin, Tim?" asked Ron.

"Ron, I tried to call but you must have your phone turned off."

"Hold it a minute, Tim. Bill and I are on to something. We figured out…"

"Ron! This is too big to wait! I know where…"

"Would you put a cork in it, Pond! Just give us another minute of solitude."

Exasperated, Tim blurted, "I know where the flash drive is!"

Ron and Bill both looked at Tim like he was some kind of demon.

"What do you mean you know where the flash drive is?" asked Ron.

"It came to me last night. I couldn't sleep due to last night's events, so I got up and watched television. A Clint Eastwood movie, titled, 'For a Few Dollars More.' was playing. I remembered that one of Corrina's entries read something like that and then it all clicked. Just like that," said Tim, snapping his fingers. "Hector loved Clint Eastwood and watching westerns. Do you remember the Perez guy telling us that, Ron?"

"Yeah, I remember. Have you been standing outside the door overhearing our conversation?"

"What? No. I just got here. I would have been here sooner, but I stopped for donuts."

"So what's the answer, hotshot?" asked a seething Ron, pissed that his young partner solved the puzzle before he had.

"What's with the attitude? I come up with the solution to all those crazy entries in Corrina's journal, and you're not thrilled. What's up with that, Ron?"

"What's the fucking answer, Tim-o-thy!" Ron roared.

"Geez, all right, all ready. Settle down, big fella. It's in a DVD between the Lonesome Dove DVD's."

"Keeping it between the isolated feathers," whispered Baxter. "By God, Ron, he's got it!"

"Let's go, fellas," yelled Ron, grabbing a chocolate-covered donut on his way out the door. It was 8:45am.

✼✼✼✼✼✼✼✼✼✼✼✼

"Mr. Driscoll, can we talk for a minute?"

It was 7:00 on Saturday morning and asking was Bruno.

Driscoll was in his exercise room, walking on a treadmill. His day started early and ended late. He claimed that exercise and no fatty foods kept him going.

"Sure Bruno. I'm surprised to see the two of you here this early. I trust it's something important you need to talk to me about."

"What would it be worth to you to have that flash drive, Cameron?"

Driscoll, hearing Bruno call him by his first name, gave him pause.

"Why do you ask, Bruno?"

"We know where the flash drive is. So what is it worth to you?"

"Are you trying to blackmail me?"

"Call it what you like, Cameron. I'll ask you one last time. What is it worth to you?"

"I'll have you both killed for this!"

"We thought you'd say something like that, Cameron, which I must say, is disappointing. But look around. Do you see anyone who will kill us? I don't see anyone. We're your killers. We're capable of killing anyone," then with a long pause, Bruno added with a snarl, "even you."

Hearing the obvious unveiled threat, Driscoll's mouth went dry. Retrieving his water bottle he had in a holder attached to the treadmill, he took a long swig. Giving credence to Bruno's words, he asked, "How much do you want?"

"A million for me and a million and a half for Jocko."

"Are you telling me that Jocko figured out where the drive is?"

"I'd be careful what you're implying with that tone, Cameron. Jocko has never liked the way you spoke to him or about him."

*Two and a half million,* thought Driscoll. *What fools these two idiots are. I would have paid twice that to get my hands on that flash drive.*

"How do I know what you're telling me is true?"

"You don't, Cameron. You'll just have to trust us."

"Okay. So how do we do this, Bruno?"

"We opened an offshore account. You wire half the money now and the other half when we turn over the drive."

"Hmm, that seems to be to your advantage. What's keeping you from taking half the money and leaving town, never to be seen or heard from again?"

"Jocko."

"What's that supposed to mean?"

"Tell him, Jocko."

"I promised Bruno that if we don't get every last dollar, I'll break his neck and yours."

"Well, we wouldn't want that now, would we, Bruno? Could you give me a hint as to how you came up with the solution?"

"No chance, Cameron," replied Jocko.

"Do you want the drive, or not?" asked an impatient Bruno.

"We'll need to wait until 8:30 before I can wire the money."

"We'll wait," announced a confident Jocko.

It was 8:40 when Bruno and Jocko left Driscoll's office and headed to Hector's house. They didn't know it but they had a five-minute head start on the FBI.

"There are cops watching the house, Bruno."

"Soon they'll be dead cops, Jocko."

# CHAPTER 50

**Hector's home, located** in the high-end Briarcliff Estates, was four miles closer to the FBI offices than it was to Driscoll's location in Little River.

The multitude of traffic signals Bruno and Jocko would engage would negate their five-minute advantage.

Ron, Tim, and Baxter reached the Falano home at 9:07. The house, located on Cypress Lane, was a sprawling brick ranch with two driveways.

A blacktopped driveway, that led to the garage, ran along the far right of the property.

The builder had placed the second, a decorative and stamped circular drive, in the middle of the property. It had a standard driveway entrance, but after 15 feet, expanded to a large circular parking area, fronting the home. A birdbath, surrounded by small bushes, sat in the middle of the circle.

Tim had pulled the FBI Tahoe into the middle drive, circled the birdbath, and stopped as close to the front door as possible. Three door slams later, they were all standing outside the vehicle, staring at the front door.

Parked out on the street were two Horry County Sheriff Deputies. One deputy exited the car and was walking toward the Tahoe, when Ron held up his badge, and announced, "It's okay, fellas, FBI."

The officer, recognizing Ron, stopped and giving a semi-salute, returned to his black and white.

The crime lab had dressed the front door in the obligatory yellow crime scene tape. Tim, stripping it away, unlocked the door and the three men entered. There was an eight-foot foyer leading into the living room. Straight ahead, on shelves, surrounding a stone fireplace, was Hector's library of DVDs.

************

No sooner had the FBI agents closed the home's front door, than did Bruno's Mercedes make the scene.

"Damn, Bruno. The FBI is here!"

"Let's take care of these guys first," said Bruno, pulling up even with the sheriff's cruiser.

Rolling down his window, Bruno asked the officer sitting in the driver seat, "Excuse me, officer, but how do you get out of this neighborhood and back onto the bypass?"

The officer, smiling at the man's inability to navigate the neighborhood, pointed back toward where they had come. He was about to explain when Bruno lifted his silenced Glock above the windowsill and shot the officer in the head. The impact of the bullet flung the dead officer sideways, and exposed his partner sitting in the passenger seat. A second shot caught his partner in the throat and a third found the officer's ear.

Bruno backed the Mercedes up about twenty feet and pulled onto the blacktopped drive. Creeping forward, the Mercedes stopped in front of the all too familiar garage doors. Exiting their vehicle, Bruno and Jocko made their way toward the door that would take them into the garage.

************

"God, he had a lot of DVDs!" exclaimed Baxter. "There must be 500 or more."

"I'd guess more," said Ron.

They were standing in the home's living room just inside the front entrance.

The DVDs were no longer occupying the bookshelves. Whoever had searched the house earlier, hoping to find the flash drive behind the neatly placed DVDs, had wheeled through the disks, with reckless abandonment, sending them flying onto the floor.

"It looks like 'Keeping it between the isolated feathers,' is a clue that has seen its day," voiced Tim.

"Yeah, I guess we have no alternative but to look through every one of these damn things that someone was nice enough to spill all over the floor," declared Ron.

"Let's get on with it," said Baxter, finding a chair and placing it amongst the DVD debris.

Tim and Ron were about to find chairs of their own when a noise from the rear of the house caught Ron's attention.

"What was that, fellas?"

"What was what?" asked Baxter, already opening and closing DVDs.

"I heard a noise," replied Ron.

Tim, looking out the front window, turned to Ron, saying, "I don't see any movement in the cruiser."

"Arm yourselves, boys. We may have company," whispered Ron.

There were, other than the front door itself, only two ways to enter the living room. One was through the dining room, on the right. The other was from the library, on the left.

Behind the back wall of the living room was the kitchen.

Bruno and Jocko had made their way into the kitchen through the garage. When they first entered, they heard the faint voices of the FBI agents, but now they heard nothing.

The sudden silence told Bruno they had lost the element of surprise.

"They know someone is here," whispered Bruno.

Having been here on two previous occasions, they knew the home's layout.

The kitchen had three doorways. One was the entrance through the garage. The other led to the dining room, and the third led to a Carolina room.

Bruno, with a simple nod of his head, directed Jocko to the doorway on the left.

Behind that doorway was the Carolina room, which had an entrance into the library.

Bruno would attack from the right via the dining room, while Jocko would strike from the library. Both men, expert killers and heavily armed, moved into position.

✳✳✳✳✳✳✳✳✳✳✳✳

It was 9:00am when Michael and Isabella pulled into the north gate of Hillcrest Cemetery and made their way to the Chapel Mausoleum.

Michael parked their vehicle next to quadrant E on the road to the left of the mausoleum. Quadrant F, where the Hall funeral would take place in three hours, was another hundred yards further to the south.

After exiting the vehicle, Michael opened the Yukon's hatch and removed a baby stroller. There would be no baby in this stroller. There would, however, be a sniper's rifle mounted with a suppressor.

Walking eastward, they, like a couple with a young child might do, leisurely pushed the stroller along the tree-lined road between sections E and F.

Upon reaching the southern-most point of quadrant F, they stopped for a moment. Directly in front of them was the eastern end of the 300-yard-long service road that connected with the western portion of the cemetery.

Ensuring that no one was in sight, Michael removed the rifle from the stroller, and carried it to a stand of oak trees lining the service road. Stepping amongst the trees, Michael found the largest and leaned the weapon against the trunk where it would go unseen.

Returning to Isabella, Michael grasped the stroller, and they continued on to where they had parked their vehicle.

"Let's drive over to the other end of the service road, Michael," suggested Isabella.

A minute later, Michael had their vehicle parked at the west entrance.

"Let's review," proposed Isabella. "You'll drop me off at the corner of quadrants, 'E' and 'F'. You will then proceed to this spot where you will wait until I signal you. After receiving my signal you will back the vehicle down the road about 250 yards and open this passenger door."

"Yes," agreed Michael. "Whereas you, once you have taken the shot, will leave the rifle and make your way up the service road. You enter this vehicle and we will exit the cemetery via the north gate. We will drive to Darlington where a private plane awaits to fly you out of the country. After which, I will never see you again."

Smiling at his sweetness, she leaned over and kissed him, saying, "I wouldn't count on that last part, Michael."

"That's a nice thought, Isabella."

# CHAPTER 51

**"What are they** doing, Ron?" whispered Tim.

"Do I look like I have x-ray eyes, partner?" Ron whispered back.

"Well, fellas," breathed Baxter, "let's put a plan together in the next ten seconds, because I believe they will come at us from the left and the right."

"There's nowhere to hide in this room," announced Tim. "Hiding behind that couch won't cut it. I hear bullets penetrate that shit. And since you don't have x-ray eyes, then you can't be Superman and those bullets will give you a bad boo-boo."

"You're right, Tim, so let's be judicious and go out the front door."

"Brilliant idea, Ron!" said Baxter, who was not ready to die today.

"I was being facetious, Bill."

"Damn it, Ron," said a disappointed Baxter. "You're picking a bad time to be playing games."

"Okay, here's the plan," said Ron, getting serious. "Bill, I'd like you to go outside but leave the front door wide open. Position yourself behind our vehicle where you'll have clear visibility into this room. When you see someone in this room, who isn't Tim or me, shoot to kill!"

"What the hell are we going to do, Ron?" asked Tim, looking at his partner like he was crazy.

"We, partner, will hide behind those two big chairs sitting in the corners."

"Are those bullet-proof chairs?" asked Tim.

"Now you're being facetious, Tim-o-thy," said Ron, with a wry grin. "Get going Bill and don't forget to leave the door open."

The room had a three-seat couch sitting in front of the fireplace, with oak end tables and a matching coffee table. Two oversized-chairs occupied the two corners of the room next to the front windows. Both had a four-foot ottoman fronting it.

"Now, listen, Tim. Wait until you hear Bill firing before you spring from behind the chair. Let's try to take them alive, but, if they decide that's not what they want to do, don't hesitate for a second to put them down."

"Gotcha, partner."

"Just remember, Tim, if it comes to a shoot-out, I'm on the opposite side. I don't want a circular firing squad with the two of us killing each other."

"Good point, Ron. I'll take the chair on the dining room side. Good luck."

They hadn't been in position more than 30 seconds before both Bruno and Jocko burst into the room with firearms held in the classic attack position.

After circling the couch and seeing no one, Jocko asked, "Where did they go, Bruno?"

"Shhh!" scolded Bruno. Then he nodded toward the oversized-chair in the corner on his side of the room.

Jocko returned the nod indicating he understood and began making his way toward the chair in the opposite corner, but as he did, he saw the open front door.

"Bruno!" he shouted. "The front door is open They went outside!"

Bruno, only two steps from the chair where Tim was hiding, stopped and made his way to Jocko's position. Giving Jocko a slight nod, they started toward the open door. They stopped just short of the foyer entrance when they saw a man appear from behind the parked SUV. He had a weapon pointed in their direction.

A split-second later they saw a muzzle flash and bullets were whizzing past their heads.

They returned fire, but it was brief as Ron and Tim both rose from behind the chairs, yelling "Drop your weapons! FBI!"

The two men eyed the two agents, but neither, as requested, dropped their guns.

"Drop the weapons, gentlemen, or we will kill you both, and that is a promise," stated Ron.

Jocko believed him – Bruno didn't. As Jocko was dropping his gun, Bruno was raising his weapon toward Tim, but Tim, remembering Ron's words, fired four rapid shots with all finding their mark.

The coroner would later confirm that any of the four shots would have ended the life of Bruno Lorenza.

Upon hearing the coroner's comment, Tim asked, "Damn! Will I be getting a bill for the bullets I wasted?"

"Naw," replied Ron, "they'll just deduct it out of your paycheck."

Jocko, mortified by his friend's violent death, was furious.

Although Jocko had dropped his gun, he still had a trick up his sleeve… in the form of a blackjack.

With guns raised and pointed at Jocko's head, both Ron and Tim closed in on the behemoth.

Jocko let the blackjack slide down his sleeve and melt into his hand.

As Ron reached out to grab his arm, Jocko swung the blackjack and caught Ron across the forehead which stopped the FBI agent dead in his tracks. It was if he had run into a wall. He crumpled to the floor, out cold.

Tim got caught off-guard when seeing his partner go down. That momentary lapse was all the time Jocko needed. Using the blackjack, he swatted Tim's gun from his hand and then, grabbing the agent by the throat, raised him into the air, and squeezed.

Tim, dangling in the air, with his legs thrashing about, appeared to be an out-of-control puppet. While his eyes bulged in fear, his hands tried, in vain, to pry Jocko's massive and powerful hand off his throat. Tim's tongue, extending from a gurgling mouth trying to scream, wiggled like a worm discovered under an overturned stone.

With his life flashing before his dimming eyes, Tim knew it was over when his bladder released its contents.

Having blacked out, Tim never heard what saved his life. If he had stayed conscious for just a few more seconds, he may have heard Bill Baxter's service revolver pumping five .38 slugs into the oversized, but powerful body of Jocko Moritz. And unlike the hits that Bruno had taken, where just a single shot would have done the job, it took all five hits to put Jocko down for the count.

It wasn't until the fourth of those five .38 slugs hit its mark did the blackjack monster release Tim from his death grip. The fifth bullet sent Jocko sprawling backward, where he landed on the DVDs. It was a fitting, but ironic end for Jocko, seeing it was he who had scattered Hector's collection across the floor a week earlier.

Baxter, himself badly shaken, had called for backup and an ambulance. He was sitting on an ottoman, gazing at the carnage that lay in front of him, when they arrived.

It took almost a half-hour to revive Ron and Tim, and to treat their injuries.

Tim, seeing his bruised neck in a mirror, looked at Baxter and said, "Damn, Bill, what took you so long to get in here!"

"I became mesmerized by the shades of red you were turning, Tim. Lost my concentration. Sorry."

"What time is it?" Ron asked, while rubbing his forehead with an icepack.

"It's 11:05, Ron," answered Robert Edge who arrived long before they had revived the two FBI agents. "I warned you guys to shoot first and then ask questions when it was convenient."

"It's Ron's fault. I took out the first guy. It was his job to take down that damn Godzilla freak."

"Sorry, partner, but I got caught up in watching your work. I would have gotten around to it… sooner or later," snickered Ron.

"How? You were on the floor looking like the loser of a bar fight," chided Tim.

Ron, ignoring Tim's dig, exclaimed, "Hey, that's two kills in less than 24 hours, Tim! You're becoming a regular Harry Callahan. We'll need to refer to you as, Dirty Tim."

"If that's the case, let's refer to Baxter as Billy 'the kid' Baxter and as for you, Ron, to paraphrase Howard Cosell, 'Down goes Lee!'"

"Tim, it's 11:10. We need to get to the funeral! You ready to travel?"

"I pissed my pants, so what do you think? Besides, do these finger marks embedded in my neck take away from my good looks?" Tim asked with a croaky voice.

"What good looks?" chorused Ron, Bill, and Robert.

Tim shot them all the bird, then said to Ron, "That welt on your head gives you some much-needed character."

Smiling at Tim's left-handed compliment, Ron said, "It looks like we both have a badge of honor we can talk about at the bar when this is over."

"Well, you need to get to this funeral," said Tim. "I need to go home to shower and change clothes. Bill, can you have one of your guys drop me at my house?"

"I believe I can find you a ride, Tim," answered a still shaken Baxter who had just killed his first man in the line of duty.

"Thanks, Bill. I'll meet you there, Ron. I need to hear what you say about Ken. If you do a good job, I'll consider having you eulogize me!"

As the two FBI agents headed out the door, Baxter shouted, "Hey, Ron! What about the flash drive?"

"You have twenty officers here, Bill. It shouldn't take you long to find it."

"I bet it's under this tub of shit," asserted Bill, while nodding toward Jocko.

"You'll need a crane to get that asshole on a gurney, Robert," suggested Tim as he and Ron left the home and went their separate ways.

With his two henchmen dead, Cameron Driscoll was out $1,125,000. It would be money that would stay in a hidden off-shore account until hell froze over.

Driscoll, however, with the flash drive now in the hands of the FBI, had much bigger problems coming his way.

# CHAPTER 52

**It took Ron** almost 40 minutes to get to the Hillcrest Cemetery. Most of the mourners had arrived and were seated under the large white tent.

The day had turned morbidly overcast with the temperature hovering in the high 30s, and the wind kicking around 10-15 mph. It felt like it was well below freezing and getting colder by the minute.

Ron stopped to express his condolences to Irene and Ken's sons and daughter who, along with grandchildren, surrounded the grieving widow. An usher escorted him to his seat on the front row, a dozen chairs to the left of Irene.

Rich Freeman was sitting to his left. Out of respect, they didn't speak, other than to say "Hello."

Glancing around the tent, Ron saw many from the Hagan Hackers golfing group in attendance. Further perusal of the tent showed it filled to near-capacity.

The Honor Guard, who would fulfill the "Honoring Those Who Served" regimen, were standing just a few feet from where Ron was sitting.

The Guard's services included carrying the flag-draped casket to the gravesite, presenting the flag to the widow, executing the 21-gun salute, and playing taps.

A solemn sounding bell, rung once, proclaimed it was the noon hour, and the program was to begin.

*************

Isabella had arrived at 11:40, fifteen minutes before Ron made his appearance. Wearing the black maternity dress and the light brown wig, she added glasses and a big brimmed black hat to enhance her disguise.

Seeing the target arrive, she watched as he spoke to the widow and the family members of the deceased. She wondered about the large reddish bump on his forehead that was clearly visible from what she estimated to be a distance of 100 feet or more.

It was not until she saw the usher take him to his seat did she realize her plan to shoot him during the 21-gun Salute was no longer viable. The site lines would be impaired by too many other heads sitting behind him.

They would have to resort to Plan B. She called Michael and when he answered, all she said was, "Plan B."

Plan B would be much more dangerous, as it didn't offer the cover the 21-Gun Salute would have provided.

Sitting in the far left seat of the last row, she watched the Honor Guard ceremony and appeared moved by it. *It was,* she reminded herself, *my misguided actions that required this gathering of sorrow.*

She remained seated until the first of the eulogies began. Rising from her chair, she passed by the few mourners who stood outside the tent.

Stepping through the headstones, she made her way down to the service road where she disappeared into the trees.

\*\*\*\*\*\*\*\*\*\*\*\*\*

Tim, showered and wearing a new suit of clothing, had been barreling down Route 544 in his Ford Escape, at 15 miles over the speed limit. His reckless speeding caused him to miss the south entrance into the cemetery. That required that he enter the cemetery at the north entrance, a few hundred yards further on.

It was 12:22 when he turned into the cemetery. Driving much slower, he made his way toward quadrant F, but, not having a map, and confused by the myriad of roadways, he made an incorrect turn. This path took him toward quadrants G and H in the western part of the cemetery.

Moments later, after realizing he was going in the wrong direction, he made another wrong turn at the Open-Air Chapel. Seeing the dirt service road fifty yards ahead on his left, he realized once again he had chosen the wrong path. While putting the vehicle in reverse, he noticed the white Yukon parked near the end of the service road. He saw a dark-haired male, wearing sunglasses, sitting behind the wheel who appeared to be using his cell phone.

Puzzled as to why the vehicle would park where there were no immediate gravesites, Tim recalled his own predicament.

*Maybe he's lost too. It's easy in this place, that's for sure.*

Not giving it another thought, Tim backed up his vehicle to the intersection where he had made the wrong turn. He sat there for a moment wondering how he would find the funeral's location when he heard the answer in the form of the 21-gun salute.

Pulling straight ahead, he found himself at the intersection of quadrants E and F, where he cursed himself for his stupidity. He made a right turn, and, displaying respect, drove slowly until he was even with the tent.

Seeing that the entire quadrant was encircled with parked vehicles along its left side, Tim was forced to park alongside the right side of the road, leaving no room for a car to pass. Knowing how cold it was, he elected to stay in the vehicle with his window down, and the heater running. Although parked on the right side of the road, he still had a clear view of the southern-facing podium and with the sound system, had no problem hearing what each speaker was saying.

As he sat there, he saw a woman, attired in black, walking away from the tent toward the service road. His impression was she had a good looking body and moved with a type of grace most women lack. However, with her back facing him, Tim couldn't see her face or that she was pregnant.

\*\*\*\*\*\*\*\*\*\*\*\*\*

The second of the six men, to eulogize Ken Hall, was speaking when Rich Freemen, leaning toward Ron, whispered, "Where did you get that knot on your forehead, Ron? It looks painful."

"Blackjack," whispered Ron in return.

"You got that playing blackjack?" asked Richie, his eyes wide in surprise.

Ron, turning in his seat, looked at Richie, saying, "You know something, Rich? I didn't realize until this very minute, although I've suspected it for some time, that you, unlike most people, aren't as smart as you look."

Richie, retaliating, said, "If I wasn't old and weak, I'd knock you on your ass, right where you sit."

Ron replied, "You must be weak-minded too, Richie, seeing that I'm already on my ass, sitting in this chair."

"Shhh," whispered a half-dozen people in their immediate vicinity.

As the speaker left the podium, the family's reverend announced that Richie Freeman had words to say.

Special Agent Colonel Ron Lee would be next.

# CHAPTER 53

**When the Honor** Guard completed their portion of the program, Isabella left her last-row seat and walked toward the back of the cemetery.

Those who witnessed her departure, assumed, being pregnant, she had trouble sitting for extended periods, or experiencing nausea, felt it best to return to the confines of her vehicle.

Having made her way through the cemetery, she now had the bumper-to-bumper mourner's cars to cover her movements toward the gravelly service road. Reaching the road, she made her way, unseen, or so she thought, a short 20 yards, before disappearing into a stand of trees.

After discarding the large hat and the sunglasses, she removed the dress to reveal she was wearing camouflage apparel. She found the rifle where Michael had hidden it and moved to the location from where she would take the shot.

As she corrected the gunsight, she set it on the current speaker, Rich Freeman, as he stood on the podium. While targeting the center of his forehead, she smiled as she remembered Ron Lee's bruise. It would make the targeted area even easier to sight.

She watched as Richie stepped down from the podium and the reverend announced that Ron Lee had a few words.

In a moment, Ron Lee would stand at the podium.

Pressing the talk button on a walkie-talkie, she spoke but a single word.

"Now."

Michael backed the Yukon down the service road until he was 60 yards from Isabella's location. Reaching across the passenger seat, he pushed open the door.

Then, from the center console, he removed a P08 Lugar with an attached silencer. It was a gift from his grandfather who had captured it from a German officer during WWII. He placed the weapon on his lap.

\*\*\*\*\*\*\*\*\*\*\*\*\*

Tim, comfortable in the warmth of his car, watched the previous speaker leave the podium and Richie Freeman step up to give his thoughts about Ken Hall.

Out of the corner of his eye, he saw the woman he had noticed earlier walking amongst the tombstones. She was now passing between parked cars and making her way toward the service road. He had a side view of her now and, although they were a distance apart, he thought she looked a little heavy around the middle.

*Too bad,* he thought, *from the rear, she had all the makings.*

He turned away to listen to Richie, but his mind wandered back to the Yukon parked at the western end of the service road. There was something about the driver.

*He looked familiar,* thought Tim. *Where had he seen him before?*

An announcement interrupted his thoughts when he heard Ron Lee's name mentioned over the loud-speaker.

Turning his attention back toward the tent, he watched as Richie descended the podium stairs. Ron, meanwhile, rose from his seat and approached the podium, stopping only for a moment to share some words with the reverend. He then made the three-step journey up to the podium where he removed his notes from his jacket pocket and placed them on the lectern.

It was at that moment that Tim remembered where he had seen the driver of the Yukon. Bolting up in his seat, he yelled, "That's the son-of-a-bitch who asked me to point out Ron at Burning Ridge!"

Blowing on the car horn, he opened the door. He stood on the vehicle's small foot space between the seat and the open door, and while making a downward push with his left arm, yelled, "Ron, get down! Get down!"

The sudden continuous blowing of the vehicle's horn had all looking to their left. Who, they wondered, was that inconsiderate bastard? Ron, hearing, over the sound of the horn, a voice he recognized, reacted instinctively. As he dove toward the floor, a bullet whizzed past, striking a tent stanchion just ten feet behind Ron's head. The pole cracked in half and a ten-foot portion of the tent sagged.

With the mourners now standing and the target impossible to see, Isabella knew the window of opportunity had been slammed shut. There would be no chance for a second attempt. Dropping the rifle, she ran from the trees and up the service road toward the nearby parked Yukon.

Seconds later, she was at the door and climbing in when Michael urgently asked, "Is he dead, Isabella?"

"No," she replied. "Someone warned him just as I pulled the trigger. He ducked out of the way."

She had lifted her left foot up onto the running board when she heard Michael say, "That's too bad, Isabella. Juan Pablo, sends his condolences."

Lifting the Lugar from his lap, Michael pointed it at the most beautiful woman he had ever made love to and shot her twice in the head.

Leaving the vehicle, he ran to the other side of the car and while closing the passenger door, shot her, although she was already dead, once more in the heart.

Returning to the driver's side, Michael sped from the cemetery, exiting at the north entrance. He had stored another vehicle in a garage a mile away. The plan was to drive to Darlington and take Isabella's place on the plane reserved for her escape to Mexico.

Ron, hearing the projectile strike the tent pole, stayed down for a brief moment before standing with his weapon in his hand.

The standing mourners, not realizing what was happening, stared at the now erect Ron, with looks of bewilderment on their faces.

The horn blowing had ceased, but now they heard someone yelling, "Ron, the shot came from the service road. C'mon!"

Leaning in toward the microphone, Ron's voice spewing urgency, said, "Sorry Irene, but I must be going. Ken was a great guy."

They all watched Ron descend the podium stairs and rush off toward the Ford Escape.

The mourners, seeing the tent sagging, Ron running off with a gun in his hand, and hearing Tim's cry of 'shots fired', began to panic. In their attempt to escape the tent, which had no chance of collapsing, they created chaos by running into and over one another.

As Ron approached the passenger door, Tim yelled, "Get in. It was Isabella! I saw her enter the service road."

Ron was only halfway in the seat as Tim floored the Escape and headed toward the road 200 feet away.

While making a screeching right turn onto the service road, they saw the taillights of the white Yukon heading north toward the cemetery's exit.

"There they go, Ron!"

"I don't think it's they, partner," said Ron, seeing a body, just 100 feet ahead, lying in the road. "Stop."

"Stop? They're getting away!"

"I don't believe Isabella is getting away, Tim. I could be wrong, but I'm betting that's her in the road."

Tim stopped the vehicle a few feet short of the body.

Exiting the vehicle, they stood over the body, quiet as church mice. She was lying on her back. Her big brown eyes, wide open, were staring upward at the graying sky. Even dressed in camouflage and having two bullets in her head and another in her chest, Isabella Sanchez was still strikingly beautiful.

Tim ended the silence, asking, "How come, Ron?"

"She failed to get the job done would be my guess, Tim. The cartel doesn't look kindly upon failure."

"She worked for the Juarez Cartel. Right?"

"That's what our records say," answered Ron.

"Who's the boss man down there?"

"His name is Juan Pablo Ledezma. I'm guessing Juan is a man of little patience. According to all accounts, Isabella was the best Flakas in all of Mexico. That, I'm guessing, didn't carry much weight with Juan, though. It's obvious that he will not tolerate a single mistake."

"What about the guy who got away?"

"I'm guessing he'll be out of the country in a few hours. Oh, while I'm thinking of it. Thanks."

"For what?"

"If you hadn't been here, she would have scattered my brains all over the cemetery grounds."

"The clean-up wouldn't be as big as you might imagine," said Tim with a grin.

"Always a wise-ass, ain't you?"

"Hey, Ron, all kidding aside, we've had a busy, but successful, 24 hours."

Ron, nodding his head in agreement, started counting on his fingers, saying as he went along, "Well, we got Officer Clyde Garrett, aka The Ghost. He killed four cops, a judge, a detective, two FBI agents, a woman's husband in New York, and then the woman herself."

"That alone is almost a whole career's worth of work, partner," said Tim.

"Yeah, but we have other trophies we can raise, partner."

"Let's hear 'em, Ron," cried Tim, already knowing what's coming.

"We got the guys who killed Hector and Corrina, the little receptionist, Maria, the Tree Amigos, and Agent Adams."

"You got any more, Colonel Lee?" asked Tim.

"Well, I can't rightly say we can take credit for this purty little lady lying here with all those bullet holes in her head and chest."

"No, we can't," agreed Tim. "We know, however, she's responsible for our buddy Ken Hall, a pair of store clerks, and for a sheriff, albeit a crooked one, down in Georgetown."

"Don't forget, partner, she died trying to kill me. We should get some credit. Don't you agree?"

"I agree, Ron. So what's next?"

"Let's go see what's on that flash drive. I have a feeling we'll be seeing Mr. Cameron Driscoll before the next sunrise."

# CHAPTER 54

**Michael was halfway** to Darlington when his phone rang.

"Hello."

*"Is Isabella with you?"*

"I'm sorry to say she is not."

*"That is unfortunate."*

"In more ways than you can imagine, Uncle Juan."

*"Oh, I don't know, I can imagine many things, nephew."*

Smiling sadly, Michael replied, "Well, she's gone."

*"So Special Agent Colonel Ron Lee still lives?"*

"He does."

*"Where are you?"*

"I'm about 30 minutes from the plane."

*"Turn around. Go do what Isabella could not, and while you are there, I think it best that we discontinue our relationship with Mr. Driscoll. Is all this understood, Michael?"*

"Yes, uncle, I understand."

*"Good. When you have taken care of business, the plane will be waiting."*

"I'll see you soon, Uncle Juan."

*"I await your safe and successful return, nephew."*

\*\*\*\*\*\*\*\*\*\*\*\*\*

Ron and Tim, after wrapping things up at the cemetery, returned to their office. It was 2:20pm, and hunger made its presence known to both men. They called a local restaurant for a delivery of steak sandwiches which they devoured in minutes.

Knowing they had found the flash drive inside a DVD appropriately titled, "True Grit," they asked a good portion of the staff, including Heather, to report to work at 5:00pm.

Bill Baxter showed up, as they were wolfing down their sandwiches, at 2:45 with a copy of the flash drive.

"What's with the copy, Bill? This is an FBI case," roared Ron, visibly upset. "No one has jurisdiction over that flash drive but the FBI!"

"Don't shoot the messenger, Ron, but SLED says otherwise."

"Well, SLED can kiss my ass!" shouted Ron, his blood already reaching its boiling point.

"SLED says Hector was working for them."

"He was a goddam FBI agent, Bill! We loaned him to SLED!"

"They took the original, Ron. What can I say? They swarmed the place as soon as the word got out about the shootout at Hector's home. When we found the drive inside the DVD, they took it and left without saying hello, goodbye, or screw you. They gave me this copy an hour ago."

"Have you looked at it, Bill?" asked Tim.

"I have."

"And?"

"It looks redacted to me, fellas."

"Redacted! How?" bellowed Ron.

"There's financial information and names of small time dealers, but nothing of people who protect Driscoll."

"What! Why would they do that, Bill?" asked Tim, now getting as riled up as Ron.

"I can't answer that question, Tim."

"I can!" exclaimed Ron. "Someone in SLED, for whatever reason, doesn't want the FBI having any knowledge of what is on that disk."

"Maybe so, but is it for their protection, or for the FBI's?"

"That's a damn good question, Bill."

"Shit, Ron, without that drive, we can't even charge Driscoll with friggin' jaywalking," stated a frustrated Tim.

Ron, trying to cool down, took a seat, and shaking his head, acknowledged what Tim had said.

"Even though Garrett told me Driscoll had hired him to kill Judge Samuels, Detective Hardy, and that cop in Hilton Head, it wouldn't hold up in court. It would be my word against a guy rotting away on a slab at the morgue."

"We can't use a 'death bed confession', Ron?"

"I don't think The Ghost was lying down on a bed looking up into Tim's eyes and spilling his conscience when Tim blew him away, Bill."

"We have nothing connecting him to drugs?"

"Hey, we know what he is, Bill, but proving it, well, that's something else again."

"Is SLED going to prosecute anyone found on that drive?" asked Tim.

"If they do, it won't be anyone of power. You can count on that," answered Ron.

"It might be interesting to know if Driscoll is aware that SLED has the drive," said Tim.

"Why? What would it matter?" asked Baxter.

"Maybe we can bluff him."

Ron, hearing Tim's suggestion, stood up and began pacing the floor.

"That, partner, might just work… if… someone at SLED hasn't already talked to him."

"Has word gotten out about Clyde Garrett, Bill?"

"No. Being a cop, we wanted to disinfect that situation before we told the public about a cop being a 'cop killer.'"

"Maybe we can use Garrett to trick Driscoll into giving himself away."

"If not him, Ron, how about those two goons at Hector's house we put to sleep this morning? Word hasn't reach the press about their identities."

"Who were they, Bill?"

"Their names were Bruno Lorenza and Jocko Moritz. Both go way back as suspected hitmen for various organizations. We have them tied to Driscoll for at least the past three years."

"So we tell Driscoll we have Garrett, Bruno, and Jocko in custody and they are all singing like canaries."

"Let's go get him, Ron!"

"Let's do just that, partner. We'll keep you posted, Bill."

"What should I do with this drive, Ron?"

"I'd say stick it up someone's ass at SLED, but I'm betting it's way too crowded with someone's head up there already. Give it to me. I can use it where we're going."

As Ron and Tim pulled out of the FBI parking lot, a dark green Chrysler 200, staying far back, followed.

\*\*\*\*\*\*\*\*\*\*\*\*\*

It was 3:30, and not having heard from Bruno, Driscoll was bemoaning the fact that a pair of dumb-asses had taken him to the tune of a million plus.

As he sat there mentally kicking himself, the buzz of the intercom interrupted his thoughts. He then heard the soothing voice of Linda Kiel, his secretary, announcing, *"There are two FBI men here to see you, sir."*

Cameron Driscoll's home sat atop a bluff in Tidewater Plantation.

Valued at over five million dollars, it overlooked House Creek, the spectacular marshlands, and further on, the Atlantic Ocean.

Adding to the magnificent view, was the Tidewater Golf Club's fourth hole. It's entire length ran along the bluff, ending with its green posing as Driscoll's backyard.

"Bring them in, Linda."

A moment later, Linda was opening the large oaken door into Cameron's office and introducing the two agents.

"Mr. Driscoll, this is Special Agent Colonel Ron Lee and Agent Tim Pond."

"Nothing special about you, Agent Pond?" asked Cameron.

"I get that a lot, Driscoll. I only take it as an affront when my wife says it."

Cameron, ignoring Tim's self-deprecating joke, did, however, take umbrage to the agent's calling him by his last name.

"It's Mr. Driscoll, if you don't mind," he said with a sneer.

"Okay, Mr. Driscoll," said Ron with an emphasis on mister. We're here to arrest you. You're charged with ordering the murders of FBI Agent Hector Falano and his wife Corrina, Judge Samuels, Detective Tom Hardy, and Sgt. Harold Sutcliff, just to name a few."

"I have no idea what you are talking about. I never heard of any of those people, Agent… I'm sorry, I've forgotten your name. Are you the special agent fella?"

"It doesn't matter that you can't remember my name, Cameron, but there are three guys down in lockup that know yours. In fact, they're the ones who sent us here.

Ever hear of Bruno Lorenza and Jocko Moritz? We caught those guys in Hector Falano's house this morning. Seems they were looking for this flash drive," Ron said, holding up the green-colored drive Baxter had brought to the office.

Driscoll's color transformed to a molten gray, but he held his composure, saying, "What's on that? Photos of Hector's family?"

"Oh, no, Cameron. This drive has all of your illicit business dealings on it. Who you pay and how much. It won't be long before the names on this disk will sing the same tune The Ghost was humming last night."

"You caught the…" muttered Cameron, stopping himself in mid-sentence.

"Yeah, maybe you know him as Officer Clyde Garrett. Does that ring a bell, Driscoll?"

Cameron didn't answer. He was searching for a way out. Something that would limit the impact.

"I have information about the Juarez cartel. What would that be worth to you?"

"Don't you mean, what would it be worth to you?"

"Okay, whatever… can we make some kind of deal?"

"You're responsible for the deaths of… ten, twelve people, that we know of, and you deal drugs to thousands of others. But you want to make a deal? Just to keep from getting the needle, you'd have to give us something incredible, Cameron. Do you know anything that we would consider… incredible?"

"I'll give you the names of Washington politicians who are taking bribes from Mexican cartels!"

"You're bluffing, Driscoll. You're not big enough to know about such things," said Ron, goading the drug czar to spill his guts.

"I know people in SLED and the FBI connected to the cartels."

It hurt to hear it, but Ron knew he wasn't lying.

"Give me a name!"

"Not until I have something in writing stating I get immunity from all charges and I'm put in the Witness Protection Program."

"You understand that if what you tell us turns out to be nothing but bullshit, they will fry your ass as fast as they can?"

"Yeah, I do."

"Okay, then let's go to FBI headquarters and make this official, but not until you give me one name," said Ron.

"Are you guys, wired?" asked Driscoll.

"No, we are not. Why?"

Ignoring Ron's question, Driscoll said, "Put your cell phones on the desk where I can see them. I don't want you recording me. If I give you a name and it's recorded, I lose any advantage I may have."

Dubious of Driscoll's claims, Ron and Tim nevertheless turned off their phones and placed them on Driscoll's desk.

"All right, you got what you wanted, now give me a name!" Ron bellowed.

*"Mr. Driscoll?"* It was Linda calling via the intercom. *"There's a man from SLED to see you, sir."*

Ron, knowing SLED withheld the unredacted flash drive, wondered why they would send a single agent here to see Driscoll.

"Tim, find cover! Get prepared."

Taking his gun from his holster, Tim moved to the right of the entrance doorway.

"Tell her to send him in, Cameron."

"What's going on?"

"Tell her to send him in!"

Pressing the response button, Driscoll, said, "Send him in, Linda."

The expected reply, didn't come.

"Again," said Ron.

"Linda? Did you hear me? I said, send him in."

Nothing.

"How many goons do you have working for you, Cameron? I hope you don't think you can shoot your way out of this."

"No! I only had Bruno and Jocko. No one else."

"If that's true, Cameron, someone wants you dead."

\*\*\*\*\*\*\*\*\*\*\*\*\*

Michael couldn't believe it when he realized the two agents were driving to the home of Cameron Driscoll.

*Damn! I believe I have a double-dip coming my way. I'll be on that plane back to Mexico City by 9:00,* his inside voice told him.

Michael Garcia was born to the sister of Juan Pablo Ledezma. Given the name of Garcia, which means 'young warrior' Michael was the only male child born to a Ledezma family member. Juan Pablo, always wanting a male child, had fathered four daughters. His only nephew, Michael, became his adopted son. He was molding Michael to be the leader of the Juarez cartel.

If Michael could carry out this assignment, his loving uncle would set him up for the rest of his life.

Arriving at the house, Michael parked in the street, blocking the driveway where the agents had parked.

Checking that he had a full clip in his Lugar, he attached a silencer, and tucked the weapon in the back of his pants. Opening the car's trunk, Michael selected a small package of C4, two tear gas canisters, and a handful of clips for the Lugar, which he tucked in his jacket pockets. Closing the trunk, he made his way to the front door.

Linda, seeing, via a monitor on her desk, the man approaching the door, waited until he pressed the doorbell that only she could hear.

"Yes, can I help you, sir?"

"Agent Garcia from SLED," said Michael holding up what appeared to be credentials but in fact was his Mexican driver's license. "I'm here to see Mr. Driscoll."

Linda, fooled by the false identification, buzzed him in.

"Mr. Cameron is with two agents from the FBI. Would you like to take a seat?"

"No, I wouldn't. Please announce I'm waiting."

"Sir, I can't…" was as far as Linda's response went before she was staring down the barrel of Michael's Lugar.

"Do it!" said Michael, while pressing the gun's barrel against the woman's forehead.

Linda, needing no further urging, pressed the talk button and in a voice filled with stress, announced, "Mr. Driscoll? There's a man from SLED to see you, sir."

There was a long pause before they heard Driscoll's reply to send him in.

"You've been a great help," said Michael, just before he put a bullet between Linda's beautiful blue eyes.

Moving to the door, he heard Driscoll's second response which had a touch of bewilderment, laced with concern.

*You should worry, Mr. Driscoll,* thought Michael.

Realizing the two FBI agents would now be on full alert after not hearing a reply from Cameron's secretary,

Michael removed the C4 from his pocket. Placing it next to the center hinge of the door, he moved to a position behind a large chair, and pulled a tear gas canister from his pocket. Ducking behind the chair, he detonated the C4.

The noise alone almost brought Linda back from the dead. The door shattered into hundreds, maybe thousands of pieces, making a hell of a mess.

Michael stood, popped the tear gas canister and tossed it into Cameron's office.

He stood there, Lugar in hand, waiting to shoot the proverbial, fish in the barrel.

# CHAPTER 55

**SATURDAY, JANUARY 26th, 2019**

**At the same** moment Michael was slapping the C4 on the door hinge, Ron was asking, "Is there another way out of here?"

"There is!" replied Driscoll. "I have an escape hatch behind that bookshelf."

"Then we better get to it. I have a feeling that door won't be there much longer."

As Driscoll headed toward the bookshelf, Ron hailed Tim, saying, "Tim! Follow us! Hurry!"

The bookshelf was behind Driscoll's desk and the button to open it was behind a book on the third shelf.

Driscoll pressed the button and the shelf, moving at what seemed a snail's pace, swung open about five feet to reveal a dark corridor.

"Where does it lead?" asked Ron.

"To the garage."

"Let's go," said Ron, pushing Driscoll into the passageway.

Tim was next to enter and Ron followed asking, "How do you close it, Driscoll?"

"There are two switches on the right wall," answered Cameron. "One will close the bookshelf, the other will light this corridor."

Ron hit both switches, which illuminated the corridor, and began closing the bookshelf.

Seeing it slowly closing, Ron pointed down the corridor, saying, "Let's get going!"

They had taken no more than a step when the C4 explosion rocked Cameron's office, and for whatever reason, halted the shelf's closing and darkened the corridor.

Ron, returning to the open shelf, tried to pull it closed but it wouldn't budge.

Then he heard the tear gas canister explode.

"Tear gas!" Ron yelled. "Get to the garage."

Moving along the passageway in the dark wasn't as easy as it should have been.

"How long is this passageway?" asked Tim.

"It runs along the side of the house, so what's that? Sixty feet, maybe?"

"Is this a straight shot?" asked Ron.

"No," answered Driscoll. "There are two turns. One left, one right. Keep your left hand on the wall. When the wall ends, that will signal the left turn. Take three more steps and turn right. The door to the garage will be 10 feet straight ahead. There's a switch on the wall to open the door."

Michael expected them to come stumbling from the room, gasping, coughing, and blinded by the tear gas. When they did, he would shoot them dead, but to his astonishment, no one came out.

*It would be impossible to remain in the room without a gasmask*, he told himself.

The gas was dissipating.

*Maybe the explosion knocked them out of commission*, thought Michael. *Maybe they are unconscious and lying on the floor. If that's the case, I'll just put a bullet or two in their heads.*

He approached the door with the Lugar at the ready. Although the gas had all but dispersed, that which lingered, stung his eyes. Stepping through the doorway, he swept the room with the Lugar. The room was empty.

There! To his left. A door!

*A bathroom*, thought Michael. *They hid in the bathroom!*

Standing a mere six feet from the door, he emptied a full clip through the bathroom door.

There was no return fire.

Reloading, he stepped to the door and swung it open.

Nothing!

"This is impossible," he screamed aloud. Then he saw it. Behind the desk was a doorway, disguised as a bookshelf.

*Damn it! A secret passage!* Michael's inner voice screamed.

The corridor served as a sound conduit, with any sounds made in the office amplified by the confines of the corridor's four walls.

Ron, hearing the soft, *pop, pop, pop* of the Lugar, whispered, "They are in the office! Move!"

Rushing to the narrow opening, Michael squeezed into the darkness. He heard voices. Raising his Lugar, he emptied another full clip down the dark corridor.

Driscoll and Tim had made the left-hand turn when the first of the Lugar's projectiles hit the far wall. Ron, lingering by a step or two, had turned the corner, but the last bullet fired barely nicked him on the right shoulder. He made no complaint to the others.

"Damn! That was close!" whispered Ron.

Seconds later they were at the doorway to the garage.

"Where's the damn switch, Driscoll?" asked Tim.

"I can't see my hand in front of my face," answered Driscoll. "It's on the wall, someplace!"

"Tim!"

"Yeah, Ron."

"Fire a shot into the ceiling. The flash should light up the walls."

Tim, doing as told, fired his Glock into the ceiling. It only lasted a brief second, but as Ron had said, the flash showed the switch to be on the righthand wall.

Tim hit the switch and nothing happened.

"It ain't working, Ron," announced Tim.

"Son-of-bitch! That damn explosion must have tripped the breaker that controls the circuits for this corridor."

"Maybe we can shoot the lock open," suggested Tim.

"It's a 500 pound steel door," said Cameron. "Unless you have a bazooka, I don't think those pee-shooters you have will do the trick."

"We ain't getting out this way, are we, Ron?"

"I don't see it happening, partner. The only way out is the way we came in."

"How many of them are there, Ron?"

"When the secretary buzzed the office, she announced there was a single man. There may, however, have been others waiting outside."

Hearing Ron mention his secretary, Driscoll shouted, "What do you think happened to Linda?"

"Quiet, you fool!" whispered Tim.

"She's as dead as Napoleon, Cameron," said Ron, being blunt, as usual.

"What should we do, Ron?"

"Let me think for a moment."

While Ron was thinking, Michael was making his way down the corridor, but stopped when he clearly heard Driscoll asking about his secretary.

When he entered the corridor, Michael saw the two switches on the wall and flipped them both with nothing happening. He now realized that a lack of power to open the escape door had thwarted their escape route.

Their only way out was through him, but that wasn't going to happen.

They were doomed to die in this dark corridor by his hand.

# CHAPTER 56

As they sat there in the dark, they heard Michael calling from somewhere in the corridor, "Mr. Driscoll, come out. My uncle sent me to take you to Mexico, where you'll be safe."

"Don't even try to go out there, Driscoll," hissed Ron, "because if he doesn't kill you, and he intends to do just that, then I will."

Driscoll, hearing Ron's words, yells, "The FBI says you are here to kill me!"

"No! No, not at all, Mr. Driscoll. You've done so much for the family, why would we kill you? Don't listen to their lies."

"He's lying, Driscoll," Ron said with emphasis. "You go out there, you'll be dead and in hell before your body hits the floor. They think you'll spill your guts to save your own skin. He is here for one reason: to kill you!"

Why don't you arrest him?" asked a confused Driscoll. "You guys are the FBI. You have him out-numbered two-to-one!

"Well, I don't think he'll lay down his weapons and come peacefully, Cameron. Maybe you haven't noticed, but it is also pitch black in here. We have this thing that when we shoot, we like the target to be visible," Ron explained with a strong dose of sarcasm. "That gives us a better chance of hitting it."

"Driscoll!" called Michael. "Are you coming?"
Silence filled the corridor.
Tim, whispering, said, "Ron, I've been thinking."
"Shit, now we are in danger."
"No, listen to me."

"I'm listening. Start talking."

"He couldn't see us if we were standing five feet in front of him. Correct?"

"If you say so, partner."

"What I was thinking is, the open bookcase allows in a limited amount of light. His silhouette against that backdrop should stand out like a sore thumb. Wouldn't you think?"

"You would be right, Tim, if the explosion hadn't blown out all the lights in Driscoll's office."

"Driscoll's office had plenty of windows. There would be natural light."

Not wearing a watch, Ron asked Driscoll for the time.

Driscoll, looking at his illuminated digital watch, responded. "It's 4:35."

"We have about 25 minutes of daylight left, Tim. If we want this done, we better do it now."

It was a good plan and it would have worked, but for Michael acting first.

Taking the second cannister of tear gas, he popped it and tossed it down the corridor where it hit the far wall and spewed the nauseous gas. As the cannister clanged along the floor toward the wall, Michael retreated to the bookshelf opening and waited.

"Damn!" Tim cried out. "More tear gas!"

"I'll get the tear gas, Tim. You blow that bastard away!"

Driscoll, getting a whiff of the gas, panicked, and in the dark ran up the corridor, yelling, "Don't shoot, it's me."

Somehow, Driscoll made it through the tear gas, and although somewhat blinded, was stumbling toward the open bookshelf.

"It's me, Driscoll. Don't shoot!"

Those would be his last words.

Michael, unable to see anyone in the corridor's darkness, did, however, see a small bluish-light bouncing in the darkness. Aiming at the light, he emptied the full clip of the Lugar. Four of the eight rounds fired found their mark. The drug king of Myrtle Beach was dead.

His illuminated digital watch had sealed his fate.

Michael had completed half of his assignment.

Ron and Tim, blinded by darkness, were unaware Driscoll had abandoned their location, until they heard his cries. They knew he was a dead man and there was nothing they could do to prevent him from meeting his destiny.

Whipping off his jacket, Ron, barely able to breathe, somehow yelled, "Follow me!"

Tim, his eyes on fire and his throat screaming for air, followed with his Glock fully loaded.

Turning the corner, Ron couldn't see the cannister of tear gas still belching its poison, but he could hear it. Holding his open jacket out in front of him, he fell to the floor and finding the cannister, wrapped it with his jacket. Tim, not realizing what Ron was doing, tripped on his partner's outstretched leg and fell to the floor, losing the hold on his weapon.

The clatter of the Glock hitting the concrete floor alerted Michael that the FBI agents were coming his way. Forgetting he had emptied his Lugar while killing Driscoll, he lost a few seconds of his advantage while he reloaded with another clip from his pocket.

Those few seconds allowed Tim to locate his weapon, and staying low, began crawling up the corridor. He had crawled no more than five or six feet when a hail of bullets flew well over his head, spraying the back wall. He couldn't see Michael through the thinning gas, but he saw the muzzle flashes of the Lugar.

Rising to a knee, Tim emptied all 17 rounds of his Glock toward the flashes. The last 10 rounds were a waste. Michael Garcia, clear heir to the control of the Juarez cartel, was dead long before Tim pulled the trigger on round 17.

Five bullets found Michael's body, including two shots to the face that virtually guaranteed there would be no open casket at his funeral.

Not knowing the effect of the barrage of hot lead sent Michaels's way, Tim reloaded and had his weapon ready to return fire.

The corridor turned dead silent.

Ron Lee ended the silence by asking, "Did you get him, Tim?"

"Damned if I know. I guess he could have ran off. How about you? Are you okay?"

"Ruined a nice jacket," answered Ron.

"That was a good idea. What made you think of that?"

"I saw rioters on television doing it."

"I guess it pays to watch the news once in a while."

"Too bad you don't watch the news. You won't get tips like that watching those porn stations."

"Oh, there you go again, making assumptions. I'll let you know I've gotten plenty of tips watching those professionals. I know for a fact that Wilma is appreciative."

"I don't want to hear about it, partner."

"Okay, but I could tell you some really interesting stuff."

"I'm sure you could, Tim. Maybe later. But for now, let's go check the body count."

After stepping over Driscoll's bullet-torn body, they reached the end of the corridor where Michael's bloodied body was blocking the opening to the office.

"Damn, partner. I think you hit him six or seven times."

"Hmm, is that all? I fired an entire clip."

"Well, unless you were shooting at the floor, the rest of the clip hit the wall. I must commend you on your firearm expertise. It is exemplary."

"I just imagined him as a target at a carnival."

"I wish I had a teddy bear I could give you," responded Ron.

"Damn shame we lost Driscoll. Being he's dead, many people who would have been sleeping at the Hotel J Reuben Long Detention Center tonight, will get to sleep in their own beds."

"Life isn't always fair, Tim."

"You know, you're right, but death, on the other hand," said Tim while pointing at Driscoll's and Michael's bodies, "just might be."

"That's an Amen, partner."

# EPILOGUE

**Combined, they had** murdered dozens of people, yet there were no trials. Ironic, though it may be, there was simply no one left to prosecute.

Cameron Driscoll, Bruno Lorenza, Jocko Moritz, Vivian Hanson, Clyde Garrett, Isabella Sanchez, and Michael Garcia were all deposed by the gun, bypassing the need for a judge and jury.

Driscoll's drug empire evaporated with his death, but everyone knew it would eventually return under new management.

Peggy Patterson buried her mother with a funeral fit for a queen. When asked why she would be so lavish for a cop killer, she replied, "She was my mother and she saved my life."

Sheila Bennington, absolved of all wrong-doing in the murder of her husband, received payment on her man's insurance policy from a reluctant insurance provider.

Diana Clayton, wife of the third police officer killed by Clyde Garrett, left the Grand Strand a destitute widow. She moved back to Pennsylvania to live with her parents.

Ron put in for a new jacket, but they rejected his claim because the jacket in question was not FBI issued.

A review of Michael Garcia's autopsy report determined the agent responsible for Garcia's death had been overzealous in his duties. Therefore, the Payroll Department would be notified to deduct the cost of the wasted ammunition from the agent's next paycheck.

When Juan Pablo Ledezma saw his nephew's body and his unrecognizable face, he swore he would avenge Michael's death.

Soon after Michael's funeral, Juan Pablo sent a five-person hit squad to Myrtle Beach to kill FBI Agent Tim Pond, the man who had killed Ledezma's beloved nephew. They were told to kill him and everyone in his family, up to, and including, his dog.

Killing Colonel Ron Lee was also attached to the assignment.

The squad members were told, in no uncertain terms, not to return until all were dead. Failure was not an acceptable option.

The cartel's hit-squad's arrival in Myrtle Beach coincided with that of a man known in dark places, as The Mamba. Like his namesake, he was beyond extremely deadly.

A traitor in Washington had passed the word to Tehran that the leader of the free world would be visiting Myrtle Beach.

The Mamba had been sent from Iran to kill one person: The President of the United States.

Only when an unlikely death occurs, does the FBI have any hint of his possible presence.

Special Agent Ron Lee and Agent Tim Pond are given the task to root out the most feared assassin in the world.

Once again there would be multiple forces testing the resiliency of FBI Agents, Lee and Pond.

# "THE COMBOS"

It is a fact that in Africa, snakes kill over 30,000 people a year, with one of the deadliest being the Black Mamba. It is not, however, the most venomous snake in Africa. That dubious distinction falls to the Puff Adder, but the Mamba is the most feared, because of its aggressive nature, its incredible speed, and its large size.

Their venom, composed of neurotoxins, will neutralize a human within 45 minutes, and if not treated, it has a 100% fatality rate.

Seeing Africa's savannahs and jungles are lacking a single Walgreens, where an anti-venom might be available, most victims succumb within hours.

There are no positives in being bitten by a Mamba, but if there were, it was the aspect of a slow death. As gruesome and painful as this may be, it allows the victim to "experience" the so-called phenomenon of "seeing one's life flashing before one's eyes."

That "experience" would not be the case if one was the target of Bahran Khan, whose reputation for killing earned him the moniker of "The Mamba."

There would be no 'life flashing' when a bullet fired from a 1000 yards turns a head into boney shrapnel. There would only be instant death as a sharp blade slits a throat, or when a simple twist of a key turns a car into an inferno.

"The Mamba" is as deadly as his namesake, but much faster.

Bahran Khan was the world's deadliest assassin, and he had a new assignment: Kill the President of the United States.

The Mamba was on his way to the United States. His final destination: Myrtle Beach, South Carolina.

************

A couple, whose final destination was also Myrtle Beach, had boarded a flight out of Houston that was bound for Atlanta. They had business to conduct in the Grand Strand. Although their business was similar to that of Bahran Khan's, its impact, if successful, would not be felt worldwide.

They were assassins, but their target was not The President of the United States. Their mission was much simpler. They were to exact revenge on the two FBI Agents responsible for the death of Michael Garcia, the beloved nephew of Juan Pablo Ledezma, the leader of the Juarez cartel.

Although her fake passport stated otherwise, the woman's real name was Maria Sanchez. She was the younger sister of the recently deceased Isabella Sanchez. Having followed her sister's footsteps as an assassin for the cartel, Maria was not yet the equal of Isabella, but she was gaining… fast. And now, a lie stoked her passion to kill. Led to believe FBI Agents Ron Lee and Tim Pond killed Isabella, she insisted on being a member of the cartel hit-squad.

Maria vowed to exact revenge, but it would be for Isabella, not for Michael Garcia.

Three other sicarios, each having traveled different routes, had made their way to the Grand Strand, including Alejandro Lopez, Maria's lover of three years.

Alejandro had been a sicario for the Juarez cartel for over seven years and was accountable for killings numbering well north of a hundred.

Together they would bring a new terror to the Grand Strand, but they would have to share the spotlight.

"The Mamba" was also on his way.

# ABOUT THE AUTHOR

**James Robert Fuller** was born in Rochester, New York in 1944. His mother moved to Buffalo, New York, shortly after he was born. There she met and married a man whose last name, an alias, was Wing. For reasons never explained, the two-year-old **James Fuller became Ronald Wing**, the name he would carry for the rest of his life. He would be 35 years old before discovering his true identity.

Growing up in Western New York, Ron spent many of his younger years living with his maternal grandparents, James and Maud Fuller, in Salamanca, New York, a small city nestled in the Allegheny foothills. It was where he had experiences that fostered his *Bay Hollow Thriller* series.

Ron married Barbara Bowman in 1967. They have two children, Jennifer and Jason and four grandchildren.

Ron worked for Bethlehem Steel in Lackawanna, New York, until 1978 as a systems analyst.

The family moved to Greenville, North Carolina, in 1978, where Ron worked for Burroughs Wellcome, a pharmaceutical company, until retiring in 1995.

Ron and Barbara moved to Myrtle Beach, South Carolina, in 2000. This is where Ron began his writing career, penning the *Bay Hollow Thrillers* which targets young adults and those older adults who are young at heart.

Customers of the *Bay Hollow* series would often ask if those stories involved Myrtle Beach. This led Ron to write the *Myrtle Beach Crime Thrillers*, using his given name on his birth certificate, **James Robert Fuller**, in honor of his grandparents.

*"The Falano Findings",* follows *"Paradise: Disturbed"* and *"The Scale Tippers"* in the adult targeted, *Myrtle Beach Crime series.*

Book four in the series, *"The Combos"* will be available in the summer of 2020.

## FALANO CHARACTERS LISTED ALPHABETICALLY
## & THEIR INITIAL CHAPTER APPEARANCE

| CHARACTER | DESCRIPTION | CHAP |
|---|---|---|
| ADAMS, PAUL | ONE OF 3 ROOKIE FBI AGENTS | 31 |
| ALBRIGHT, HARRY | SPECIAL AGENT WHO IS JEALOUS OF RON LEE | 27 |
| ANDERSON, MICHAEL | BUREAU CHIEF OF MIAMI FBI | 3 |
| BAXTER, CPT. BILL | COMMANDER OF HORRY COUNTY STATE POLICE | 2 |
| BEERMUENDER, FRED | A WITNESS TO THE SHOOTING AT BURNING RIDGE | 28 |
| BELLAMY, PATTY | HORRY COUNTY DEPUTY CORONER | 38 |
| BENNINGTON, JESSE | MURDERED STATE TROOPER | 1 |
| BENNINGTON, SHEILA | WIFE OF JESSE BENNINGTON | 2 |
| BLAKE, TOM | A STATE TROOPER DETECTIVE- TARGET OF GHOST | 32 |
| BRADDOCK, JIM | HEAD OF FBI IN MYTLE BEACH OFFICE | 13 |
| CAMPBELL,JOSH | GOLDFINCH FUNERAL HOME EMPLOYEE | 44 |
| CLAYTON, DIANA | JACK CLAYTON'S WIFE | 20 |
| CLAYTON, JACK | MURDERED HORRY COUNTY POLICEMAN | 20 |
| CORA, MIKE | DRISCOLL HITMAN | 5 |
| DARBY, MOLLY | CLOSE FRIEND OF SHEILA BENNINGTON | 4 |
| DEAN, SGT MAX | ON DUTY DEPUTY AT GEORGETOWN HEADQUARTERS | 23 |
| DELGADO, CPT LUIZ | COMMANDER OF EL MORRO CASTLE PRISON | 3 |
| DRISCOLL, CAMERON | HEAD OF S.C. DRUG RING | PROLOG |
| EDGE, ROBERT | THE HORRY COUNTY CORONER | 15 |
| FALANO, CORRINA | WIFE OF HECTOR FALANO | 5 |
| FALANO, HECTOR | FBI/SLED UNDERCOVER NAME OF RAUL RUIZ | 5 |
| FISHER, SALLY | BELK'S SALESPERSON WHO RECOGNIZES ISABELLA | 34 |
| FRAN | HARRY ALBRIGHT'S SECRETARY WHO LIKES TO TALK | 27 |
| FREEMAN, RICH | GOLFER WHO DOES ISABELLA A FATAL FAVOR | 26 |
| GARCIA, MICHAEL | ISABELLA'S DRIVER | 26 |
| GARRETT, CLYDE | HORRY COUNTY SHERIFF DEPUTY | 6 |
| GHOST, THE | WORKING NAME OF MYSTERY MAN | 14 |
| GONZALEZ, MARIA | ALIAS USED BY ISABELLA SANCHEZ | 24 |
| GUGINO, FRANK | AN ALIAS USED BY BRUNO LORENZA | 17 |
| HALL, KEN | AN INNOCENT BYSTANDER MISTAKEN FOR LEE | 26 |
| HANSON, VIVIAN | MOTHER OF PEGGY PATTERSON | 9 |
| HASKINS, MARGE | RECEPTIONIST AT HORRY COUNTY MORGUE | 15 |
| HASTINGS, HELEN | BELK'S SALESPERSON WHO SELLS WIGS TO ISABELLA | 34 |
| HEATHER | RON'S & TIM'S SECRETARY | 30 |
| JULIO, ED | AN ALIAS USED BY JOCKO MORITZ | 17 |
| KIEL, LINDA | DRISCOLL'S SECRETARY | 54 |
| LAMB, FOREST | GEORGETOWN CHIEF OF POLICE | 18 |
| LEDEMA, JUAN PABLO | LEADER OF THE JUAREZ CARTEL | 54 |
| LEE, COLONEL RON | FBI SPECIAL AGENT PARTNERED WITH AGENT TIM POND | 2 |
| LESLIE,CPT. JIM | U.S. ARMY WHO RECRUITS RAMON RUIZ | 3 |
| LORENZA, BRUNO | DRISCOLL'S #1 HITMAN | PROLOG |
| LOWE, AL | A WITNESS AT BURNING RIDGE | 28 |
| LUCAS, SAM | BELK'S MANAGER | 37 |
| MALONE, CARL | HORRY COUNTY SHERIFF LUNCHES WITH BENNINGTON | 1 |
| MANNY | OWNER OF MANNY'S DELI | 1 |
| MARIA | THE TREE AMIGOS RECEPTIONIST | 21 |
| MAURY, BOB | HORRY COUNTY SHERIFF LUNCHES WITH BENNINGTON | 1 |
| MILLER, SAMUEL | ONE OF 3 ROOKIE FBI AGENTS | 31 |
| MOLE | SOMEONE IN FBI OFFICE WORKING FOR DRISCOLL | 27 |
| MORITZ, JOCKO | BRUNO'S SIDEKICK & VICOUS KILLER | PROLOG |